The godde[...] [...] [...] barian swordsman — for his life . . .

The Empire of Rome is threatened with disaster by a barbaric sorcerer who raises mindless killers for the earth itself . . .

The last survivor of Atlantis is called upon to do battle against a human-eating creature only he can brave — to save a race of giants . . .

Robert E. Howard provides weird surprises in a tale of a Spanish opportunist, a "lost" Aztec city, and a centuries-old mage — in what may be the last story REH ever wrote . . .

The sexiest woman on the planet has never lost in her sadistic duels with men . . .

and other all-new tales of menace, high adventure and derring-do, written especially for this volume!

SWORDS AGAINST DARKNESS

edited by andrew j. offutt

ZEBRA BOOKS

KENSINGTON PUBLISHING CORP.

ZEBRA BOOKS

are published by

Kensington Publishing Corp.
475 Park Avenue South
New York, NY 10016

Third printing: April, 1990

Printed in the United States of America

Contents

FOREWORD

They tell me a Texican named Robert Ervin Howard started it. I disagree; I think an Achaean named Homer did.

Howard, nearly 2800 years later, reduced it, raised it, brought it into the twentieth century — and created a new sub-genre of fantasy.

Some of us call it heroic fantasy. Some call it epic fantasy, although the two aren't always synonymous. Some call it sword and sorcery, a phrase invented by a practitioner named Fritz Leiber. There is usually a fantasy element, and there is usually a hero (bearing in mind that "hero" isn't a sexist word — only "heroine" is!). So — heroic fantasy: hf.

It can be said to appeal to all ages, though thousands and thousands of people above age twenty are closet fans of hf. Either you're crazy about it, can't resist it, or think it's nonsense — or *pretend* to. It hardly ever gets good reviews, because high adventure fiction in which the mood is *not* existential futilism and the good guy usually prevails (without federal aid) isn't lit'rature. You know, Literature: like . . . Homer, or *The Three Musketeers,* which has outlived all the parasites who, as "critics," sneered at that novel and its creator, Dumas.

I was a closet hf fan for years, before I Came Out. I'm doing penance for all those years. Hopefully this book of *new* stories is also a good deed for the genre and its lovers, both readers and writers.

Whatever it's called, some of us are hopelessly in love with it, even when it's done in manner rotten, as it too frequently is. All of us who love to read it (and watch old Errol Flynn movies and think what a shame that Basil Rathbone never played a Howard sorcerous villain) and those of us who *can't help* writing it are the very people Conan Doyle was referring to when he wrote

> I have wrought my simple plan
> If I give one hour of joy
> To the boy who's half a man,
> Or the man who's half a boy.

I am . . . one of the above. So is Manly Wade Wellman, a great huge bear of a man a hundred and eighty-leben years old who looks fifty. Change the sexes in Doyle's poem and realize that Leigh Brackett and Andre Norton are women who are half girls, lovers of hf or s&s: high adventure with a touch of the outré.

Poul Anderson is one of us boy-men too, and he summed it up darned well in his reply to the letter I sent him, asking for a story:

"Well, I'd pretty much sworn off . . . especially with all the work to do there is lying on this desk. However you hit me in a weak spot; there are so few opportunities to do any sword and sorcery these days. So, all right . . ."

That's it. His weak spot. *We can't help it.*

Writing heroic fantasy is *fun* — though not so easy as too many people think. We *love* to write it, as we love to read it. Yet though Howard the Master is reprinted again and again, few markets exist for new tales of barbarians and Atlanteans, Romans and Parthians, Egyptians and Conquistadors, swordsmen and sorcerers. That's why Anderson set aside the science fiction he was working on and wrote a Viking tale for this book, for us . . . for himself! That's why Wellman, one of my boyhood favorites, took time out from those totally different stories of the hill country he's been doing, to write one of the sort that thrilled me long ago — and still does. It is about the very last survivor of sunken Atlantis — and some giants who are *not* inimical, for a pleasant change.

Imagine my thrill at being able to tell these guys that a market existed and they were wanted and needed! Imagine my delight at writing out checks to them and to the others whose stories fill this book (with more words than the publisher asked for, meaning I overspent). Imagine my thrill at getting to read never-before published stories in this genre, fresh off the typewriter — free!

9

You know and I know that I didn't really bring Poul out of hf retirement — but I'm going to claim I did. In Manly's case it's true. In Proctor's case, I became his first s&s sale — from a Texan who should e'en now be measuring his shoulders for the mantle of Howard. Andre Norton had been sick and was behind in everything, and said no, and I asked three times. This overworked silver tongue prevailed: there will be a long Norton novelet in the second volume of this series. When we were in Providence, Rhode Island for the first World Fantasy Convention at which he won his overdue award, *Manly* asked *me, twice,* if he could do another story for Volume Two. "Yessir," I said, and probably genuflected. After all, the man was writing fiction before I was hatched and is two hundred and ninety-leben years old.

There are nine stories in this book, most of them novelets, a favorite length. You can get your teeth into the tale, live with it, and unlike all too many novels, it ends while your interest is still high. Two are definitely what I'd call "Howardesque"; two are sort-of; four are . . . *different.*

Let it be known that I asked four — no, five — women for tales of heroic fantasy with a female protagonist. None could or would. I think it can be done; I also think 999 out of a thousand *male* writers couldn't. (Though Anderson's novel *The Winter of the World* must have blown the minds of a lot of female chauvinist sows who thought they had him pegged!) Contributor Bruce Jones, who's scripted and drawn *Red Sonja* (among a lot of other things) for the Marvel line of magazines, has done all right, I think . . . for a male . . . .

Lord, I hope you like these stories; this book. I love 'em all; I even like the ones I turned down. If you do, talk it up, go back and buy another copy (frame the magnificent cover painting by another man who can't help himself; you don't want to deface *this* copy); we'll need the business in order for there to be a Volume Three.

Thanks, you nine writers. Thanks, readers. Thanks, Zebra Books. Thanks, Homeros of Chios — or Smyrna. Thanks, Robert Howard. And thanks, Roberta.

Introduction to "Nekht Semerkeht"
by Robert E. Howard & Andrew J. Offutt

It is all too well known that after ten or so years of creating such marvelously enduring characters as Conan and Kull and Solomon Kane and Cormac mac Art and Francis X. Gordon, Robert E. Howard shot himself to death in 1936.

Over the years his popularity has risen and expand-ed until many people have realized more profit from Conan the Cimmerian than Howard ever did. New Howard manuscripts and partial mss have persisted in turning up until some wonder aloud if Glenn Lord, the man who acts on behalf of the Howard literary estate, is secretly writing the partials in the sub-basement of a vast dark castle in Pasadena, Texas, which is so unlikely-named a town that Lord must have made it up.

It isn't true. Like all of us, Howard outlined, partially outlined, began, and even first-drafted all sorts of stories that he never finished. The tale that follows is one such. Partway through the original ms, it becomes first draft; a couple of pages later it becomes little more than outline. Nor was it titled. It's possible REH would have called it The Feeders from the Sky *or* North of the Rio Grande *or* Black Pits of Tlasceltec. *My job, accepted as an honor and a delight, was to edit-revise where necessary and, in accord with the brief outline, finish the story. It's Howard's plot. Most of it is Howard's writing.*

I admit to you that I might well have sliced a chunk of the longish philosophizing just after the opening action scene. But there is a reason it belongs there intact, in REH's words.

In a letter to August Derleth dated May 9, 1936, Howard expressed his sympathy for recent deaths in Derleth's family and went on: "When a man dies young he misses much suffering, but the old have only life as a possession and somehow to me the tearing of a pitiful remnant from weak old fingers is more tragic than the looting of life in its rich full prime. I don't want to live to be old. I want to die when my time comes, quickly and suddenly, in the full tide of my strength and health."

In that same letter he confessed that "I haven't written a weird story for nearly a year, though I've been contemplating one dealing with Coronado's expedition on the Staked Plains in 1541."

13

He soon began that story, in a dark mood, and he wrote in a great deal about instinct and the reason for seeking to live on and on. He never finished the story, probably the last one he ever worked on. Well before that year was out, he had killed himself . . . in the full tide of his strength and health.

Dear God I hope this is close to the way he'd have done it.

NEKHT SEMERKEHT
by
Robert E. Howard and Andrew J. Offutt

"And what I am sure of is that there is not any gold or any other metal in that country." —Coronado

The snap of a bowstring broke the stillness, and was followed by the shrill scream of a horse death-stricken. The Spanish animal reared, the feathered end of the arrow quivering high behind its foreleg, and went down in a headlong plunge. Its rider sprang free as it fell, to alight on his feet with a dry clang of steel. He staggered, empty hands flung wide, fighting to regain his balance. His matchlock had fallen several feet away and the match had gone out.

15

He drew his broadsword and looked about him, trying to locate the beady black eyes he knew glittered at him from somewhere in the close-set greasewood bushes that edged the rim of the dry wash to his left. Even as he sought the slayer of his steed, the man appeared — he rose erect and sprang over a low shrub almost in one movement. A vengeful yell of triumph quivered in the late afternoon stillness.

An instant they faced one another, separated by more than the fifty foot stretch of tawny sand — the New World and the Old personified in the two men.

About them, from horizon to horizon, the naked plains swept away and away to mingle in the faint ocean-like haze that hovered along the turquoise rim of the sky. No bird cried, no beast moved. The dead horse lay motionless. In all that vast expanse these two men were the only living, sentient beings; the tall, grey-bearded man in tarnished steel and the copper-skinned brave naked in his beaded loin-clout, black eyes burning redly under the square-cut bang of his black mane.

Those fierce eyes flickered toward the matchlock, lying out of reach and useless, and the red glints grew more lurid. The Chiricahua — known to the Spaniards as *llanero*, plainsmen, had learned the deadliness of the "white" men's guns. But now he was sure the advantage was with him. His left hand gripped a short, stout bow of bois d'arc, backed with sinew; in his right was the flint-headed arrow of dogwood. The stone-headed hatchet remained at his girdle; he had no intention of coming within the sweep of the long sword that glimmered dully in the rays of the westering sun.

For an instant the tableau held motionless, while he swept his fierce gaze over his enemy. He knew flint darts would splinter on the white man's armour — but no vizor covered the bearded face. Yet, he was unwilling to waste a single arrow, each of which represented hours of tedious toil.

Cat-like he glided toward his prey, not in a straight line but springing lightly from side to side, to confuse the other, to make him shift his position and so catch him at the end of a motion, where he could not dodge the leap of winged death at him. The brave did not fear a sudden sword-swinging rush. The steel-clad man could never match his own fleetness of foot. The white was at his mercy and he could kill in his own way, without risk.

With a short fierce cry he stopped short, whipped up the bow and jerked back the arrow — just as the white man plucked a pistol from his belt and fired point-blank.

The arrow whined erratically skyward. The bow slipped from the warrior's hands as he went to his knees, choking. Blood gushed between the fingers that clutched at his muscular breast. He sank down in the sand, still glaring his hate. Glazing eyes fixed on his slayer in a last spasm of despairing hatred. The white man had always something in reserve, something unknown and unguessed. The warrior saw the armored man looming above him like a grim god of steel, implacable and unconquerable, with bleak and pitiless eyes. In that gleaming figure the brave read the ultimate doom of his entire race.

Weakly, as a dying snake hisses, he reared his head, spat at his slayer, and slid back dead.

Hernando de Guzman sheathed his sword. He reloaded the clumsy wheel-lock pistol and replaced it beside its mate, reflecting briefly that it was well for

17

him that this particular *llanero* had not been familiar with the shorter arms.

The Spaniard sighed as he looked down at his dead horse. Like many of his race, he had a fondness for fine horses and displayed toward them a kindliness he seldom showed to human beings — if ever. He made no move to secure the ornately decorated saddle and bridle. In the miles he must cover, afoot now, he would find exhaustion enough without further burdening himself. The matchlock he secured. With it resting on his shoulder he stood motionless, seeking to orient himself.

A feeling that he was already lost had been tugging at him for the last hour, even with his horse under him. Veteran though he was, Hernando de Guzman had wandered farther afield than was wise, in vain pursuit of an antelope whose flaring white scud, gleaming in the sunlight, had led him like a will-o'-the-wisp over sand hills and prairie. He had tried to keep the location of the camp in his mind. He feared that he had failed; no landmarks interrupted these plains that swept without break from sunrise to sunset. An expedition, driving its own sustenance on the hoof, was like a ship groping its way across an unknown sea, its only chance of survival resting in its self-sufficiency. A lone rider was like a man adrift in an open boat, without food or water or compass. And a man *afoot* ...

A man alone and afoot was as good as dead, unless he could swiftly reach his companions. Briefly exploring the shallow gully in hopes of finding a horse, de Guzman knew he could not. The Chiricahua had not taken to horse-riding. Steeds strayed or stolen from the Spaniards were used as food, though Hernando had heard of a terrible tribe to the north whose warriors were already horsemen.

18

Choosing the direction he hoped was right, he took up his march. Lifting his morion, he ran his fingers through damp, greying locks, but the heat of the sun made him replace it. Years of wearing armor had accustomed him to the weight and heat of the steel that encased him. Later it would add to his weariness, but it might stand him in good stead if he met other roaming warriors of the plains. The presence of the lone brave he had slain proved that a whole clan abode somewhere in the vicinity.

The sun dipped toward the western horizon. Across its staring red eye he moved, a pigmy in the midst of the illimitable plain that mocked him in its grim vastness and silence. De Guzman walked.

The sun seemed to poise on the desert rim before it rushed from sight and sent a thin streamer of crimson running north and south around the horizon. The sky seemed to expand, to deepen with the sunset. Already in the east the hot volcanic blue was paling to the steel of Toledo swords.

De Guzman stopped and dropped the butt of his matchlock to the earth. It rang on that hard ground, and left no imprint. When he looked back the way he'd come, he was unable to trace his own route over the short springy grass. He had left no footprints. He might have been a phantom, drifting futilely across a sleeping, indifferent land. The plains were impervious to human efforts. Man left no trace on them; he marched, fought, struggled and died cursing the gods that betrayed him — but the plains dreamed on, with no more trace of his passing than he left on the surface of the sea.

"Gold," muttered de Guzman, and he laughed sardonically.

He had come a long way since his horse fell. If he

19

were going in the right direction, he'd have approached the camp near enough to hear the shots the men would be firing to guide him back. He heard nothing. He was lost. He knew not in which direction to turn. The plains had claimed him for their own. His bones, bred of the wheat and oil and wind of Old Spain, would bleach on the dreary expanse with the bones of the Chiricahua and horse, coyote and rattlesnake.

I am dead.

The thought stirred in him no religious or senti-mental horror. Spain was far away, a dream-like memory, a land of Cockaigne that had once been real, in the golden glow of youth and desire, but now had no more reality than a ghost-continent lost in a sea of mist.

"Spanish blood's no more sacred than any other," he muttered.

Aye. Blood was only blood, and he had seen oceans of it spilled: Spanish blood, English blood, Huguenot blood, Inca blood and Aztec, the royal but hardly purple blood of Montezuma dripping from the parapets of Tenochtitlan . . . blood running ankle-deep in the plaza of Cajamarca, about the slipping, frantic feet of doomed Atahualpa.

But the will to live burned fiercely in de Guzman's breast, the blind black instinct toward life that had no relation to intellect or reason. As such, de Guzman recognized and obeyed it. He had taken many lives; he strove to keep his own, this man who had no illusions concerning existence. He knew what all men knew who had bared its core, and he licked his lips and said it now, for no ears save his own:

"The game is not worth the candle."

We men rationalize the blind instinct of self-preser-

vation and we build glib air-castles to explain why it is better to live than to die, while our boasted — but ignored! — intellect is in every phase a negation of life! Ah, but how we civilized men hate and fear our "animal" instincts! As we hate and fear every heritage from the blind, squalling pit of primordial beginnings that bred us.

Dogs, apes, even elephants, he knew, obeyed instincts and lived only because instinct bade them. De Guzman had kept to himself what he had long since decided: Man's urge toward life was no less blind and reasonless. But, abhorring his kinship with those creatures that had the misfortune not to be made in the Deity's image — having no prophets to declare it! — he fondled his favorite delusion.

Oh, of course we are guided solely by reason, even when reason tells us it is better to die than to live! It is not the intellect we boast that bids us live — and kill to live — but the blind unreasoning beast-instinct.

Hernando de Guzman did not try to deceive himself into believing there was some intellectual reason, then, why he should not give up the agonizing struggle and place the muzzle of his pistol to his head; quit an existence whose savor had long ago become less than its pain. Mother of God, if by some miracle I find my way back to Coronado's camp and even at last to Mexico or fabled Quivira . . . there is no reason, none, to believe life would be any less sordid or more desirable than it was before I came tramping northward in search of the Seven Cities of Gold.

"Gold," he muttered again, with a satiric twist of lip. A scar writhed on his sun-darkened face. "The gold we seek is death!"

But . . . that blind instinct bade him fight for life,

21

strive on to its last gagging gasp, to live in spite of hell or the actions of his fellow men. It burned as strongly in this man's powerful body now as it had in that long-past youth when he'd fought shoulder-to-shoulder with black-hearted Cortez and saw the plumed hordes of Montezuma roll in like a wave to engulf the desperate handful that defied them — and stole their lives.

"To live!" de Guzman challenged, lifting a fist whose bony knuckles were accustomed to jutting about a weapon for the slaying of men. "To live! Not for love, not for profit, or ambition, or a *cause!*" He spat, for all those noble concepts were wisps of mist, phantoms conjured up by men to explain the unexplainable. To *live*, because in his being there was implanted (too deeply) a blind dark urge to live, and he knew that it was in itself question and answer, desire and goal, beginning and end, and the answer to all the riddles of the universe.

"The game's not worth the candle! Ah . . . but to keep it lit . . . "

The Conquistador laughed sardonically, and shouldered his matchlock, and prepared to take up his futile march — into ultimate oblivion and silence.

It was then that he heard the drum.

Even, deliberate, unhurried, the drum's hollow voice rolled across the plain, mellow as the booming of waves of wine on a golden coast.

De Guzman paused, poised, an image of steel as he strained his ears. The sound came from the east, he decided — and it was no *llanero* drum! No, this was exotic, *alien*, like a drum he had heard that night he'd stood on a flat roof in Cajamarca and watched the myriad fires that were the great Inca army, twinkling

22

through the night — while nearby the passionless voice of Bastard Pizarro spun black webs of treachery and infamy.

He closed his eyes, rubbed a hand across them; opened them. Listened with his head tilted sidewise, wondering if the heat and silence were already melting his brain and giving birth to phantasies . . .

No! This was no mirage framed in sound. Steady as the pulse in his own temple it throbbed and throbbed. The sound touched obscure chords in his brain until his whole being thrummed with that call of mystery. For a moment dead ashes flickered into flame, as if his youth were for the moment revived. Encompassed in that mellow sound were allure and . . . magic. For the moment he felt again as he had so long ago when with hot eager hands he gripped a ship's rail and watched the fabled golden coast of Mexico loom out of the morning mist, calling him with the lure of adventure and plunder that was like the blast of a trumpet of gold, ringing down the wind.

The moment passed, but a pulse in his temple beat swift staccato so that Hernando laughed at himself. Without pausing to argue the matter inwardly, he turned and strode eastward, toward the sound of the drum.

The sun had set; the brief twilight of the plains glowed and faded. The stars blinked forth, great white, cold stars, indifferent to the tiny shining figure plodding across the shadowless vastness. The sparse bushes crouched like nameless beasts waiting for the wanderer to stumble and fall. The drum pulsed steadily on and on, booming golden wavelets of sound across the wasteland. It roused memories, long faded and alien, of exotic flaming gardens of great blossoms, steaming jungles, tinkling fountains . . . and always an undertone of golden drops tinkling on an aureate paving.

Gold!

Again he was following its siren call; the same, old, threadbare quest that had led him around the world over resentful seas, through worse jungles, and through the smoke and flame of butchered cities. Like Coronado, sleeping somewhere on this endless plain and wrapped in fantastic dreams, de Guzman was following the call of gold — and one as tangible as that which maddened Francisco's dreams.

Mad Francisco! Seeking vainly for the cities of Cibolo, with lofty manses and glittering treasures, where even the slaves eat from golden dishes! De Guzman's parched, thirst-swollen lips smiled bitterly. In future years, he reflected, Coronado must become a symbol for the chasing of will-o'-the-wisps. Historians yet unborn, wise with the arrogant wisdom of hindsight, would mock him for a visionary and a fool. *His name will become a taunt for treasure-seekers.*

Why? With what reason? Why should we Spaniards not search for gold in this land north of the Rio Grande? Why refuse to credit the story of Cibolo? They are no more incredible than the tales of Mexico were, less than a generation ago. As much reason to believe in Cibolo as there was to believe that Peru existed, before Pizarro sailed! But . . . the world judges by failure or success. Coronado is of that same hard-headed breed as Pizarro and Cortez . . . and me. But they found gold, and will go down in history as — what? Robbers and plunderers? Coronado has found no gold and will be remembered as a credulous visionary and believer in myths, a chaser of nonexistent rainbows.

Unless he finds it!

24

De Guzman laughed, laughed as he strode, and his laughter was not pleasant, for it embodied his personal opinion of the human race, which was not flattering.

Through the night he walked, following the mellow booming of the drum that should not have been. It grew subtly louder as he paced on.

The small hours of morning found his feet weighted not with steel but with lead and sleep filling his eyes like dust so that he must blink constantly. But he was aware of a vague bulk looming among the stars on the eastern horizon. Lights twinkled that might have been stars, but that he believed to be fires. Nor was the drum far off now; he caught minor notes and undertones he had not heard before. Too there were strange soft rustlings and murmurings, like the swish of the skirts of the cacao-eyed Aztec women, or the low soft gurglings of their laughter that tinkled among the silvery fountains in the gardens of Tenochtitlan before Spanish swords reddened those gardens with fountains of blood. Why should a drum speak with such voices in this naked, northern land, bringing the lures and mysteries of the faraway south?

On either hand now he could make out the faint outlines of a long ridge. He had made a slow gradual descent, barely aware. He knew that he had entered a broad and shallow valley, probably one marking the course of a sunken river. The ridges drew nearer as he advanced, and their height increased.

Just before dawn he stumbled upon a small stream that ran southeastward as all streams seemed to run, in this land. Willows and cottonwoods among straggling bushes grew thick along the banks. The weary Spaniard drank deeply and lay there near the water's edge, waiting for dawn. Once more the drum pulsed — and

25

ceased. A single watch-fire now twinkled amid the dark bulk before him. Silence lay over this ancient unknown land north of the Rio Grande.

With the first streak of milky light in the east, de Guzman stared up at the towers and flat roofs of a walled city. Though he had roamed too far and seen too many incredible sights to be greatly surprised at anything, he lay there wondering at the fantastic sight. A *walled . . . city!*

It was built of adobe, like the pueblos far to the west, but there the resemblance ended. These walls were sheathed in an enamel-like glaze that was decorated with intricate designs in blue and purple and crimson. Though the city was not large in extent, the houses, three or four stories in height, did not resemble the beehive huts of the pueblos. The whole city was dominated by a towering structure that gleamed in the dawn-light. Atop it a truly enormous gong imitated the sun while reflecting its rays in a blaze of yellow fire. That structure was similar to a teocalla, save that it was topped by a dome.

De Guzman blinked at that. He had seen nothing like it, in Peru or Yucatan or Mexico. The architecture of the whole city was baffling, obviously allied to that of the Aztecs and yet curiously unlike, as if Aztec hands had reared what an alien brain conceived.

The incredible city rose in a broad fan-shaped valley, which narrowed and deepened to the east — or rather the cliffs reared higher, for the valley floor remained level. Thousands and perhaps millions of years ago a great river had sliced its channel through the plain and plunged out of sight to leave the V-shaped valley. Cliffs walled it on three sides and towered steeply at their apex. The city faced eastward, toward the valley's broad mouth, where the ridges diminished until they vanished.

Wondering, de Guzman studied the whole of city and valley with a soldier's gaze. Any enemy must approach from the west — but there was no barrier to guard the city in that direction, where the dwindling ridges were more than a mile apart. The stream entered the broad mouth and wound past the walls at a distance of a few hundred yards, before it plunged into a cavern in the cliff. Beyond the city, to the southeast, it wriggled through a checkerboard of irrigated fields in which he recognized maize, grapes, berries, melons, and nut-trees. The soil of these barren plains was fertile, needing only water to produce food in abundance. And here there was water.

His gaze swerved when a small gate opened in the city's southeast wall. Smallish brown people emerged to enter the fields for the day's work, well-formed men clad in loincloths and women whose short sleeveless tunics left bare the left breast and fell scarcely below mid-thigh.

As he lay watching, the Spaniard heard a rumbling to the west. It was a sound he knew. Jerking his head about to peer through the intertwining willows, he saw a cloud of dust rising in the valley's mouth. Within the dust, a long low black line grew rapidly as it advanced. The line became a swiftly rolling mass that he soon saw was formed of shaggy dark animals with huge, horned heads. It was a stampede of the plains cattle, buffalo! The fieldworkers ran for the gate, which swung open to receive them. The beasts plunged on blindly, perhaps a thousand of them. Heads appeared along the walls of the city. A trumpet blared brazenly. De Guzman frowned. He had seen buffalo stampede — but never to charge so blindly toward rearing walls!

Three hundred yards from those walls, the animal horde split as on an unseen barrier to flow away to the north and south. Some crashed through the willows and splashed madly across the stream, though not near the unseen watcher. And then he saw the cause of the stampede. Man!

The beasts' dividing unmasked Chiricahua, *llaneros*; surely they numbered three hundred in their warpaint, all bearing bows or lances in addition to knives and a few war clubs. These fleet barbarians had driven the bison before them and, running behind and among them fleet-footed and untiring as wolves, had used the galloping herd as their cover to come within bow-shot of the city.

De Guzman was very glad he had kept his cover in the bushes among the willows.

Yelling barbarically the nigh-naked men raced for the gate, with a recklessness he did not associate with their clan. *Drugged with* tizwin, *sure*, he mused, watching the ferocious attack through narrowed eyes hard as black diamonds. But . . . why was there no shower of arrows from the wall, no shouted alarums? Not so much as one arrow keened to meet the shrieking plainsmen.

Then . . . from those shining walls . . . *something* came, and a cold hand seemed to trail its fingers up de Guzman's spine. A shifting, writhing cloud of some eerie bluish *mist* rolled over the wall's top. It lowered at once, like a great bird swooping on prey. As if possessed of eyes and some impossible intelligence, it floated out and down over the charging Chiricahua.

Pale blue mist settled over the warriors like the sky descending in a pale shroud.

Where there had been the shrieking of warcries, silence closed like a fist. The sudden quiet was no less eerie than the mist itself. De Guzman gritted his teeth and did not realize he was holding his breath in the absolute funereal silence. He stared, nape prickling, seeing naught but the eddying, roiling, pale blue . . .

The azure mist dispersed. He saw them again. Fifteen score ruddy-skinned men of the plains, seconds ago war-yelling and blood-mad, lay now where they had fallen almost instantly under the cloud. Naked bodies gleamed like copper in the rising sun; feathers stirred forlornly in a slight breeze.

The mist returned to the city like a heeling dog once the hunt was done.

The flesh of Hernando de Guzman crawled. Sweat was a clammy chill within his armor. A *mist* . . . three hundred men . . . three hundred corpses. *This was necromancy!*

Now, stately men came calmly from the city's gate onto that plain of silent death. Tall and sinewy they were, with plumes nodding above their helmets. Loinclouts that were oddly *pleated* stirred as the men walked so that beadwork caught the sunlight in constant flashes. Staring, de Guzman felt the old blood-stir of the Conquistador, for those strange helms gleamed in the sun, too . . . shining as only pure gold could glint!

With businesslike efficiency, the tall warriors fastened ropes to the heels of the fallen braves. All were dragged into the city, a process that consumed two hours or more. De Guzman's stomach rumbled as the great gates closed. The small one opened. Again the workers entered the fields. Hernando de Guzman lay among the willows, pondering.

Necromancy.

And gold.

He had slaked his thirst, aye — but he was ravenously hungry. Yet he hesitated to reveal himself to these people, who were manifestly possessed of some gift of the devil. Though the Spaniard had long doubted the existence of a Lord of Evil, he recognized diabolatry when he saw it. He lay still, pondering.

Despite all, he was still weary from yesterday's travails. He slept.

He awoke with a start.

A girl or young woman had parted the willows and was gazing down at him from wide eyes the color of that drink wealthier Aztecs had made of the shiny brown cacao beans. Though she was clad only in the scanty white tunic of the field hands, it seemed *wrong* on her; she seemed not the sort of woman who should be wearing so lowly a garment. Surely rustly silks and scintillant jewels were more appropriate to her tallish, well formed body. The scanty tunic she wore left few of her generous contours wholly concealed. About her was an Aztec look . . . *Aztec? Here?*

De Guzman felt a quickening of his pulse as he had when he saw the gold helmets of her strange city. The grey in his beard was no indication of the fire that burned in the Conquistador's veins. This vision from the unknown city of sorcerous death was not unlike the strange, exotic women who had intoxicated him in his youth, when he first followed the iron captains to hot, unknown lands.

Stammering in her surprise, she spoke: "Wh- who are you?"

30

She spoke in the language of the people of Quetzl-coatl, of people well south of here, though he only just recognized it in its alien enunciations. Splinter city of the Aztecs? The mother city of the Aztecs?

The grey in de Guzman's beard was also no indication of his reflexes or swiftness. He was on his feet in an instant, armor and all, and his hand closed on her wrist even as she began to recoil. Her water jar dropped. The young woman stared up at him, wide dark eyes mirroring amazement more than fear.

A subtle perfume filled his nostrils and his head reeled — momentarily, for de Guzman controlled de Guzman. "How is it such a woman as you labors in the fields?"

Either his faulty, badly-pronounced Aztec was not clear to her or she ignored his question. "I know what manner of man you are! You are of those who slew Montezuma and destroyed his kingdom . . . one of those who ride beasts called . . . horses, and make thunder and red flame of death flash out of a metal war-club!"

Eager fingers traced over his dented breastplate. Her touch on his bearded face sent tingles of pleasure through his iron frame. But he smiled a sardonic smile. *What new thing is there for me to learn about women, who cannot remember how many these arms have held?* Yet his instincts drew him to her, and he neither resisted nor questioned them.

"Word came here," she said, in the soft voice of recollection, staring at his cuirass. "Word of the slaughter south, in Mexico . . . I was but a baby then. Men doubted . . . but no more tribute came from Montezuma, and —"

"*Tribute!*" The word was startled from him.

31

"Tribute? From Montezuma, the emperor of all Mexico?"

"Aye. He and his fathers paid tribute to *Nekht Semerkeht* for long centuries . . . slaves, gold, pelts."

"Nekht Semerkeht?"

It had a strange, alien ring, this name that was not Aztec. Surely he had heard it afore . . . where? When? Dimly, its echo reverberated in the shadowy halls and recesses of de Guzman's mind. An association flickered: the harsh odor of gunpowder and the reek of spilt blood.

"I have seen men like you!" she was saying, "When I was ten, I wandered outside the city and the Chiricahua captured me." She heaved a pensive sigh and her left breast shuddered. De Guzman gritted his teeth. "They sold me to the Lipans, who traded me to the Karankawas — they dwelt on the coast far to the south, and are cannibals. Once a great war-canoe with wings came gliding along the coast, and the Karankawa braves went forth in their dugouts and loosed arrows at it. There were men on deck, like you. I remember! They turned great hollow logs of metal toward the canoes and thundered them into pieces. I was confused and terrified, and I ran away. I came to a camp of the Tonkewas, who brought me home again — for they are our servants." She gazed into his eyes. "What — is your name, man of metal? Now I see you are not *all* metal, as I thought then . . . "

He told her and listened to her turn his name about her tongue, lisping in her attempts at pronouncing the words.

"And who are you?" he demanded. He had not released her wrist; now his steel-sheathed arm slipped about her supple waist. She started and made to draw away, but could not without a struggle; she did not struggle. *A clever girl,* he mused.

"My name is Nezahualca," she said, and with hauteur, "I am a princess."

"Oh?" He covered his amusement. "What are you doing in slave's clothing?" he asked, plucking at the garment as if to call her attention to it. Having thus lifted the tiny skirt, he held back his smile — and left his hand where it was.

Fine dark eyes filled suddenly with tears, and she spoke to his chest. "I forgot. I am a slave, a toiler in the fields — I bear the marks of the overseer's whip!" She turned lithely and wriggled, as if to show him. "I, the daughter of kings, whipped like a common slave!"

Staring at the flesh she exhibited, de Guzman saw no weals. *She knows what she's about,* he mused, *and a boy would be taken in.* Good! Perhaps this clever slave-princess was as much the opportunist as he was.

She swung back to speak rapidly, passionately. "Listen, Ernano d'goozm. I, Nezahualca, am daughter of a line of kings. Nekht Semerkeht rules in Tlasceltec, and below him reigns the governor — the *tlacatecatl,* Lord of the Fighting Men. My lover Acampichtli was an officer in his command. It was my desire that Acampichtli become governor, naturally."

De Guzman nodded. *Naturally. So you schemed* . . .

"We intrigued. I have — I *had* power here in Tlasceltec. But *Nekht Semerkeht* learned, and was not pleased; *he* must choose who rules, *under* him. My lover was given to the Feeders From The Sky. I was degraded thus, to the status of a public slave, like the Totonacs my ancestors brought with them centuries ago when they came northward."

33

Ah. Her people were *Aztecs, then. They came up here, long ago — centuries!*

"*Nekht Semerkeht* came to Tenochtitlan centuries and centuries ago. He reigned there for a space, then gathered together many of the recently wedded young people and brought them far north, here to found this city."

"About which those left in Tenochtitlan were far from happy!"

"At the loss of fighting men, aye. But the king was again king in Tenochtitlan, Ernano d'goozm. For *Nekht Semerkeht ruled* there — *he is powerful.*"

"Call me Hernan-Do . . ." He trailed off. Now he remembered where he'd heard that strangely alien name!

Nekht Semerkeht! A cry from the blood-bubbling lips of an Aztec priest as he fell in the darkness during the terrible battle on *noche triste.* It was as if in his last extremity, desperate, he invoked a demon or devil rather than a god. De Guzman remembered, too, the vague references far to the north . . . here! He'd assumed it was from such tales had grown the stories of Cibolo. And he had thought it mere legend! But . . . the name was not Aztec.

"Who is Nekht Semerkeht?" He added "Princess Nezahualca" to please and win her.

She gestured vaguely, eastward. "He came from the blue ocean, long ago. He is a mighty mage, mightier than the priest of the Toltecs. Alone he came, but soon he was ruler of Mexico! Yet he wanted his own city, and he came north to — ah! Listen to me, iron man!" Very excitedly:

"*Nekht Semerkeht* does not know of your race! Even his magic cannot prevail against the thunder

34

of your war-club. Help me to slay him, him who has ruled *generations*. I am who I . . . was, and warriors there are who will still follow me. I can gather a few in a chamber of the temple, and open a gate to you in the night, and lead you into the temple. The sub-overseer who guards the slaves at night is a young man, and he loves me. He will do anything I ask. Together, you and I . . ."

He nodded. De Guzman recognized the loud knock of opportunity, and he knew when to open wide the door to it. If he took time to give it thought, his head would swim. "Aye," he said. "But bring me food." It was a brief test, his peremptory "command." *The iron war-club will hold a princess in line as well as a mage . . . little girl!*

She blinked, stiffened slightly — and nodded. "I will leave food among the bushes. Now I must get water and return to the gardens before I am missed."

"And does Nezahualca love this young man who loves her?" he asked, tugging her a bit closer. *A daughter of kings, eh . . . and golden helmets!*

She spoke evenly, gazing into his eyes, her bosom against his armor. "Nezahualca would be princess again . . . no! *Queen*, of Tlasceltec! And beside her will be the most powerful man in Tlasceltec; he who rids the city of *Nekht Semerkeht.*"

He gave her wrist a final squeeze. "Aye. Bring the food, Queen-to-be. And show me which gate."

"It must be the slave gate," she said, and when he sighed, she gave him a slow, level-eyed smile. "Once, Hernando, you shall enter by the Gate of Slaves. And so shall I, *once* more!"

All that day he lay hidden among the bushes beneath the willows, and he had much to think on, while he saw to his weapons. For two reasons he waited until well after dark to be sure he was not seen, and to give her time to grow apprehensive lest he not come. Nezahualca needed him, as he needed her, for once the mage met his belated end she would be the symbol of power here . . . *the power I will hold!*

He watched cloud and moon approach each other with the patience of a warrior with much scarlet past, and — now — a golden future. Then the moon swam in a cloud, and across the silent gardens ghosted one lone man until he came to the Gate of Slaves. Little more than a door in the wall, it opened at once to his tap. He smiled inwardly at that — but noted her control too. Limned in the faint flow of a tiny hand-cresset, dressed for the last time in her scanty garment, she made no mention of her long wait. Beside her was a young man, little more than a boy, and de Guzman recognized the trappings of a sub-overseer.

Nezahualca caught his hand in slim fingers; his armored gloves were in his belt. "Come! My warriors wait!" She gave him the briefest of introductions to Chaculcun.

Our *warriors wait,* de Guzman mused, but said nothing. She led him through narrow streets and shadowy courtyards to a side door in the great temple that gleamed in the moonlight like the outer walls. Along a dark corridor they moved then, until they came to a dim-lit chamber. Ten men waited — in complete silence.

Nezahualca's sharp cry broke the stillness. De Guzman saw, too; each of the ten warriors of Tlasceltec sat

36

rigid in his chair, staring at nothing . . . with unseeing eyes. "They're —"

The glim was extinguished by a puff of air from no visible source. Dim as the room had been, now it was in total darkness. De Guzman heard Chaculcun's gasp just before Nezahualca shrieked. The Spaniard reached for her — and a strong jerk tore his matchlock from his hand. A curse escaped the startled man but like a cat he flowed aside, at the same time unsheathing his sword with a steely scrape in the blackness. He stood tense and waiting in complete silence and darkness.

Those ten men are dead, Hernando thought, striving to be trebly alert in all senses. *I've seen enough dead men to know. But . . . I saw no marks . . .*

A small hand touched his. Instantly his other arm rose, but he arrested the automatic sword-slash; this was a woman's slim hand. The fingers closed supplely about his. He followed their gentle tug, gliding as noiselessly as possible in his armor. His guide made no sound, not even the whisper of feet on stone. The Spaniard kept his sword ready, but close to his body that it might noisily strike no wall. Through a doorway he was led; along a corridor in which his own *clink-clink* sounds seemed ghostly and thunderous. On he was conducted, and on . . .

From well behind him, a woman screamed out a stricken cry that echoed along stone-lined corridors. The voice was Nezahualca's.

Smitten by a grisly thought, de Guzman turned his wrist and ran his fingers along the wrist of his guide's hand. Soft, smooth womanly wrist . . . gave way a few inches above to a hairy, wiry arm! Even as he shuddered the treacherous fingers tightened on his,

37

with terrible strength. A peal of demoniac laughter clove the air and ululated along the corridor. De Guzman's hair stirred beneath his helm.

Gagging with horror, he swept his blade around to smite blindly with all his strength. Instinct guided the blade, and the horrid guffaw broke off into an agonized gurgle. The fingers leaped reflexively from his wrist and *something* thrashed and flopped in the darkness at his feet.

The Spaniard turned hurriedly back, his flesh crawling. That nameless abomination with the delicately slim hands of a woman had not been leading him anywhere he wished to be. His sword scraping the wall to his right and his hand trailing along it on the left, he moved back along the pitch-black corridor. His sword found space; he turned that way. Soon his hand slipped from stone onto what felt like metal, and he found a door. It opened easily. The faintest glimmer of far-off light led him to his left.

Realizing he'd be able to see any approach, he sheathed his sword as he walked. He drew both pistols. Into growing illumination he strode, until he emerged onto a sort of gallery overlooking a large chamber at a lower level. At a wooden rail, he looked down to where a voice rose, dry and passionless as mummy's dust.

A canopy and back hid the occupant of a throne of deepest midnight ebony, but he knew someone — or something — sat there, speaking. His or its minions had worked swiftly, for here too were Chaculcun and Nezahualca. Stark naked, the young man hung suspended from a golden chain that was attached to the ceiling and to gyves on his ankles. Immediately beneath him, a gold brazier huffed up clouds of azure mist that from time to time obscured him to the waist.

De Guzman's teeth grated; he knew that mist, and thought he knew now why Nezahualca's warriors were dead, without marks.

She lay face up on a gem-encrusted altar of gold, spreadeagled in a supine X, and she was as naked as the youth who had loved her. Slender gold chains confined her wrists and ankles. Dilated with fear, her lovely eyes stared wildly upward. The Spaniard saw that directly above her a circular opening holed the great chamber's dome to reveal a disk of blue-black night sky besprent with stars.

From the black throne the voice spoke without passion; calm it was, and merciless its words. "You were a fool to place trust in some outlander with his little thunder-stave. Its power is less than mine by many times, silly little slave who was a princess. He was easily bereft of his thunder-club, and a child of darkness has by now led him to the pit of the rattle-snakes. All for naught, silly little Neza. You had your life, and easy work in the fields; now your flesh will provide a delicacy for the Feeders From The Sky."

An awful cry of despair and fear broke from the young woman's throat.

De Guzman glanced about, backed from the rail, and hurried to the stairway down. He descended with each hand clamped around a pistol. As he reached the lower landing, he heard Nezahualca's awful cry, and a sound like that of a sail in the wind — or the dry rustle of great wings. The Conquistador hurried to an arched doorway.

Mother of God! He was staring at a nightmare

39

shape that had descended through the orifice in the dome. This awful dragon-like monster from the air's upper reaches was too obviously the source, in its millennia of raids on these lower levels, of the grisly tales of vampires and harpies. Aye, it was as Coronado insisted: all legends have their roots in fact.

It looks mortal enough, de Guzman thought. He stepped through the archway and took aim, using the pistol in his left hand, since there was time: the darkling bloodsucker with its fifteen-foot wings was staring down at its intended victim, as a man looks upon a particularly fine cut of meat set before him. The pistol's roar was as of ten in the stone-walled chamber . . . and as effective. Its head blasted, the monster reeled. One claw tore the naked skin of the young woman's upper thigh. Then the Feeder From The Sky slipped, shuddered, and tumbled to the floor,

Without pausing, de Guzman half-wheeled to face the canopied ebon throne.

A man had risen from the seat of blackness. Though the Conquistador had slain two grotesque monstrosities this night and fully expected to see another, his flesh crawled. The man was *old* . . . but de Guzman's shudder and swallow were in reaction to the sheer ages-old but ageless *evil* in the luminous dark eyes.

"Well-done," the robed man said calmly, *"fool!* Soon others will come flapping from the sky — to find your pulsing jugular awaiting them!"

De Guzman knew this man was many centuries old, and evil by nature and desire, and possessed furthermore of arcane powers — and his long bony hand was rising . . .

40

"This fool has two pistols," de Guzman said, and fired point-blank.

Nekht Semerkeht reeled with a choking cry and the rising hand ceased its gesture to clutch at his chest. As he staggered back, dread eyes staring in shock at the Spaniard, the latter marveled at the ease of his quest and his chore. Then Nekht Semerkeht vanished, *into the wall.*

While de Guzman stared at the blank wall that had swallowed his enemy, Nezahualca called out weakly. Instantly the Spaniard gave his head a jerk and sprang to the altar. A glance upward showed him more than one shape wheeling downward betwixt him and the stars. His hands trembled while he loosed chains of solid gold, noting that her thigh's blood had crusted already; the claw-cut was not deep.

"What makes that mist?" he demanded, as she sat up.

"*Hurry!* He's escaped through his private passage, and others come!" she said in the voice of a frightened child, and only after he had shaken her violently did she point at a great hamper. "The dust, in that — a handful slays an army!"

"*Move,* girl," he bade her, and moments later he was upending the hamper into the golden brazier beneath Chaculcun's corpse. "Those bloodsucking devils will find a fine surprise this time, rather than a feast. Now — lead me to him!"

"This way," she called, taking up a cresset. "Hurry!"

Without a backward glance at the man who had loved her and was dead amid a vast new cloud of azure mist, she led de Guzman from the chamber. He paused to slam a huge brazen door before following through strange corridors that were Aztec and yet

41

not *quite* Aztec. Their emergence into a long, broad hall brought him to a halt. He stared.

The long walls were lined with the upright bodies of men, not statues, though they were surely of stone. Toltecs there were, Aztecs, Totonacs, Tonkewas and Lipans and the Chiricahua of the plains, as well as warriors of tribes unfamiliar to the Spaniard; plumed men he knew instinctively had lived and died before the father of the father of Montezuma, perhaps earlier than the days of the Cid.

Presiding over them all in this eerie place was the huge seated statue of a man whose head seemed to combine the features and shape of both pig and donkey. And before and beneath the statue was a smooth stone table, and behind it sat Nekht Semerkeht. Staring at de Guzman were those eyes that reflected evil that had endured across untold centuries. On the thin lips of the wizened face was a slight smile of seeming self-mockery. His red-stained hand pressed against his breast. With his other hand, the ancient ruler of Tlasceltec gestured.

"Come; join me, join Nekht Semerkeht of Egypt, in whom Sethis has resided these tens and tens of centuries. And you, hairy-faced barbarian, have conquered. I am dying, of a weapon that ends prowess and cleverness and will harden man all the more."

"Better to join you than *those*," de Guzman said, and plucked the cresset from Nezahualca's hand. She stood still, gazing at the man who'd made her a slave. De Guzman set the glim on the stone table. "Attempt to wreak aught of your evil necromancy on me, Nekht Semerkeht, and you die the sooner."

"A few more moments are important to me, now the millennia of life end. Sit in peace, and tell me of the world you've seen."

"Nekht Semerkeht of Egypt . . . an Egypt long dead, I'll wager!"

"And win the wager. It was the Ptolemies that drove me from Thebes and Egypt itself. Though I taught these simple people how to measure and record time, I have lost track of the centuries. My galley was wrecked off the coast of Mexico. My arts were strong then, as many in my own land had learned — but they grew stronger still. Making myself Lord of Mexico was not difficult . . . but I wearied of ruling silly tribesmen, and came northward to create my own city here. As I have done. I have heard how your race slew Montezuma, in greed." His chuckle became a cough; he clutched his chest. "Here in this city are greater treasures than ever Cortez thefted from Tenochtitlan."

"I have come for them."

"To take oversea to your thrice-greedy rulers?"

De Guzman's smile was not reflected in the eyes that remained fastened coldly on the Egyptian godman. "I have had enough of that. *I* have come for Tlasceltec's treasure . . . and its princess who shall sit its throne . . . and for Tlasceltec itself!"

"Ah, a *worthy* man then, who like me — and Neza there, make no mistake — thinks first of himself. Good!" Nekht Semerkeht coughed, spoke effortfully. "At least it is no mercenary bought with money or that false foolishness called 'patriotism' that has slain me, who have lived so many lifetimes. But come, tell me of the world unknown to these children."

And so Hernando de Guzman sat and conversed

43

with a man who had lived uncounted centuries, a man in whose spirit was incorporated that of a god of ancient Egypt. The cresseted glim between them flickered lower — and almost de Guzman succumbed to unseen, unspoken sorcery. It was when he moved a leg he realized a web of magic was rising about him; the leg felt immersed in thick honey.

"Monster!" he snarled suddenly, interrupting the other in mid-sentence. "Ye do sorcery on me!" Lurching forward as though in quicksand, de Guzman struck Nekht Semerkeht's hand — the reddened hand pressed against his bulletholed chest.

Instantly the sensation of being caught in cloying, sticky honey left the Conquistador's limbs — but as instantly the Egyptian was rising to reveal that beneath the table he had held a curved sword.

"Silly child!" he cried, coming round the table in a rush and hiss of dark robes. "Fool who's lived perhaps twoscore years! Ye broke my hold on ye, but not me — think ye that pellet of metal could slay *Nekht Semerkeht?*"

Only by allowing himself to fall backward off his backless chair did de Guzman save himself from a lunging stab — and only by slamming a foot into a robed leg did he stop the Egyptian from carving him where he lay. Armor clanged and screeched on stone as he rolled desperately. Then the Conquistador was on his feet with sword in hand. He wished now he had had the sense to reload his pistols!

The curving blade of the other was white flame about the Spaniard's guard, and with every desperate parry of clanging sword he felt the awful heat of a blade of magic. No lunge he made found flesh, though he was able to keep that other sword from

44

him. Once it struck his chestplate, and he groaned at the terrible heat.

Nekht Semerkeht's back was to the cresset when it guttered. In the instant the flame went out, de Guzman made a mighty sideward leap and then another forward, smiting desperately to strike down this dark fiend before the blackness betrayed him to the sword of fire. Blade rang on blade and sparks danced. Both men cried out, de Guzman at the searing heat that nearly forced open his fingers. But the man from the past staggered back — and a long diminishing cry apprised de Guzman of the trap set for him: it was to have been he hurtling through that trapdoor, not Nekht Semerkeht! Before the door crashed shut, de Guzman heard the angry rattling of many vicious serpents, far below.

Panting, sweating, the Conquistador found Nezahualca in the dark. "Surely he is not impervious to the bites of a dozen rattlesnakes!"

"I — hope not," she said, and clutched at him.

De Guzman smiled in the dark, for he held the new ruler of Tlasceltec — and thus he held Tlasceltec!

Out of that accursed hall of the dead they hurried, and enormous doors crashed ringingly shut behind them. They fled through dark corridors that were no longer ruled by Nekht Semerkeht and his creatures.

On the morrow, Nezahualca, who strangely had been known by no man before de Guzman, announced to the people of that long accursed city that Nekht Semerkeht was at last no more, and that she was their rightful sovereign, and that the savior of them all would be her viceroy. As she turned to gesture to him, de Guzman smiled and pushed into his belt the pistol that had been his insurance, lest she suffer a last-instant change of mind about making that announcement.

These people had never seen or heard the flash and roar of gunpowder; the governor provided a marvelous opportunity for de Guzman to display his power. The governor had been comfortable, ruling under Nekht Semerkeht's direction, and was hardly prepared simply to yield to an outlander and the mere girl who but yesterday had been a slave in the fields.

De Guzman fired once. The governor and his sword slid and tumbled down the steps of the temple. A thousand knees bent to the man beside the princess who had just become a queen.

Hernando de Guzman looked down to find her gazing at him. He smiled. "Give them my title," the soldier ordered the daughter of kings. "I am to be called . . . *Conquistador!*"

And so it was done. None knew, a few days later, that the "indisposition" that kept their ruler from their sight was a split lip and a great bruise on her cheek, in addition to de Guzman's other marks on less visible portions of her anatomy, for never had he been a patient man or a gentle lover.

When she again emerged it was to announce that the army would begin training, and that there were certain substances in the earth the Conquistador wanted found and mined. He had no doubts that charcoal and sulfur and potash were obtainable hereabouts. If Coronado or more Chiricahua arrived before Tlasceltec's walls, they would find no easily murdered primitives but gunpowder aplenty and men who knew how to use it. Nor did her people know that beneath her queenly robes she wore a slave's shift, and it torn, though belted tightly enough to remind her constantly that she was the woman of the Conquistador, who ruled in Tlasceltec.

De Guzman's life had just begun; Nezahualca's slavery had not ended.

Yet that same night the Conquistador saw a man approaching him, in his sleep. The eyes of that dark-robed man were full of naught but malice and evil and the knowledge of centuries. Desperately de Guzman essayed to draw sword; then in that weirdness of the dream state he recognized that he was dreaming, and sought to awake. He could not.

"No outlander rules *my* city," Nekht Semerkeht told him. "The red men of the plains come upon you, murderer, power-greedy fool, and you shall not escape their knives and axes!"

In the dream, de Guzman watched the ancient mage, a patch of brown on the chest of his robe. Laboriously he climbed into the temple's tower. There he took up a great mallet and, staggering, began to smite again and again the huge gong suspended there. The reverberations were as brazen thunder that boomed again and again at de Guzman's head like a physical force — and at the walls of the city. He saw cracks appear, saw a section crumble, topple. And he watched the shrieking, naked men of the plains come bounding copper-skinned into *his* city. His city, whose rule was the culmination of his life of opportunism and greed and slaying.

He awoke, sweating and gasping . . . to the sound of shrieking and screaming and, over all, the repeated booming notes of the enormous bronze gong.

It must be said of Hernando de Guzman that he slew over a dozen of the yelling attackers even as he fell, and too that he drove his sword up into the belly of the man whose club jellied his head against the bottom step of the temple of Tlasceltec.

Only when every man and woman and child had been butchered, so that naked and moccasin-clad feet slipped in gore, did the azure mist come billowing from the temple. Every attacker soon joined those he had slain, in swift death. The last of them saw the robed man atop the temple steps, gesturing at the skies, and sought to loose an arrow at him. But the mist was too swift, and Tlasceltec became a city of the dead — save for Nekht Semerkeht.

Still he gestured and muttered, uttering incantations that were more ancient than the tongue in which he unleashed them, a tongue no longer spoken.

At last he ceased. Reeling, he slipped to his knees. "In a city of the dead, I die. But . . . in dying . . . I take my slayer with me . . . and my city!"

Nor did Coronado nor anyone else find the fabled city of Cibolo, which was in truth Tlasceltec north of Mexico, placed on the bosom of the earth by Nekht Semerkeht — who, in passing, took it with him.

Introduction to "The Tale of Hauk"
by Poul Anderson

If the language of this story isn't the way scholars think the tales of Scandinavia should be translated — they're wrong. If you don't fall promptly in love with the language — you're wrong.

Aside from that, Poul Anderson has written twenty or eighty million books and stories, won several meaningful awards, kept several magazines alive, been convention Guest of Honor and the S.F. Book Club's selection seemingly dozens of times, been president of Science Fiction Writers of America, created whole solar systems, gotten better and better year after year, and is somehow a nice, decent human being. And good company.

You probably already knew all that. Know too that he is loved in many places by many people. Your editor is only one of them.

THE TALE OF HAUK
by
Poul Anderson

A man called Geirolf dwelt on the Great Fjord in Raumsdal. His father was Bui Hardhand, who owned a farm inland near the Dofra Fell. One year Bui went in viking to Finnmark and brought back a woman he dubbed Gydha. She became the mother of Geirolf. But because Bui already had children by his wife, there would be small inheritance for this by-blow.

Folk said uncanny things about Gydha. She was fair to see, but spoke little, did no more work than she must, dwelt by herself in a shack out of sight of the garth, and often went for long stridings alone on the upland heaths, heedless of cold, rain, and rovers. Bui did not visit her often. Her son Geirolf did. He too was a moody sort, not much given to playing with others, quick and harsh of temper. Big and strong, he went abroad with his father already when he was twelve, and in the next few years won the name of a mighty though ruthless fighter.

Then Gydha died. They buried her near her shack, and it was whispered that she spooked around it of nights. Soon after, walking home with some men by moonlight from a feast at a neighbor's, Bui clutched his breast and fell dead. They wondered if Gydha had called him, maybe to accompany her home to Finnmark, for there was no more sight of her.

Geirolf bargained with his kin and got the price of a ship for himself. Thereafter he gathered a crew, mostly younger sons and a wild lot, and fared west. For a long while he harried Scotland, Ireland, and the coasts south of the Channel, and won much booty. With some of this he bought his farm on the Great Fjord. Meanwhile he courted Thyra, a daughter of the yeoman Sigtryg Einarsson, and got her.

They had one son early on, Hauk, a bright and lively lad. But thereafter five years went by until they had a daughter who lived, Unn, and two years later a boy they called Einar. Geirolf was a viking every summer, and sometimes wintered over in the Westlands. Yet he was a kindly father, whose children were always glad to see him come roaring home. Very tall and broad in the shoulders, he had long red-brown hair and a full beard around a broad blunt-nosed face whose eyes were ice-blue and slanted. He liked fine clothes and heavy gold rings, which he also lavished on Thyra.

Then the time came when Geirolf said he felt poorly and would not fare elsewhere that season. Hauk was fourteen years old and had been wild to go. "I'll keep my promise to you as well as may be," Geirolf said, and sent men asking around. The best he could do was get his son a bench on a ship belonging to Ottar the Wide-Faring from Haalogaland in the north, who was trading along the coast and meant to do likewise overseas.

Hauk and Ottar took well to each other. In England, the man got the boy prime-signed so he could deal with Christians. Though neither was baptized, what he heard while they wintered there made Hauk thoughtful. Next spring they fared south to trade among the Moors, and did not come home until late fall.

Ottar was Geirolf's guest for a while, though he scowled to himself when his host broke into fits of deep coughing. He offered to take Hauk along on his voyages from now on and start the youth toward a good livelihood.

"You a chapman — the son of a viking?" Geirolf sneered. He had grown surly of late.

Hauk flushed. "You've heard what we did to those vikings who set on *us*," he answered.

"Give our son his head," was Thyra's smiling rede, "or he'll take the bit between his teeth."

The upshot was that Geirolf grumbled agreement, and Hauk fared off. He did not come back for five years.

Long were the journeys he took with Ottar. By ship and horse, they made their way to Uppsala in Svithjodh, thence into the wilderness of the Keel after pelts; amber they got on the windy strands of Jutland, salt herring along the Sound; seeking beeswax, honey, and tallow, they pushed beyond Holmgard to the fair at

Kiev; walrus ivory lured them past North Cape, through bergs and floes to the land of the fur-clad Biarmians; and they bore many goods west. They did not hide that the wish to see what was new to them drove them as hard as any hope of gain.

In those days King Harald Fairhair went widely about in Norway, bringing all the land under himself. Lesser kings and chieftains must either plight faith to him or meet his wrath; it crushed whomever would stand fast. When he entered Raumsdal, he sent men from garth to garth as was his wont, to say he wanted oaths and warriors.

"My older son is abroad," Geirolf told these, "and my younger still a stripling. As for myself — " He coughed, and blood flecked his beard. The king's men did not press the matter.

But now Geirolf's moods grew ever worse. He snarled at everybody, cuffed his children and housefolk, once drew a dagger and stabbed to death a thrall who chanced to spill some soup on him. When Thyra reproached him for this, he said only, "Let them know I am not yet altogether hollowed out. I can still wield blade." And he looked at her so threateningly from beneath his shaggy brows that she, no coward, withdrew in silence.

A year later, Hauk Geirolfsson returned to visit his parents.

That was on a chill fall noontide. Whitecaps chopped beneath a whistling wind and cast spindrift salty onto lips. Clifftops on either side of the fjord were lost in mist. Above blew cloud wrack like smoke. Hauk's ship, a wide-beamed knorr, rolled, pitched, and creaked as it beat its way under sail. The owner stood in the bows, wrapped in a flame-red cloak, an uncommonly big young man, yellow hair tossing around a face akin to his father's, weatherbeaten though still scant of beard. When he saw the arm of the fjord that he wanted to enter, he pointed with a spear at whose head he had bound a silk pennon. When he saw Disafoss pouring in a white stream down the blue-gray stone wall to larboard, and beyond the waterfall at the end of that arm lay his old home, he shouted for happiness.

Geirolf had rich holdings. The hall bulked over all else, heavy-timbered, brightly painted, dragon heads arching from rafters and gables. Elsewhere around the yard were cookhouse, smokehouse, bathhouse, storehouses, workshop, stables, barns, women's bower. Several cabins for hirelings and their families were strewn beyond. Fishing boats lay on the strand near a shed which held the master's dragonship. Behind the steading, land sloped sharply upward through a narrow dale, where fields were walled with stones grubbed out of them and now stubbled after harvest. A bronze-leaved oakenshaw stood untouched not far from the buildings; and a mile inland, where hills humped themselves toward the mountains, rose a darkling wall of pinewood.

Spearheads and helmets glimmered ashore. But men saw it was a single craft bound their way, white shield on the mast. As the hull slipped alongside the little wharf, they lowered their weapons. Hauk sprang from bow to dock in a single leap and whooped.

Geirolf trod forth. "Is that you, my son?" he called. His voice was hoarse from coughing; he had grown gaunt and sunken-eyed; the ax that he bore shivered in his hand.

"Yes, father, yes, home again," Hauk stammered. He could not hide his shock.

55

Maybe this drove Geirolf to anger. Nobody knew; he had become impossible to get along with. "I could well-nigh have hoped otherwise," he rasped. "An unfriend would give me something better than strawdeath."

The rest of the men, housecarls and thralls alike, flocked about Hauk to bid him welcome. Among them was a burly, grizzled yeoman whom he knew from aforetime, Leif Egilsson, a neighbor come to dicker for a horse. When he was small, Hauk had often wended his way over a woodland trail to Leif's garth to play with the children there.

He called his crew to him. They were not just Norse, but had among them Danes, Swedes, and English, gathered together over the years as he found them trustworthy. "You brought a mickle for me to feed," Geirolf said. Luckily, the wind bore his words from all but Hauk. "Where's your master Ottar?"

The young man stiffened. "He's my friend, never my master," he answered. "This is my own ship, bought with my own earnings. Ottar abides in England this year. The West Saxons have a new king, one Alfred, whom he wants to get to know."

"Time was when it was enough to know how to get sword past a Westman's shield," Geirolf grumbled.

Seeing peace down by the water, women and children hastened from the hall to meet the newcomers. At their head went Thyra. She was tall and deep-bosomed; her gown blew around a form still straight and freely striding. But as she neared, Hauk saw that the gold of her braids was dimmed and sorrow had furrowed her face. Nonetheless she kindled when she knew him. "Oh, thrice welcome, Hauk!" she said low. "How long can you bide with us?"

After his father's greeting, it had been in his mind to say he must soon be off. But when he spied who walked behind his mother, he said, "We thought we might be guests here the winter through, if that's not too much of a burden."

"Never — " began Thyra. Then she saw where his gaze had gone, and suddenly she smiled.

Alfhild Leifsdottir had joined her widowed father on this visit. She was two years younger than Hauk, but they had been glad of each other as playmates. Today she stood a maiden grown, lissome in a blue wadmal gown, heavily crowned with red locks above great green eyes, straight nose, and gently curved mouth. Though he had known many a woman, none struck him as being so fair.

He grinned at her and let his cloak flap open to show his finery of broidered, fur-lined tunic, linen shirt and breeks, chased leather boots, gold on arms and neck and sword-hilt. She paid them less heed than she did him when they spoke.

Thus Hauk and his men moved to Geirolf's hall. He brought plentiful gifts, there was ample food and drink, and their tales of strange lands — their songs, dances, games, jests, manners — made them good housefellows in these lengthening nights.

Already on the next morning, he walked out with Alfhild. Rain had cleared the air, heaven and fjord sparkled, wavelets chuckled beneath a cool breeze from the woods. Nobody else was on the strand where they went.

"So you grow mighty as a chapman, Hauk," Alfhild teased. "Have you never gone in viking . . . only once, only to please your father?"

"No," he answered gravely. "I fail to see what manliness lies in falling on those too weak to defend themselves. We traders must be stronger and more war-skilled than any who may seek to plunder us." A thick branch of driftwood, bleached and hardened, lay nearby. Hauk picked it up and snapped it between his hands. Two other men would have had trouble doing that. It gladdened him to see Alfhild glow at the sight. "Nobody has tried us twice," he said.

They passed the shed where Geirolf's dragon lay on rollers. Hauk opened the door for a peek at the remembered slim shape. A sharp whiff from the gloom within brought his nose wrinkling. "Whew!" he snorted. "Dry rot."

"Poor *Fireworm* has long lain idle," Alfhild sighed. "In later years, your father's illness has gnawed him till he doesn't even see to the care of his ship. He knows he will never take it a-roving again."

"I feared that," Hauk murmured.

"We grieve for him on our own garth too," she said. "In former days, he was a staunch friend to us. Now we bear with his ways, yes, insults that would make my father draw blade on anybody else."

"That is dear of you," Hauk said, staring straight before him. "I'm very thankful."

"You have not much cause for that, have you?" she asked. "I mean, you've been away so long . . . Of course, you have your mother. She's borne the brunt, stood like a shield before your siblings —" She touched her lips. "I talk too much."

"You talk as a friend," he blurted. "May we always be friends."

They wandered on, along a path from shore to fields. It went by the shaw. Through boles and boughs and falling leaves, they saw Thor's image and altar among the trees. "I'll make offering here for my father's health," Hauk said, "though truth to tell, I've more faith in my own strength than in any gods."

"You have seen lands where strange gods rule," she nodded.

"Yes, and there too, they do not steer things well," he said. "It was in a Christian realm that a huge wolf came raiding flocks, on which no iron would bite. When it took a baby from a hamlet near our camp, I thought I'd be less than a man did I not put an end to it."

"What happened?" she asked breathlessly, and caught his arm.

"I wrestled it barehanded — no foe of mine was ever more fell — and at last broke its neck." He pulled back a sleeve to show scars of terrible bites. "Dead, it changed into a man they had outlawed that year for his evil deeds. We burned the lich to make sure it would not walk again, and thereafter the folk had peace. And . . . we had friends, in a country otherwise wary of us."

She looked on him in the wonder he had hoped for.

Erelong she must return with her father. But the way between the garths was just a few miles, and Hauk often rode or skied through the woods. At home, he and his men helped do what work there was, and gave merriment where it had long been little known.

Thyra owned this to her son, on a snowy day when they were by themselves. They were in the women's bower, whither they had gone to see a tapestry she was weaving. She wanted to know how it showed against those of the Westlands; he had brought one such, which hung above the benches in the hall. Here, in the wide quiet room, was dusk, for the day outside had become a tumbling whiteness. Breath steamed from lips as the two of them spoke. It smelled sweet; both had drunk mead until they could talk freely.

"You did better than you knew when you came back," Thyra said. "You blew like spring into this winter of ours. Einar and Unn were withering; they blossom again in your nearness."

"Strangely has our father changed," Hauk answered sadly. "I remember once when I was small, how he took me by the hand on a frost-clear night, led me forth under the stars, and named for me the pictures in them, Thor's Wain, Freyja's Spindle — how wonderful he made them, how his deep slow laughterful voice filled the dark."

"A wasting illness draws the soul inward," his mother said. "He . . . has no more manhood . . . and it tears him like fangs that he will die helpless in bed. He must strike out at someone, and here we are."

She was silent a while before she added: "He will not live out the year. Then you must take over."

"I must be gone when weather allows," Hauk warned. "I promised Ottar."

"Return as soon as may be," Thyra said. "We have need of a strong man, the more so now when yonder King Harald would reave their freehold rights from yeomen."

"It would be well to have a hearth of my own." Hauk stared past her, toward the unseen woods. Her worn face creased in a smile.

Suddenly they heard yells from the yard below. Hauk ran out onto the gallery and looked down. Geirolf was shambling after an aged carl named Atli. He had a whip in his hand and was lashing it across the white locks and wrinkled cheeks of the man, who could not run fast either and who sobbed.

"What is this?" broke from Hauk. He swung himself over the rail, hung, and let go. The drop would at least have jarred the wind out of most. He, though, bounced from where he landed, ran behind his father, caught hold of the whip and wrenched it from Geirolf's grasp. "What are you doing?"

Geirolf howled and struck his son with a doubled fist. Blood trickled from Hauk's mouth. He stood fast. Atli sank to hands and knees and fought not to weep.

"Are you also a heelbiter of mine?" Geirolf bawled.

"I'd save you from your madness, father," Hauk said in pain. "Atli followed you to battle ere I was born — he dandled me on his knee — and he's a free man. What has he done, that you'd bring down on us the anger of his kinfolk?"

"Harm not the skipper, young man," Atli begged. "I fled because I'd sooner die than lift hand against my skipper."

"Hell swallow you both!" Geirolf would have cursed further, but the coughing came on him. Blood drops flew through the snowflakes, down onto the white earth, where they mingled with the drip from the heads of Hauk and Atli. Doubled over, Geirolf let them half lead, half carry him to his shut-bed. There he closed the panel and lay alone in darkness.

"What happened between you and him?" Hauk asked.

"I was fixing to shoe a horse," Atli said into a ring of gaping onlookers. "He came in and wanted to know why I'd not asked his leave. I told him 'twas plain Kilfaxi needed new shoes. Then he hollered, 'I'll show you I'm no log in the woodpile!' and snatched yon whip off the wall and took after me." The old man squared his shoulders. "We'll speak no more of this, you hear?" he ordered the household.

Nor did Geirolf, when next day he let them bring him some broth.

For more reasons than this, Hauk came to spend much of his time at Leif's garth. He would return in such a glow that even the reproachful looks of his young sister and brother, even the sullen or the weary greeting of his father, could not dampen it.

At last, when lengthening days and quickening blood bespoke seafarings soon to come, that happened which surprised nobody. Hauk told them in the hall that he wanted to marry Alfhild Leifsdottir, and prayed Geirolf press the suit for him. "What must be, will be," said his father, a better grace than awaited. Union of the families was clearly good for both.

Leif Egilsson agreed, and Alfhild had nothing but aye to say. The betrothal feast crowded the whole neighborhood together in cheer. Thyra hid the trouble within her, and Geirolf himself was calm if not blithe.

Right after, Hauk and his men were busking themselves to fare. Regardless of his doubts about gods, he led in offering for a safe voyage to Thor, Aegir, and St. Michael. But Alfhild found herself a quiet place alone, to cut runes on an ash tree in the name of Freyja.

When all was ready, she was there with the folk of Geirolf's stead to see the sailors off. That morning was keen, wind roared in trees and skirled between cliffs, waves ran green and white beneath small flying clouds. Unn could not but hug her brother who was going, while Einar gave him a handclasp that shook. Thyra said, "Come home hale and early, my son." Alfhild mostly stored away the sight of Hauk. Atli and others of the household mumbled this and that.

Geirolf shuffled forward. The cane on which he leaned rattled among the stones of the beach. He was hunched in a hairy cloak against the sharp air. His locks fell tangled almost to the coal-smoldering eyes.

"Father, farewell," Hauk said, taking his free hand.

"You mean 'fare far,' don't you?" Geirolf grated. "'Fare far and never come back.' You'd like that, wouldn't you? But we will meet again. Oh, yes, we will meet again."

Hauk dropped the hand. Geirolf turned and sought the house. The rest behaved as if they had not heard, speaking loudly, amidst yelps of laughter, to overcome those words of foreboding. Soon Hauk called his orders to begone.

Men scrambled aboard the laden ship. Its sail slatted aloft and filled, the mooring lines were cast loose, the hull stood out to sea. Alfhild waved until it was gone from sight behind the bend where Disafoss fell.

The summer passed — plowing, sowing, lambing, calving, farrowing, hoeing, reaping, flailing, butchering — rain, hail, sun, stars, loves, quarrels, births, deaths — and the season wore toward fall. Alfhild was seldom at Geirolf's garth, nor was Leif; for Hauk's father grew steadily worse. After midsummer he could no longer leave his bed. But often he whispered, between lung-tearing coughs, to those who tended him, "I would kill you if I could."

On a dark day late in the season, when rain roared about the hall and folk and hounds huddled close to fires that hardly lit the gloom around, Geirolf awoke from a heavy sleep. Thyra marked it and came to him. Cold and dankness gnawed their way through her clothes. The fever was in him like a brand. He plucked restlessly at his blanket, where he half sat in his short

63

shut-bed. Though flesh had wasted from the great bones, his fingers still had strength to tear the wool. The mattress rustled under him. "Straw-death, straw-death," he muttered.

Thyra laid a palm on his brow. "Be at ease," she said.

It dragged from him: "You'll not be rid ... of me ... so fast . . . by straw-death." An icy sweat broke forth and the last struggle began.

Long it was, Geirolf's gasps and the sputtering flames the only noises within that room, while rain and wind ramped outside and night drew in. Thyra stood by the bedside to wipe the sweat off her man, blood and spittle from his beard. A while after sunset, he rolled his eyes back and died.

Thyra called for water and lamps. She cleansed him, clad him in his best, and laid him out. A drawn sword was on his breast.

In the morning, thralls and carls alike went forth under her orders. A hillock stood in the fields about half a mile inland from the house. They dug a grave chamber in the top of this, lining it well with timber. "Won't you bury him in his ship?" asked Atli.

"It is rotten, unworthy of him," Thyra said. Yet she made them haul it to the barrow, around which she had stones to outline a hull. Meanwhile folk readied a grave-ale, and messengers bade neighbors come.

When all were there, men of Geirolf's carried him on a litter to his resting place and put him in, together with weapons and a jar of Southland coins. After beams had roofed the chamber, his friends from aforetime took shovels and covered it well. They replaced the turfs of sere grass, leaving the hillock as it had been save that it was now bigger. Einar Thorolfsson kindled his father's ship. It burned till dusk, when the horns of the new moon stood over the fjord. Meanwhile folk had gone back down to the garth to feast and drink. Riding home next day, well gifted by Thyra, they told each other that this had been an honorable burial.

The moon waxed. On the first night that it rose full, Geirolf came again.

A thrall named Kark had been late in the woods, seeking a strayed sheep. Coming home, he passed near the howe. The moon was barely above the pines; long shivery glades of light ran on the water, lost themselves in shadows ashore, glinted wanly anew where a bedewed stone wall snaked along a stubblefield. Stars were few. A great stillness lay on the land; not even an owl hooted, until all at once dogs down in the garth began howling. It was not the way they howled at the moon; across the mile between, it sounded ragged and terrified. Kark felt the chill close in around him, and hastened toward home.

Something heavy trod the earth. He looked around and saw the bulk of a huge man coming across the field from the barrow. "Who's that?" he called uneasily. No voice replied, but the weight of those footfalls shivered through the ground into his bones. Kark swallowed, gripped his staff, and stood where he was. But then the shape came so near that moonlight picked out the head of Geirolf. Kark screamed, dropped his weapon, and ran.

Geirolf followed slowly, clumsily behind.

Down in the garth, light glimmered red as doors opened. Folk saw Kark running, gasping for breath. Atli and Einar led the way out, each with a torch in one hand, a sword in the other. Little could they see beyond the wild flame-gleam. Kark reached them, fell, writhed on the hard-beaten clay of the yard, and wailed.

"What is it, you lackwit?" Atli snapped, and kicked him. Then Einar pointed his blade.

"A stranger — " Atli began.

Geirolf rocked into sight. The mould of the grave clung to him. His eyes stared unblinking, unmoving, blank in the moonlight, out of a gray face whereon the skin crawled. The teeth in his tangled beard were dry. No breath smoked from his nostrils. He held out his arms, crook-fingered.

"Father!" Einar cried. The torch hissed from his grip, flickered weakly at his feet, and went out. The men at his back jammed the doorway of the hall as they sought its shelter.

"The skipper's come again," Atli quavered. He sheathed his sword, though that was hard when his hand shook, and made himself step forward. "Skipper, d'you know your old shipmate Atli?"

The dead man grabbed him, lifted him, and dashed him to earth. Einar heard bones break. Atli jerked once and lay still. Geirolf trod him and Kark underfoot. There was a sound of cracking and rending. Blood spurted forth.

Blindly, Einar swung blade. The edge smote but would not bite. A wave of grave-chill passed over him. He whirled and bounded back inside.

Thyra had seen. "Bar the door," she bade. The windows were already shuttered against frost. "Men, stand fast. Women, stoke up the fires."

They heard the lich groping about the yard. Walls creaked where Geirolf blundered into them. Thyra called through the door, "Why do you wish us ill, your own household?" But only those noises gave answer. The hounds cringed and whined.

"Lay iron at the doors and under every window," Thyra commanded. "If it will not cut him, it may keep him out."

All that night, then, folk huddled in the hall. Geirolf climbed onto the roof and rode the ridgepole, drumming his heels on the shakes till the whole building boomed. A little before sunrise, it stopped. Peering out by the first dull dawnlight, Thyra saw no mark of her husband but his deep-sunken footprints and the wrecked bodies he had left.

"He grew so horrible before he died," Unn wept. "Now he can't rest, can he?"

"We'll make him an offering," Thyra said through her weariness. "It may be we did not give him enough when we buried him."

Few would follow her to the howe. Those who dared, brought along the best horse on the farm. Einar, as the son of the house when Hauk was gone, himself cut its throat after a sturdy man had given the hammer-blow. Carls and wenches butchered the carcass, which Thyra and Unn cooked over a fire in whose wood was blent the charred rest of the dragon-ship. Nobody cared to eat much of the flesh or broth. Thyra poured what was left over the bones, upon the grave.

Two ravens circled in sight, waiting for folk to go so they could take the food. "Is that a good sign?" Thyra sighed. "Will Odin fetch Geirolf home?"

That night everybody who had not fled to neighboring steads gathered in the hall. Soon after the moon rose, they heard the footfalls come nearer and nearer. They heard Geirolf break into the storehouse and worry the laid-out bodies of Atli and Kark. They heard him kill cows in the barn. Again he rode the roof.

In the morning Leif Egilsson arrived, having gotten the news. He found Thyra too tired and shaken to do anything further. "The ghost did not take your offering," he said, "but maybe the gods will."

In the oakenshaw, he led the giving of more beasts. There was talk of a thrall for Odin, but he said that would not help if this did not. Instead, he saw to the proper burial of the slain, and of those kine which nobody would dare eat. That night he abode there.

And Geirolf came back. Throughout the darkness, he tormented the home which had been his.

"I will bide here one more day," Leif said next sunrise. "We all need rest — though ill is it that we must sleep during daylight when we've so much readying for winter to do."

By that time, some other neighborhood men were also on hand. They spoke loudly of how they would hew the lich asunder.

"You know not what you boast of," said aged Grim the Wise. "Einar smote, and he strikes well for a lad, but the iron would not bite. It never will. Ghost-strength is in Geirolf, and all the wrath he could not set free during his life."

That night folk waited breathless for moonrise. But when the gnawed shield climbed over the pines, nothing stirred. The dogs, too, no longer seemed cowed. About midnight, Grim murmured into the shadows, "Yes, I thought so. Geirolf walks only when the moon is full."

"Then tomorrow we'll dig him up and burn him!" Leif said.

"No," Grim told them. "That would spell the worst of luck for everybody here. Don't you see, the anger and unpeace which will not let him rest, those could be forever unslaked? They could not but bring doom on the burners."

"What then can we do?" Thyra asked dully.

"Leave this stead," Grim counselled, "at least when the moon is full."

"Hard will that be," Einar sighed. "Would that my brother Hauk were here."

"He should have returned erenow," Thyra said. "May we in our woe never know that he has come to grief himself."

In truth, Hauk had not. His wares proved welcome in Flanders, where he bartered for cloth that he took across to England. There Ottar greeted him, and he met the young King Alfred. At that time there was no war going on with the Danes, who were settling into the Danelaw and thus in need of household goods. Hauk and Ottar did a thriving business among them. This led them to think they might do as well in Iceland, whither Norse folk were moving who liked not King Harald Fairhair. They made a voyage to see. Foul winds hampered them on the way home. Hence fall was well along when Hauk's ship returned.

The day was still and cold. Low overcast turned sky and water the hue of iron. A few gulls cruised and mewed, while under them sounded creak and splash of oars, swearing of men, as the knorr was rowed. At the end of the fjord-branch, garth and leaves were tiny splashes of color, lost against rearing cliffs, brown fields, murky wildwood. Straining ahead from afar, Hauk saw that a bare handful of men came down to the shore, moving listlessly more than watchfully. When his craft was unmistakable, though, a few women — no youngsters — sped from the hall as if they could not wait. Their cries came to him more thin than the gulls'.

Hauk lay alongside the dock. Springing forth, he cried merrily, "Where is everybody? How fares Alfhild?" His words lost themselves in silence. Fear touched him. "What's wrong?"

Thyra trod forth. Years might have gone by during his summer abroad, so changed was she. "You are barely in time," she said in an unsteady tone. Taking his hands, she told him how things stood.

Hauk stared long into emptiness. At last, "Oh, no," he whispered. "What's to be done?"

"We hoped you might know that, my son," Thyra answered. "The moon will be full tomorrow night."

His voice stumbled. "I am no wizard. If the gods themselves would not lay this ghost, what can I do?"

Einar spoke, in the brashness of youth: "We thought you might deal with him as you did with the were-wolf."

"But that was — No, I cannot!" Hauk croaked. "Never ask me."

"Then I fear we must leave," Thyra said. "For aye. You see how many have already fled, thrall and free alike, though nobody else has a place for them. We've not enough left to farm these acres. And who would buy them of us? Poor must we go, helpless as the poor ever are."

"Iceland — " Hauk wet his lips. "Well, you shall not want while I live." Yet he had counted on this home-stead, whether to dwell on or sell.

"Tomorrow we move over to Leif's garth, for the next three days and nights," Thyra said.

Unn shuddered. "I know not if I can come back," she said. "This whole past month here, I could hardly ever sleep." Dulled skin and sunken eyes bore her out.

"What else would you do?" Hauk asked.

"Whatever I can," she stammered, and broke into tears. He knew: wedding herself too young to whoever would have her dowryless, poor though the match would be — or making her way to some town to turn whore, his little sister.

"Let me think on this," Hauk begged. "Maybe I can hit on something."

His crew were also daunted when they heard. At eventide they sat in the hall and gave only a few curt words about what they had done in foreign parts. Everyone lay down early on bed, bench, or floor, but none slept well.

Before sunset, Hauk had walked forth alone. First he sought the grave of Atli. "I'm sorry, dear old friend," he said. Afterward he went to Geirolf's howe. It loomed yellow-gray with withered grass wherein grinned the skull of the slaughtered horse. At its foot were strewn the charred bits of the ship, inside stones that outlined a greater but unreal hull. Around reached stubblefields and walls, hemmed in by woods on one side and water on the other, rock lifting sheer beyond. The chill and the quiet had deepened.

Hauk climbed to the top of the barrow and stood there a while, head bent downward. "Oh, father," he said, "I learned doubt in Christian lands. What's right for me to do?" There was no answer. He made a slow way back to the dwelling.

All were up betimes next day. It went slowly over the woodland path to Leif's, for animals must be herded along. The swine gave more trouble than most. Hauk chuckled once, not very merrily, and remarked that at least this took folk's minds off their sorrows. He raised no mirth.

But he had Alfhild ahead of him. At the end of the way, he sprinted into the yard. Leif owned less land than Geirolf, his buildings were smaller and fewer, most of his guests must house outdoors in sleeping bags. Hauk paid no heed. "Alfhild!" he called. "I'm here!"

She left the dough she was kneading and sped to him. They hugged each other hard and long, in sight of the whole world. None thought that shame, as things were. At last she said, striving not to weep, "How we've longed for you! Now the nightmare can end."

He stepped back. "What mean you?" he uttered slowly, knowing full well.

"Why —" She was bewildered. "Won't you give him his second death?"

Hauk gazed past her for some heartbeats before he said: "Come aside with me."

Hand in hand, they wandered off. A meadow lay hidden from the garth by a stand of aspen. Elsewhere around, pines speared into a sky that today was bright. Clouds drifted on a nipping breeze. Far off, a stag bugled.

Hauk spread feet apart, hooked thumbs in belt, and made himself meet her eyes. "You think overhighly of my strength," he said.

"Who has more?" she asked. "We kept ourselves going by saying you would come home and make things good again."

"What if the drow is too much for me?" His words sounded raw through the hush. Leaves dropped yellow from their boughs.

She flushed. "Then your name will live."

"Yes —" Softly he spoke the words of the High One:

"Kine die, kinfolk die,
and so at last oneself.
This I know that never dies:
how dead men's deeds are deemed."

"You will do it!" she cried gladly.

His head shook before it drooped. "No. I will not. I dare not."

She stood as if he had clubbed her.

"Won't you understand?" he began.

The wound he had dealt her hopes went too deep. "So you show yourself a nithing!"

"Hear me," he said, shaken. "Were the lich anybody else's —"

Overwrought beyond reason, she slapped him and choked, "The gods bear witness, I give them my holiest oath, never will I wed you unless you do this thing. See, by my blood I swear." She whipped out her dagger and gashed her wrists. Red rills coursed out and fell in drops on the fallen leaves.

He was aghast. "You know not what you say. You're too young, you've been too sheltered. *Listen.*"

She would have fled from him, but he gripped her shoulders and made her stand. "Listen," went between his teeth. "Geirolf is still my father — my father who begot me, reared me, named the stars for me, weaponed me to make my way in the world. How can I fight him? Did I slay him, what horror would come upon me and mine?"

"O-o-oh," broke from Alfhild. She sank to the ground and wept as if to tear loose her ribs.

He knelt, held her, gave what soothing he could. "Now I know," she mourned. "Too late."

"Never," he murmured. "We'll fare abroad if we must, take new land, make new lives together."

"No," she gasped. "Did I not swear? What doom awaits an oathbreaker?"

Then he was long still. Heedlessly though she had spoken, her blood lay in the earth, which would remember.

He too was young. He straightened. "I will fight," he said.

Now she clung to him and pleaded that he must not. But an iron calm had come over him. "Maybe I will not be cursed," he said. "Or maybe the curse will be no more than I can bear."

"It will be mine too, I who brought it on you," she plighted herself.

Hand in hand again, they went back to the garth. Leif spied the haggard look on them and half guessed what had happened. "Will you fare to meet the drow, Hauk?" he asked. "Wait till I can have Grim the Wise brought here. His knowledge may help you."

"No," said Hauk. "Waiting would weaken me. I go this night."

Wide eyes stared at him — all but Thyra's; she was too torn.

Toward evening he busked himself. He took no helm, shield, or byrnie, for the dead man bore no weapons. Some said they would come along, armored themselves well, and offered to be at his side. He told them to follow him, but no farther than to watch what happened. Their iron would be of no help, and he thought they would only get in each other's way, and his, when he met the overhuman might of the drow. He kissed Alfhild, his mother, and his sister, and clasped hands with his brother, bidding them stay behind if they loved him.

Long did the few miles of path seem, and gloomy

74

under the pines. The sun was on the world's rim when men came out in the open. They looked past fields and barrow down to the empty garth, the fjordside cliffs, the water where the sun lay as half an ember behind a trail of blood. Clouds hurried on a wailing wind through a greenish sky. Cold struck deep. A wolf howled.

"Wait here," Hauk said.

"The gods be with you," Leif breathed.

"I've naught tonight but my own strength," Hauk said. "Belike none of us ever had more."

His tall form, clad in leather and wadmal, showed black athwart the sunset as he walked from the edge of the woods, out across plowland toward the crouching howe. The wind fluttered his locks, a last brightness until the sun went below. Then for a while the evenstar alone had light.

Hauk reached the mound. He drew sword and leaned on it, waiting. Dusk deepened. Star after star came forth, small and strange. Clouds blowing across them picked up a glow from the still unseen moon.

It rose at last above the treetops. Its ashen sheen stretched gashes of shadow across earth. The wind loudened.

The grave groaned. Turves, stones, timbers swung aside. Geirolf shambled out beneath the sky. Hauk felt the ground shudder under his weight. There came a carrion stench, though the only sign of rotting was on the dead man's clothes. His eyes peered dim, his teeth gnashed dry in a face at once well remembered and hideously changed. When he saw the living one who waited, he veered and lumbered thitherward.

"Father," Hauk called. "It's I, your eldest son."

75

The drow drew nearer.

"Halt, I beg you," Hauk said unsteadily. "What can I do to bring you peace?"

A cloud passed over the moon. It seemed to be hurtling through heaven. Geirolf reached for his son with fingers that were ready to clutch and tear. "Hold," Hauk shrilled. "No step farther."

He could not see if the gaping mouth grinned. In another stride, the great shape came well-nigh upon him. He lifted his sword and brought it singing down. The edge struck truly, but slid aside. Geirolf's skin heaved, as if to push the blade away. In one more step, he laid grave-cold hands around Hauk's neck.

Before that grip could close, Hauk dropped his useless weapon, brought his wrists up between Geirolf's, and mightily snapped them apart. Nails left furrows, but he was free. He sprang back, into a wrestler's stance.

Geirolf moved in, reaching. Hauk hunched under those arms and himself grabbed waist and thigh. He threw his shoulder against a belly like rock. Any live man would have gone over, but the lich was too heavy.

Geirolf smote Hauk on the side. The blows drove him to his knees and thundered on his back. A foot lifted to crush him. He rolled off and found his own feet again. Geirolf lurched after him. The hastening moon linked their shadows. The wolf howled anew, but in fear. Watching men gripped spearshafts till their knuckles stood bloodless.

Hauk braced his legs and snatched for the first hold, around both of Geirolf's wrists. The drow strained to break loose and could not; but neither could Hauk bring him down. Sweat ran moon-bright

76

over the son's cheeks and darkened his shirt. The reek of it was at least a living smell in his nostrils. Breath tore at his gullet. Suddenly Geirolf wrenched so hard that his right arm tore from between his foe's fingers. He brought that hand against Hauk's throat. Hauk let go and slammed himself backward before he was throttled.

Geirolf stalked after him. The drow did not move fast. Hauk sped behind and pounced on the broad back. He seized an arm of Geirolf's and twisted it around. But the dead cannot feel pain. Geirolf stood fast. His other hand groped about, got Hauk by the hair, and yanked. Live men can hurt. Hauk stumbled away. Blood ran from his scalp into his eyes and mouth, hot and salt.

Geirolf turned and followed. He would not tire. Hauk had no long while before strength ebbed. Almost, he fled. Then the moon broke through to shine full on his father.

"You . . . shall not . . . go on . . . like that," Hauk mumbled while he snapped after air.

The drow reached him. They closed, grappled, swayed, stamped to and fro, in wind and flickery moonlight. Then Hauk hooked an ankle behind Geirolf's and pushed. With a huge thud, the drow crashed to earth. He dragged Hauk along.

Hauk's bones felt how terrible was the grip upon him. He let go his own hold. Instead, he arched his back and pushed himself away. His clothes ripped. But he burst free and reeled to his feet.

Geirolf turned over and began to crawl up. His back was once more to Hauk. The young man sprang. He got a knee hard in between the shoulderblades, while both his arms closed on the frosty head before him.

He hauled. With the last and greatest might that was in him, he hauled. Blackness went in tatters before his eyes.

There came a loud snapping sound. Geirolf ceased pawing behind him. He sprawled limp. His neck was broken, his jawbone wrenched from the skull. Hauk climbed slowly off him, shuddering. Geirolf stirred, rolled, half rose. He lifted a hand toward Hauk. It traced a line through the air and a line growing from beneath that. Then he slumped and lay still.

Hauk crumpled too.

"Follow me who dare!" Leif roared, and went forth across the field. One by one, as they saw nothing move ahead of them, the men came after. At last they stood hushed around Geirolf — who was only a harmless dead man now, though the moon shone bright in his eyes — and on Hauk, who had begun to stir.

"Bear him carefully down to the hall," Leif said. "Start a fire and tend him well. Most of you, take from the woodpile and come back here. I'll stand guard meanwhile . . . though I think there is no need."

And so they burned Geirolf there in the field. He walked no more.

In the morning, they brought Hauk back to Leif's garth. He moved as if in dreams. The others were too awestruck to speak much. Even when Alfhild ran to meet him, he could only say, "Hold clear of me. I may be under a doom."

"Did the drow lay a weird on you?" she asked, spear-stricken.

"I know not," he answered. "I think I fell into the dark before he was wholly dead."

"What?" Leif well-nigh shouted. "You did not see the sign he drew?"

"Why, no," Hauk said. "How did it go?"

"Thus. Even afar and by moonlight, I knew." Leif drew it.

"That is no ill-wishing!" Grim cried. "That's naught but the Hammer."

Life rushed back into Hauk. "Do you mean what I hope?"

"He blessed you," Grim said. "You freed him from what he had most dreaded and hated — his straw-death. The madness in him is gone, and he has wended hence to the world beyond."

Then Hauk was glad again. He led them all in heaping earth over the ashes of his father, and in setting things right on the farm. That winter, at the feast of Thor, he and Alfhild were wedded. Afterward he became well thought of by King Harald, and rose to great wealth. From him and Alfhild stem many men whose names are still remembered. Here ends the tale of Hauk the Ghost Slayer.

*Introduction to "The Smile of Oisia"
by Geo. W. Proctor*

Proctor is a warm, extraordinarily nice youngish
guy who says he's been trying for years to get editors
to publish his name as "Geo." OK, Geo.

He's also been in love with heroic fantasy and has
been writing it for years. Yet this is his first profes-
sionally published "straight" hf story, and we're
both pleased, because we are fast friends and have
shared roofs, bottles, headaches, and nigh-intermin-
able games of Spades, which is sort of like Hearts,
which is sort of like Bridge.

Asked to make a novelet of a short chapter in a
novel your editor had seen in ms., Proctor did — and
sent this story along with it. The requested tale was

returned with some embarrassment. This one's better; this one's Good. Howardesque, it is also Different, with a whale of an original scene, between mortal and im-, that we won't give away here.

Proctor is a Texican, married to a Texican even warmer and nicer than he is. Their fellow Texican, Howard, would enjoy reading this story.

THE SMILE OF OISIA
by
Geo. W. Proctor

Cuculin, city of cities, sprawled over the Isthmus of Rantajur like a courtesan poised seductively atop a bed of satins and silks awaiting her lover of the night. But the men wooing Cuculin's favors numbered ten thousand more than those seeking the amorous affections of a street wench; the city opened her arms to a never-ending procession of trade vessels sailing to and from the Ringed Sea under the flags of Upper and Lower Diadinia's coastal ports.

A coveted prize for the edacious eyes of more than one Diadinian ruler set on expanding the interests of his empire or fattening the coffers of a kingdom,

Cuculin muscled herself against invasion with an army a hundred thousand strong and a naval fleet manned in equal strength. And, locked securely behind the fortification of two solid granite walls and the heavily guarded chambers of the Palace of Kings, was Cuculin's brain, Jalitatus.

Jalitatus, emperor of this vital city-state, by necessity secluded himself with a company of advisors and necromancers within the protection of the palace, to scheme the intrigues of state and plot the course of Cuculin's defenses.

But the city's heart did not beat within those impenetrable walls of the Palace of Kings. Cuculin's life blood was commerce. The heart that pumped that precious flow was the city's wharf district, servicing a harbor filled with ships from a score of nations.

Within the core of this district was the warehouse of Fifhar the shipowner. So it was that summer morn in the thirteenth year of the Cycle of the Ram that Fifhar came to the wharfs to tally a shipload of wares arrived from distant Ubal. Thoughts of profits from jungle ivory, copra, and pearls fled the shipowner's mind when he entered his business chambers.

There on the floor was a dead man.

Naked to the waist, the master clerk, Brumus, was strapped arm and leg to an overturned chair. The man's chest was a mass of oozing red. No skin remained there, only an intricate criss-cross pattern of fine razor slashes where flesh had been cut, then ripped away inch by inch. These were the wounds of torture, slow agonizing torment — but not death.

Death was a single, jagged gash severing the man's throat from ear to ear. Blood still flowed from the deep, horrible wound. A crimson lake pooled around the clerk's head.

Fifhar backed away. His stomach churned violently. Brumus's death had not been the handiwork of an ordinary assassin. The man had lived to feel every tortuous slash, even the last deadly one.

A taunting laugh floated through the room.

The shipowner pivoted sharply to the curtained doorway behind him. His bony hand dipped into his robes, jerking free a broad-bladed dagger. No one was there!

Again the bodiless laugh came, mocking him. Its cold, mirthless tones transformed Fifhar's blood to ice. Trembling, he cautiously turned, his knife thrust before him to meet an attack. There was no assailant, only the empty room and dead Brumus.

"Fifhar," a voice called behind him.

He swirled, wrenching the dagger above his head ready to plunge twelve inches of cold steel into the breast of man or demon. The plummeting blade froze in mid-air. Neither a man nor a demon stood in the entrance, but a woman. Her green eyes were wide, but held no trace of fear, though their gaze clung to the blade hovering but mere inches from the whiteness of her breast. The delicate beauty of her face was undisturbed by the slightest quivering of intimidation.

"Cyreanna!" Nervous relief spread over the shipowner's tension-wrought face. His shaking hand slowly returned the knife to the sheath hidden within his robes. The flame-haired woman was well known to him. A lesser sorceress, Cyreanna had cast his star charts and horoscopes for the past year.

"You're lucky to be alive, girl!" he said, wiping

away the sweat beaded on his brow. "I thought you to be the butcher who killed poor Brumus there."

Cyreanna's gaze followed Fifhar's pointing finger to the dead clerk. Her lips twisted, attempting to hide a cold smile. "I am."

Fifhar's jaw dropped, but before he could utter a sound, a slim dirk pressed against his Adam's apple.

"Forget the knife!" the woman hissed. "Ere your fingers touch the hilt, I will slit your gullet!"

His eyes bulging in fear, the shipowner nodded.

Triumph danced in Cyreanna's eyes. "I want the Mask of Karmik."

"Mask?" Fifhar blinked with puzzlement.

"Your clerk said the same. Even an hour under the caress of my blade couldn't loosen his tongue. His death was hard, Fifhar, but it was nothing compared to the fate I've prepared for you." The treacherous woman jabbed the dagger tip under his chin. Blood welled from a pinprick and trickled down the man's throat. "There's a spell that binds the soul to the body. You won't die, though you will suffer wounds that would have killed a hundred men. The pain, think of the pain, Fifhar! I am Vadean, a people who consider torture the highest art!"

"My life . . . spare my life," the shipowner pleaded. "I will talk."

Cyreanna eased the pressure of her dirk. "The truth and your life is yours."

"Theopoditus . . ." Fifhar gasped, " . . . Jalitatus placed the mask with Theopoditus."

"Theopoditus?" Cyreanna pondered aloud. "Are you sure?"

"Yes. It was originally assigned to me, but only last night Jalitatus placed the mask with Theopoditus.

The man is blessed with the fortune of the gods," the shipowner assured her. "It's rumored that Theopoditus has bartered his soul to dark Kraal. No doubt he has. The whoreson is low born, yet he receives the finest consignments in all Cuculin. When other merchants' ships flounder on still seas, his vessels know only favorable winds. Forty of the city's ships have been torched by pirates this year, yet Theopoditus has never lost a dinghy to corsairs. The man's luck is uncanny."

"Aye," Cyreanna mused, " 'tis uncanny."

Without the batting of her long eyelashes, her slim wrist whipped out like a striking cobra. The sliver of steel she guided with deadly accuracy traced a deep line across Fifhar's extended throat.

The man staggered back. His round eyes widened with bewilderment. His hands clutched his neck in a vain attempt to stop the torrent of blood gushing from his throat. His mouth opened, but only an incoherent gurgle passed over his quivering lips. Then he fell, his body twitching for a moment before death took its full toll.

Stopping to wipe her dagger on the shipowner's robes, Cyreanna studied the two dead men. It would be cleaner to dispose of the bodies, she realized. But time was short and there was much to accomplish if the Mask of Karmik was to be hers before a new day dawned over the city.

On that same morning, Theopoditus sat within the opulence of his summer villa perched on a plateau of the Newtka Mountains, elevating the merchant above Cuculin's teeming masses and the heat-churned odors of the metropolis.

"Superb! Absolutely beautiful! Never has such a divine nymph graced this world!" Theopoditus' obese frame quivered with excitement beneath his silken robes of purples and reds. His slightly bulging eyes darted to the man beside him. "Is she not perfect?"

Kartorka-Shyn, priest in the Temple of Oisia, Goddess of Chance and Fortune, eased the black hood of his cape from his bald head. He glanced at the girl standing before the seated merchant. "She will not suffice."

"Don't be foolish! Never have I provided you with such a beauty." Theopoditus waved away the priest's comment and returned his gaze to the lithe girl. "A bit slim for some, I suppose. But I dare say, most men would claim her a goddess come to earth. Disrobe, my lovely Velita, and display your charms for my priestly friend."

Strands of the girl's soft, mouse-brown hair trembled as if stirred by a sudden, chilling breeze. Her wide, almond eyes rose to the toad of a man perched on the edge of the divan. Revulsion shuddered through her body. She yearned for the warm halls of her father's house in Iro. She ached for the comfort of family and friends.

But she did not protest or question the command. She was a slave. In the year since her abduction from her father's gardens, the slavers' discipline had taught her submission. Iro belonged to the past; belonged to a young girl who was but a memory. She resigned herself to the humiliation cast upon her by cruel Fate. Obediently, her fingers unclasped a single brass brooch pinned to the shoulder of her white tunic.

Sinking back into the plush cushions of his couch, Theopoditus stared over the bejeweled steeple of his fingers. His hungry eyes caressed the supple nakedness of this, his latest offering to the Goddess Oisia. Velita's eyes drifted to the floor to avoid the indignity of his lecherous leer. A mass of shining brown hair tumbled over her bare shoulder, misting around the firm, uptilted cones of her young breasts.

"A virgin," the merchant sighed with more than a touch of regret. "If it weren't for the matter at hand, I'd be hard-pressed not to keep her as a concubine."

"What does *She* care of virgins? I said the girl will not suffice. Have her sent away," Kartorka-Shyn repeated, irritation creeping into his voice.

"Won't . . ." Theopoditus began his objection.

But the priest cut him off, his voice grating like a rasp on steel. "There's no time for idle prattle. Either send her away, or I'll find another who is more willing to listen. Perhaps Shiva, the jewel merchant!"

Theopoditus paled visibly at the mention of a rival who had attempted his murder on seven occasions. His pouchy jowls aquiver, he waved the girl from the room. His eyes dropped to his lap, sparing himself the piercing blackness of Kartorka-Shyn's scowl.

"Better, much better." A pleased smile twisted across the priest's thin lips. "Now we can discuss what must be done to insure your continued prosperity."

The merchant nodded, but did not speak, nor did his eyes rise to Kartorka-Shyn.

"There is only one who will satisfy my wishes tonight," the priest continued, walking across the room to peer out a window to the city below. "The woman called Cyreanna must be sacrificed to Oisia."

"Cyreanna? The sorceress?" Theopoditus gasped, his Adam's apple twitching with a rush of panic.

"A ninth-level witch!" Kartorka-Shyn spat, twisting around to face the merchant. "A power-hungry snipe, whose magic is nothing more than sleight of hand!"

"But she has won the hearts of the people. To kill her would bring questions." Theopoditus wrung his hands, losing a ruby ring in the folds of his robes.

"Murders and questions walk hand in hand. And what is popularity among the citizens of Cuculin?" the priest answered, pausing for an instant. "Nothing! Nothing more than a passing breeze that fades and is replaced by another. The people will mourn Cyreanna's death one day and amuse themselves with another favorite the next."

"No. It's too dangerous." Theopoditus shook his head. "The risk is too great. Why not continue as we have these past five years? Who cares if a slave girl dies? Why risk the wrath of the people and detection? Forget Cyreanna, Kartorka-Shyn. You will use the slave I've purchased."

"Risks? What do you know of risks, fat man?" the priest shouted his rage. "I serve Oisia, Goddess of Chance! She is a fickle deity who does not care for mortals to meddle in her affairs. Her smile can easily be transformed to a frown. Yet, for five years, I've called her forth to seek favors in the name of Theopoditus the merchant."

89

"And you have been well paid for your risks," Theopoditus said, feebly attempting to assert himself. "Half the treasures and riches I have amassed have gone to you."

"Gold and jewels," Kartorka-Shyn snorted in contempt. "There is more in this world than riches, fool!"

A nervous spasm twitched the tautness of the priest's left cheek. The young witch's influence wove its way into high places. Doors he had labored years to open, she slammed in his face with no more than a smile and a suggestive sway of her hips in the direction of Cuculin's lords. Cyreanna had to die!

The merchant tried another approach. "There isn't time to prepare for Cyreanna's abduction. Deeds such as this should be well planned. There are too many things that could go wrong."

"Given a full cycle to scheme, you would still bungle such a task," the priest snapped, "But the sugar to bait the trap for our street fly already lies within your house in Cuculin . . . the Mask of Karmik."

"How do you know?" Theopoditus's eyes jerked up to the priest. "I can't touch that. The mask is a gift from Emperor Jalitatus to the king of Telneaus."

"Cease your whimpering and listen," Kartorka-Shyn hissed his impatience. "You have no choice in the matter, if you wish me to bargain with Oisia in your behalf. Will you do as I say, or shall I seek out the gem merchant?"

"I'll do as you say." Theopoditus swallowed hard.

"Good. The Mask of Karmik is legended to endow its wearer with the abilities of the ancient sorcerer." The priest smiled with decided relish. "Cyreanna hungers for such power. She will be unable to resist the opportunity to possess it."

90

Kartorka-Shyn paused, reaching into his black robes to produce a parchment. "You will return to your house in Cuculin and prepare for tonight. These are your instructions. Follow them to the word!"

The priest tossed the rolled paper into the merchant's lap, pivoted, and walked from the room without waiting for a reply. Theopoditus sat motionless, staring at the departing man. Then he reached down, unrolled the parchment, and read.

A broad grin of white teeth flashing across his dark face, Hweir drew the curtains to the back room of the Silver Wolf Inn. The boisterous revelry of Cuculin's rogues and less desirable elements filling the caravansary muffled to a muted rumble. He turned to his lone companion.

The fiery-haired woman's eyes rose to the sooty-skinned Kessak. "Nalcon? The name is unfamiliar."

"A prince of Paldrid, my dear Cyreanna," Hweir answered, lightly stroking the thin moustache that drooped far below the corners of his mouth. "Second born of King Arkon and brother to Aecon, the present ruler of that northern kingdom."

"Aye! I've seen the man. He seems too thin and soft to be much use to us," Cyreanna pondered. "I would prefer another such as you, my man of Kesha. One bred among the warrior tribes of the Karpetha steppes. This Paldridian has the appearance of a poet or minstrel."

"Appearances are often deceptive." Hweir's obvious pleasure from her compliment set a single braid of jet hair swaying from his shaven scalp. "Nalcon's slim frame is tempered with the muscles of a young ox.

91

His sword arm is quick and true. On more than one occasion our blades have faced common foes."

"That he meets your approval is all the assurance I need." The beautiful enchantress smiled, easing her cloak's green hood over a tumbling cascade of flaming red hair. "Now convince him it would serve his interest to work with us tonight."

"An easy task! Pride runs in Nalcon's royal veins. There's no pride in an empty purse," the dark Kessak answered. "Just see that you have the hundred diels waiting for him when we've completed the deed."

"I will," she nodded, stepping to the man. Admiration glowed in the emerald pools of her eyes. "When the Mask of Karmik is mine, we shall return to my house and Nalcon shall have his hundred gold pieces. And you shall be rewarded as only a woman can reward her champion."

Cyreanna leaned forward. Her taunting, red lips brushed against Hweir's. "Tonight at the eleventh hour, I will await you outside the house of Theopoditus."

The Kessak's massive arms closed around the temptress for a deeper taste of the wine of love she promised. "For such a reward, I would steal into the Palace of Kings and bring you the crown from Jalitatus's head."

"I ask for no such suicide, only the Mask of Karmik . . . and you." Cyreanna wiggled free of his embrace and stepped to the curtain.

She blew him a kiss . . . and disappeared behind the drapery.

"Both will be yours by the twelfth hour this night," Hweir said to himself. His broad, black hand parted the curtain to watch the woman weave through the inn and step outside into the growing dusk. Then he stepped back into the main room of the caravansary.

"May Cuculin be thrice damned!" a thundering voice vented its rage.

Hweir turned to his right and grinned, locating the source of the vehement outrage. Nalcon pushed his way through the inn's patrons. The Paldridian's shoulder-length blond hair flowed behind him as if tossed by a tempest. His face blistered with anger.

"Misfortune plagues a friend and you stand there grinning like a misbegotten Kessak mongrel!" Nalcon threw up his arms in despair upon reaching the dark man's side. "Is there no comfort in this city?"

The man of Kesha shook his head. "Surely life is not as black as you would paint it."

"Black as Kraal's heart!" The yellow-haired Paldridian cursed. "This morning I was to parley with Fifhar the shipowner. The man sent word he had need of a bodyguard. When I arrived to talk with him, his warehouse was crawling with city guards. Fifhar and one of his servants had been killed but an hour earlier. Nor had anyone glimpsed the scoundrel that slit their throats!"

"Would seem the shipowner was right," Hweir answered. "He indeed had need of a bodyguard!"

"Aye . . . *had!* But he hasn't *now!*" Nalcon grunted with dismay. "Even the gaming tables were ill-fated for me this night!"

The Kessak's black eyes dropped to a pair of dice the Paldridian held in his open palm.

"I purchased them in the bazaar this afternoon in the hope they would change my luck in the dice ring," Nalcon continued. "Now I haven't the price of a cup of wine — not even a copper for a flagon of ale!"

"*I* have." Hweir's grin broadened. He clasped his friend's shoulder with a black hand. "Put away the dice. It is well known that Paldridians are born with bad luck on their shoulders when it comes to gaming. You've no need for luck this night. I have a fine prospect to weight your purse with a hundred gold diels!"

With a sigh, the fair-haired man dropped the dice into an empty pouch on his side, watching the Kessak move to a table. "I know that tone, old friend. When a man of Kesha speaks lightly, it's more than dangerous . . . "

"Here, sit!" Hweir kicked a stool toward his companion. He waved a maid to him, ordering not Cuculin's thin, bitter ale, but the finest sweet wines from Nalcon's homeland.

Noting well how his dusky friend endeavored to cater to his tastes, the blond Paldridian dropped to the seat. "Tell me of this scheme for quick gold."

Hweir did.

Nalcon found it no more to his liking than the other less than legal ventures in which his friend had entangled him in the past. But when, in the midst of their haggling, Nalcon's empty belly growled like the grumbling bellow of an Yzasitan camel, both men knew resistance was at an end. Black Kessak and royal-blooded Paldridian would draw their swords together this night; and who for the better reason, the body of a flame-haired temptress, or the stomach of a hungry man?

"Witches! Dead Wizards! May your children be twisted gnomes, my black friend!" Nalcon hissed his curse, while clinging to the shadows veiling him and his two companions. "If we live . . . "

"Later!" Cyreanna snapped, her impatience stirred

by the moment. "We've no time for empty words!"

"We'll have the mask and be gone before the passing of an hour," Hweir added. "All that stands between us is that wall and the tower."

"And two guards patrolling the grounds," the man of Paldrid interjected, refusing to be convinced of the simplicity of the scheme. "The tower itself; what demon does Theopoditus have lurking there?"

After an uneasy silence, the beautiful redhead answered, "The tower *is* guarded . . . but the sentinel is neither man nor demon. Beyond that, I can not see."

"We're wasting time," the sooty-skinned Hweir interrupted the exchange. He stepped from the shadows to face the wall. "How high do you make it?"

"Fifteen feet," Nalcon replied.

"Grapnel?" the Kessak motioned to the hook and line slung over his shoulder.

"Too much noise," Nalcon said with a shake of his yellow-maned head. "Have you ever been a tumbler?"

Without waiting for an answer, the Paldridian trotted to the wall, silently studying its height. When he turned back to his companions, he crouched and stooped a bit at the shoulders. Nalcon's long arms drooped between his open legs, his fingers interlocking to form a stirrup.

A thin smile of amusement played over Hweir's lips, realizing what his friend intended.

Quickly stripping away his sword and slipping the rope and hook from his shoulder, Hweir of Kesha handed them to the girl at his side. Taking a firm stance on the cobblestone street, he nodded. Nalcon returned the nod. Hweir bolted forward. He heard the blond grunt when his booted foot slammed into the stirrup of his friend's hands. Then the Kessak's full attention

95

was directed to the top of the wall. Nalcon heaved and catapulted his companion upward.

Hweir's mark was short. Instead of landing atop the granite barrier, his fingers barely managed to catch its edge. He hung motionless for a moment or two. Regaining his breath, he pulled himself up.

Signalling Cyreanna to the wall, Nalcon took the extra sword she carried and tossed it to the man atop the wall. After a moment to allow the Kessak to arm himself, the blond sent up the grapnel. A black hand shot out and snatched the hook from the air; a heartbeat later, Hweir had attached it to the wall.

Cyreanna scurried up first, with Nalcon at her heels.

Theopoditus's home was palatine. A neatly manicured garden of exotic flowers and shrubs brought from the far reaches of Diadinia surrounded it. The tower they sought formed a corner of the multi-level house. There was no outside entrance to the spire, except for a single round window near its peak. An interior light clearly outlined the dimensions of the aperture.

"Down flat!" Hweir commanded in an urgent hiss.

Without questioning, Nalcon and Cyreanna dropped to their stomachs and froze. The footsteps of two men approached from below, then passed, unaware of the three intruders above.

"All clear." The Kessak pushed up to a crouch. The black braid of his hair whipped like a snake from his shaven head. "After me."

The grapnel and line once more coiled around his shoulder, Hweir leaped from the wall. A soft thud sounded as he landed on the garden's thick carpet of grass. Two more thuds followed and Nalcon and Cyreanna were beside him.

"Shall we play it as the cards fall?" Hweir whispered to the slim Paldridian.

"Nay, I've sworn off gambling," Nalcon grunted with disgust. "I prefer a sure thing . . . say, an ambush."

The dark-hued Kessak waved an arm toward the house, signaling Nalcon to take the lead.

In a running crouch, the yellow-haired man shot across the garden, vanishing into the shadows at the foot of the tower. Directing Cyreanna behind a fronded shrub, the Kessak followed his companion. There was the soft whisper of steel escaping leather sheaths. Broadswords in hand, they waited.

When the two guards stepped around the tower on another round of the garden, Nalcon emerged from the shadows. He tapped one on the shoulder and gave the unsuspecting man a hard-swung, back-handed mouthful of sword pommel. With definitely less dramatic flair, but equally effective results, Hweir swung his blade like a club. Its broad flat edge slammed into the back of the other guard's skull. The two sentries crumpled to the ground, unconscious.

"Aren't you going to slit their throats?" Cyreanna demanded upon rejoining them.

"No need," Hweir answered. "We'll be away from here long before either of these awakens."

Cyreanna dropped to her knees beside the fallen guards. Moonlight glinted from a dirk in her hand. Before either man could react, she slashed twice in rapid succession. Dark rivers spouted on the unconscious men's throats.

Neither Hweir nor Nalcon spoke, their eyes turning away from the life flowing from the guards' necks.

"Don't act like squeamish maidens," the red-haired woman spat with contempt. "You've both seen dead

97

men before. What's done is done. Now for the task at hand."

A low growl of displeasure rumbled deep in Nalcon's throat. He twisted from the girl, his gaze climbing the tower. "The window is no more than a pigeon hole from here. It's at least forty feet up and this wall is polished marble. No way to get either a handhold or footing."

"That's why I had Hweir bring the grapnel and line," Cyreanna answered. "Your task is to scale the tower. Mine is to get the rope up there. Hweir!"

The Kessak responded, handing her hook and line. Waving the men back, she placed the rope at the foot of the tower. Her arms slowly moved through the air above the coils, her hands gesturing now and then. Chanting in a voice too soft for either of the men to understand, she eased back a bit. Her arms rose above her head. The line quivered and trembled as if life had suddenly been breathed into it. The hook rose first, like some mishapen serpent. Upward it drifted, the rope uncoiling and writhing behind it.

"A touch of magic from a sorceress can't be scoffed at." Hweir winked at his companion.

"A cheap trick," Nalcon replied. "I'd be more impressed if she'd breathe life into those guards again."

A metallic clink sounded above, drawing their attention back to Cyreanna. The grapnel neatly lipped the window ledge. Nalcon reached out and tugged at the rope. It held.

"I'll make the climb," Hweir offered.

Nalcon refused to release the line. "I'd prefer you down here to guard my escape route . . . and her."

The Kessak drew his sword in answer and stepped away from the rope. Nalcon smiled, grasped the line, and began pulling himself upward. Hand over hand, his legs entwined around the rope trailing behind, he worked, pausing now and then to glance at his two companions watching his progress.

The climb took less than two minutes and was accomplished with less drain on his energies than Nalcon of Paldrid had expected. The circular window was another problem in itself. The opening was small, presenting a tight squeeze for even his slim body and an excellent opportunity for attack by whatever inhuman guard lay within.

Reaching upward, he grasped the ledge with one hand, released the rope, and grabbed the ledge with the other hand. For a moment, he dangled there, his fingers clutching the polished stone. Unable to secure a footing on the side of the tower, he relied on his arms to pull him up to peer into the aperture.

Within was a small candle-lit chamber. The room was bare, except for a single pedestal that stood at its center. A richly finished ebony box lay atop the pedestal, its lid opened to reveal the shining silver mask of the long-dead wizard Karmik.

Cyreanna's inhuman guard was nowhere in sight.

Carefully, Nalcon lifted the grapnel and tossed it inside the chamber. Still no guard! Pulling himself up, he wiggled head first through the confining opening. He sighed a prayer of relief once inside, thanking Fate that the would-be sorceress below had seen wrong. But he drew his sword, just on the possibility Cyreanna was correct.

His steel-blue eyes darted around the circular chamber while he edged toward the pedestal. Aside from the window, the only means of egress was a wooden door to his right. With one eye on that door, he examined the mask. It was a full facial mask with intricate designs flowering over the cheeks that reminded him of the painted faces of the black-skinned savages inhabiting the rain forests of Lower Diadinia. The interior of the ebony case was gold. Four sculptures of gold scorpions surrounded the mask. Each was a perfect replica of their living and deadly counterparts that inhabited the Great Desert. If the scorpions represented the wizard's fate, Nalcon did not know. However, each of the golden insects was worth a small fortune.

His gaze returned to the mask.

Despite its grotesque markings and rather tortured expression, there was a compelling beauty about it; an expert craftmanship that demanded to be touched and felt. The Paldridian's hand rose to caress its shining surface.

A movement caught his eyes. Nalcon jerked his fingers back, staring into the box, unsure whether the movement had been real or imagined. Cautiously, he extended the tip of his broadsword toward the silver mask. The tail of one of the scorpions came alive, lashing its death-laced stinger at cold steel.

Nervous relief suffused every cell of his body. He had discovered the guard of the wizard's mask. Not some ingenious mechanism, but a real scorpion. Painted gold, with the gold interior of the case molded around its legs, the insect provided the perfect sentry for the mask. Or almost perfect. Had the poisonous creature not tensed at his approach, it would have served its purpose and he would have lost his life.

Nalcon used the tip of his sword to flip shut the lid to the wooden box. Securing the lock, he sealed mask and guard within, both to be dealt with after he made good his escape.

Metal grating against stone ripped through the silence of the room. He twisted, tempered steel leveled to deliver death. But he faced no opponent, only the snaking rope and the receding grapnel, that danced around on the floor for an instant — then flew out the window when the line jerked with increased violence.

Panic gripped him. He ran to the aperture and peered below.

Neither Hweir nor Cyreanna was in sight. The hook and rope were on the ground and an unidentifiable man stood beside them. The man's head turned upward and Nalcon jerked back. He was too late.

"Kartorka-Shyn, there's another one in the tower!" a voice that was unmistakably that of Theopoditus the merchant called out.

Kartorka-Shyn! The name railed through the Paldridian's brain. What business did the priest of Oisia, Goddess of Fortune and Chance, have in the house of Theopoditus? Oisia was the deity of gamblers, not merchants. And where in all of Cuculin were Hweir and Cyreanna?

"Forget him!" a rasping voice ordered from outside. "Tak and Lithon will see to him. We've other work to attend in the cellar."

No longer bothered with the worry of discovery, Nalcon poked his head back out the window. Below he saw the answer to his last question. Either dead or unconscious, both his companions were being carried toward the front of the house by slaves. Theopoditus and the black-robed priest followed after them. Still another two men emerged from the shadows at the foot of the tower, brandishing tulwars and cursing up at him.

101

Unsure of what had happened, or what was presently occurring outside, Nalcon was sure of only one fact at the moment — the window offered no avenue of escape. Tucking the ebony case under his belt, he strode across the chamber and tested the wooden door. It was stuck.

One well-placed kick remedied the situation, nearly jarring the door from its rust-eaten hinges.

On the other side, stone steps spiraled downward into darkness. Time did not permit the Paldridian to consider where the stairs led. It was either descend or remain trapped in the tower. He took the only route open to him, running down the steps two at a time.

Ten full circles downward, the stairs abruptly ended and another wooden door barred his way. This time, Nalcon did not bother attempting to open it by hand. He simply lashed out full force with his boot. The door swung open.

The room he entered brought an amused smile to his lips. Thin, silken veils hung like canopies from the ceiling and covered the walls. Silk and satin pillows were scattered over tiles of arabesque design. A fog-like cloud of incense floated languorously through the air.

The room's only occupant sat on a thick pile of pillows near the Paldridian. She wore nothing more than a startled expression and a transparent veil of pink silk around her waist.

The girl's large, round, almond eyes blinked in confusion at least three times before she finally forced herself to utter, none too surely, "Oh! Who . . . who are you?"

"A thief in the night, lovely lady." Nalcon of Paldrid grinned and bowed slightly. "I wish that time permitted me the opportunity to dally longer, but I fear it can not be."

Nalcon froze in mid-stride. The door at the opposite end of the room suddenly was beset with a barrage of pounding fists. The urgent voices of two men called out, demanding that the door be opened. The brown-haired girl slid from her bed of pillows and trotted obediently toward the entrance. She barely managed to maintain her balance when Nalcon grabbed one of her slim wrists and jerked her back to him.

"Don't struggle and I'll not hurt you," the Paldridian commanded. Her soft, liquid eyes widened in fear. "I have no want to harm you, but I need your help. Your friends outside have every intention of running me through, unless you'll aid me."

She blinked in confusion. "What do you want of me?"

"Just stand here and do as I say." The blond intruder nodded, edging her toward the door and reaching out with his sword to slip back the latch.

The door swung inward. The two men he had seen from the tower stood there, tulwars raised and ready. Wrapping his left arm tightly around the girl's waist and backstepping a bit, Nalcon raised the point of his blade to the graceful, white arch of her neck.

"I suggest you make this as easy as possible." Nalcon's gaze darted between the two men. "Either drop your weapons, or I'll kill her."

The ploy was a good one. However, neither of the men seemed interested in the fate of such a blossom of pulchritude. Both charged through the entrance, fully intent on impaling him on those wickedly curved blades, and the girl in the process.

His human shield now useless, Nalcon shoved her aside. She tumbled and fell to the tiled floor. There would be bruises in the morning to remind her of their nocturnal meeting, but better bruises than death, he thought.

Taking a wide stance, his sword leveled at the closest of the two attackers, Nalcon waited until the last moment before their blades met. In a movement that took the man completely off guard, the Paldridian lowered his longsword and side-stepped the charge. The tulwar gouged empty air. Nalcon's foot lashed out, knocking the legs out from under his first assailant and depositing him on the floor with a fleshy thud that drove the air from the man's lungs.

Simultaneously, the Paldridian's broadsword arced upward to parry a full, over-the-head slash from the second swordsman. Steel met steel in a resounding cacophony. Sparks flashed under the bone-jarring impact. The man's eyes widened, enraged that his skull-splitting blow had been blocked with such ease.

That one instant of surprise and anger was all Nalcon needed. His wrist twisted slightly. He ducked beneath the crossed blades. The tip of his sword flicked over the curved tulwar and drove home, sinking into his opponent's throat.

The man's eyes blinked as if he were unable to comprehend what had occurred. The tulwar dropped from his fingers. He staggered back a step or two, then collapsed to the floor, dead.

A rustle sounded behind the man of Paldrid.

Nalcon swirled, his blade leaping out and parrying a thrust intended for his back. The man was no better a swordsman than his companion. With that same rotating motion of his wrist, Nalcon slipped his steel through the man's defenses and skewered into his opponent's chest. The man crumpled to the tiles, blood flowing from his pierced heart.

Wiping his sword on one of the pillows scattered on the floor, Nalcon resheathed the blade. He started toward the opened exit before Theopoditus could send more of his household guards to reclaim the purloined mask.

"Where are you going?" the girl cried to him. "You can't leave me here! I'll be punished for this!"

"I can't take you with me." He shrugged, turning back to her. "That is, unless you can manage one of these swords."

"In my country, women are trained in the ways to please men, not murder them." Her gaze drifted to the guards on the floor. She added with a proud grin, "Although, I am a virgin . . . "

"You tempt me, but I'm afraid it is not to be." He smiled, then asked abruptly, "How well do you know the house?"

"I was here a month before Master Theopoditus moved his household to his summer villa," she answered. "Why?"

"Can you lead me to the cellar?" Nalcon pressed, with the hope of locating Hweir and Cyreanna.

"There is an entrance in the kitchens," she nodded. "I can show you . . . if you'll take me with you."

"First, the cellar." He waved an arm for her to lead on.

"Good!" Her eyes sparkled with delight. She scurried to him, nearly losing that one thin veil she wore. "I am called Velita."

"Nalcon of Paldrid," he bowed slightly and once more waved his arm toward the door.

Taking his hand, she led him into the corridor outside. Down a dimly lit hall and a flight of stairs they moved, careful that their steps were light. A lesser hallway and another staircase and they stood within the kitchens. Several bowls of burning oil lit the room like a thousand candles.

"The cellar's this way." Velita motioned him toward a line of ovens and pointed to the floor. "The tile lifts."

A brass ring was inset in the white tile. Kneeling, Nalcon gripped the ring and pulled. The tile, set on a pair of well-oiled hinges, swung upward with ease. An effluvium of soured wine and dust assailed his nostrils. A wooden staircase led into the darkness below.

"A wine cellar?" His head twisted to the girl. "Is this the only cellar?"

Velita's gaze drifted to the floor and she nodded.

"It's not what I'm seeking," he grunted with disgust. "Are you sure that this is . . . "

A muffled scream rose from below, stopping him before he could complete his question. His eyes darted to the girl. Another scream muffled its way from the wine cellar.

"Wait here. If I don't return within the half hour, go back to your room," Nalcon whispered, apprehension coursing through his body. "A beating is better than death."

Confusion clouded her face, but Velita did not protest. She nodded again, watching the blond man of Paldrid draw his sword, then disappear into the cellar.

At the foot of the wooden stairway, Nalcon paused, allowing his eyes to accustom themselves to the murkiness of the underground chamber. He stood amid a narrow corridor lined on each side with row upon row of wine kegs stacked from floor to ceiling. A rat squeaked its objections to the intruder, then scurried away, its claws scraping against the kegs as it fled.

106

There was another scream, sounding closer now. It was followed by a string of colorful profanities in the unmistakable voice of the dark-skinned Kessak. Someone shouted and Hweir's curses were abruptly cut off.

Broadsword leveled against the darkness, Nalcon moved down the corridor of wine kegs, following the direction of the voices. One foot, then the other, he walked as if to disturb the dust covering the floor would betray his position.

The point of his blade tapped stone. Reaching out in the darkness, the Paldridian's fingers brushed against a wall that dead-ended the cellar. Perplexed by the barrier, Nalcon turned to retrace his steps, in the hope of discovering some avenue that had eluded him in the blackness.

A voice came again, neither cursing nor that of Hweir, but a deep, droning voice. Easing back to the wall, Nalcon pressed his ear to the stone. No sound penetrated the rock. The wall was solid, concealing no hidden chamber behind a false facade.

The monotonous droning increased. Cocking his head from side to side, Nalcon reoriented himself to the sound. It came from below, from under his feet!

Sinking to his knees, he felt out blindly with his left hand. His fingers fumbled against the brass ring he knew would be there. Like its counterpart in the kitchen, the ring opened a false tile. Nalcon inched it upwards, just enough to peer through a slight crack.

Below was yet another subterranean vault. Unlike the wine cellar, torches hung from its walls, their flickering light luminating the chamber with the brightness of the kitchens above. Directly below the trapdoor, at the foot of a wooden ladder, stood Theopoditus. The fat man brandished a long, needle-pointed dagger

107

toward Hweir, who was chained spread-eagle to the right wall of the room. An angry lump on the Kessak's dark forehead had swollen his left eye shut and a thin trickle of blood ran from the corner of his mouth. Hweir's one good eye glared with hatred, but no sound passed over his lips.

"Oisia, Goddess of Chance . . . Oisia, Goddess of Fortune . . . " the droning voice continued its chant.

Opening the trapdoor a bit further, Nalcon found its source. The priest Kartorka-Shyn knelt at the far end of the chamber, his head raised and his arms uplifted. Before him was a massive block of stone. Atop it — Cyreanna, naked and bound hand and foot. The woman's emerald eyes flashed with fear, her gaze darting between Kartorka-Shyn and the helpless Hweir.

" . . . Tonight your servants call. Tonight the feast is laid before you. Oisia, Goddess of Chance, Oisia, Goddess of Fortune," the priest called out, his hands weaving gestures in the air.

Nalcon sucked in his breath. His body tensed to swing wide the trapdoor and drop through the opening. Then he froze, his brain refusing to accept what his eyes saw.

A shadow at the foot of the block of stone darkened, thickening, as if taking on a mass of its own. It grew, widening like a small pool. It bubbled and boiled, vapors rising in a black cloud that abruptly transformed to white. Writhing and churning within itself, the cloud took form, as though molded by unseen hands.

Then it solidified.

Never could Nalcon describe the vision that stood beside the altar as a woman!

She was a Goddess. Clothed only in a mist of everchanging light, she stood there, her beauty defying the mudane limits of Nalcon's brain. An unearthly silence filled the chamber. Even Cyreanna, whose lips writhed in terror, could find no voice for her screams.

A humorless smile brightened the goddess' face. Her gaze leisurely surveyed the chamber, alighting on Cyreanna.

"Oisia," Kartorka-Shyn whispered with the heart of reverence.

"Is this your offering?" she asked, but did not ask. Her voice was as cold and forbidding as the frozen mountains of the north and as warm and gentle as a lover's caress.

The priest nodded, stammering, "Her life . . . in exchange for . . . continued blessings . . . for Theopoditus . . . the merchant."

"Agreed." The Goddess Oisia smiled, her hand rising toward Cyreanna.

The red-haired woman twisted and struggled, but could not escape the confines of her bonds.

Nalcon forced himself to move, breaking the icy fingers of fear gripping his muscles. Throwing the trapdoor open, he leaped down, thudding heavily into the back of the merchant.

The impact sent Theopoditus to the floor of the chamber, his dagger careening across stone. Before the merchant could even recover his breath, the Paldridian rolled to his feet, his sword raised toward the goddess in challenge.

"A gnat with a bee's sting!" Oisia grinned, her eyes rising to the intruder.

There were no irises in those eyes, no whites, only eerie orbs of churning topaz!

She laughed, pointing a single finger at Nalcon's blade. There was no explosion, no ball of consuming

109

fire. The sword simply wilted, tempered steel transformed to parchment. The goddess's mirth rose. Her laughter reverberated through the chamber. Her hand once more lifted to Cyreanna to claim her tribute.

"Goddess of gamblers!" Nalcon shouted in desperation. "Goddess of Chance! Are your names but jests?"

Oisia's hand halted. Her head turned back to the Paldridian.

His knees threatening to give way, his body chilled with terror, Nalcon forced himself to continue. "Where is the sweet risk of the gamble?"

"What do you propose, gnat?" Oisia's gaze was as piercing as cold steel.

Nalcon swallowed hard. "A wager! Life. . . or death. The highest stake a mortal can offer. The lives of the girl, my chained friend, and myself, against those of the priest and the merchant!"

Kartorka-Shyn's eyes widened in horror. His lips moved, but uttered no sound. Theopoditus squirmed on the floor, unable to regain his footing. Panic raced through his fat frame.

"The game?" the goddess asked.

"These," Nalcon answered, reaching into his money pouch and extracting the pair of dice he had placed there earlier in the evening.

Hweir moaned in total helplessness.

"Agreed." Oisia nodded, the topaz orbs of her eyes flashing with specks of gold. "Give me the dice."

"Our pact!" Kartorka-Shyn cried out, suddenly finding his tongue. "Our pact!"

"The girl lives. There is no bargain. And this mortal's wager amuses me," Oisia replied, lifting the two carved bone cubes from Nalcon's palm.

Her fingers closed around the dice and opened. The

110

common dice were replaced by two cube-cut rubies, each facet inlaid with delicate gold figures.

"Examine them," she commanded, returning the dice to the Paldridian. "The death-head is my sign. The jester represents the fool who wagers against Chance herself. Each die has equal facets of death and fool, equal odds for you and me."

Nalcon rolled the cubes on his palm. Each was intricately decorated with three skulls and three harlequins.

"Are they weighted?" Hweir called out. "Are they weighted?"

Nalcon appeared to ignore his dark-skinned friend, but rolled the dice again, testing them for load. He could not tell.

"The game is simple," the goddess explained. "You and your companions are free if you roll two fools. You are mine if I roll two death-heads."

"And if I roll the skulls?" Nalcon asked, thumbing the cubes in an attempt to locate a load. He still could not.

"You lose," Oisia replied. "As I lose should I toss the fools. Is the game agreeable?"

Nalcon eyed the ruby dice in his hand and nodded his approval.

The goddess's smile grew. She lifted a finger to touch Cyreanna's bonds. They snapped. The naked woman scuttled from the stone altar and shrank back against the wall near Hweir. Her eyes darted between man and goddess.

"An appropriate gaming table," Oisia's hand waved over the altar. "And in a gesture of fair play, I give you first toss."

An ice floe ran through Nalcon's spine, while the rest of his body was parched like the sands of the Great

111

Desert. Perspiration beaded on his forehead. He closed his fist around the dice. Silently he did as all Diadinian gamblers do; he began a prayer to Oisia. Then he stopped, realizing his prayer would not be answered this night.

"Well, mortal, do we play?" Oisia insisted.

"Paldridians are born with bad luck on their shoulders," Hweir moaned under his breath, remembering the adage he had found humorous but a few hours ago.

Gulping down a lungful of air, Nalcon shook the dice, then shook them once more for luck — and tossed.

The jewels chimed like glass as they hit atop the altar. They rolled in helter-skelter fashion across the stone. Abruptly one die settled and a jester smiled up at mortal and deity. Nalcon's heart eased its throbbing a bit, only to resume its heavy hammering when the second cube stopped, topped by the grin of death.

Hweir sighed behind him, whether in relief or desperation, the man of Paldrid was unable to judge.

The Goddess of Chance smiled. She reached down and scooped the dice from the altar. With no display at all, she tossed. The rubies skidded across the stone in a topsy-turvy dance that matched the pounding of Nalcon's temples. A jester and skull of shining gold stared up as the dice halted.

"Your throw, mortal," Oisia mused.

Palms slick with sweat and fingers atremble, Nalcon pulled the dice to him and closed his hand around their translucent redness. With no god to call upon for aid, he simply shook the cubes and tossed. Hweir's gasp chorused his own. A death-head popped up on the first die. A nervous smile spread over the Paldridian's lips when it was accompanied by a fool.

With no more ceremony than before, Oisia gathered

the rubies and rolled them. Again she tossed a jester and a skull.

The full weight of the odds he faced leadening his arm, Nalcon retrieved the dice for the third time, shook and tossed. The first cube stopped dead, refusing even one tumble. Its skull grinned up to mock him. However, the other die danced wildly across the altar, teetering on the edge of the stone for an instant, then falling to the floor. Neither Nalcon nor Oisia moved.

"Do you wish another toss, or take it as it lies?" the goddess questioned.

"Another roll!" the Kessak urged, straining against his chains.

Nalcon's heart missed a beat. "As it is."

Both man and goddess peered over the edge of the altar. Their gazed was returned by that of a harlequin.

"A wise choice," Oisia grunted, snapping her fingers. The stray die rose to her hand.

She shook the ruby cubes this time. Their muted chiming filled the room like a death rattle. She threw. The dice spun and tumbled, rolling over the stone. A jester peered up, accompanied by another fool when the second cube settled.

"It seems it is a night for fools." Oisia smiled, her hand pointing to Hweir. Chains dropped away from the Kessak's wrists and ankles. "And it seems a portion of my prize has escaped."

Nalcon glanced behind him. Theopoditus was gone.

"He will not evade his fate," the goddess said simply, easing the ruby dice across the altar to Nalcon. "Take these as a reminder of the night Oisia smiled on you."

Without speaking, the Paldridian scooped up the cubes and deposited them in his pouch. His gaze returned to the Goddess of Chance and Fortune. She

113

now held Kartorka-Shyn by the back of his neck. The priest's feet dangled helplessly in the air.

"Begone now, ere I decide you somehow managed to cheat me," the goddess commanded.

When a deity commands, mortals obey. Nalcon, Hweir, and Cyreanna ran to the back of the chamber and clambered up the wooden ladder leading to the wine cellar. A scream, the soul of terror itself, rose from the lower chamber as Nalcon closed the trapdoor, sealing priest and goddess below. His eyes clamped shut and he held them that way for more than a few moments. But he knew not even a lifetime could blot out the scene he had glimpsed in the flickering torches below.

"The Mask of Karmik?" Cyreanna's hands shook his shoulder. "Did you get the mask?"

"We've trod the paths of gods tonight. Is the mask all you can think of?" the Paldridian snapped.

"I came for the mask and I want it!" the woman demanded, yanking the ebony box from his grasp. "That's better. Now let's be out of here before Oisia has a change of mind."

Hweir agreed, running toward the stairs at the end of the cellar and the light filtering down from above. Both Cyreanna and Nalcon followed, nearly stumbling over each other as they darted up the stairs. All three halted dead in their tracks when they reached the kitchens. Theopoditus, backed by four guards armed with tulwars, stood at the doorway Nalcon and Velita had used to enter the room.

"There they are! Kill them!" The merchant's arm waved the guards forward.

Brandishing their blades, the four men ran toward the trio. Both Nalcon and Hweir reached for their own swords. Their sheaths were empty, Nalcon's blade now a useless scrap of paper on the floor of the chamber below and Hweir's lost when he was first taken captive by the priest and merchant.

Abruptly the four swordsmen skidded to a stop less than ten feet from the trio of thieves. Fear masked their faces. Theopoditus's own face turned as white as the tiles on which he stood. He trembled for a moment, then turned and ran into the interior of the house. Following the course of their leader, the four guards twisted around and bolted from the room.

A movement to his side caught Nalcon's eyes. He glanced over his shoulder. Oisia floated in the air above the opened wine cellar. Without a word or motion, the Goddess of Chance drifted after the fleeing merchant, her bare feet elevated at least a foot from the kitchens' tiles.

"She claims the last portion of her winnings." Hweir managed a smile, despite his swollen eye and split lip.

"And the time has come to claim our own rewards." Nalcon nodded, turning to the woman at his side.

There was no woman at his side. The fire-haired Cyreanna was gone.

"Apparently my love has decided to slip away without paying her debts," Hweir shrugged.

Nalcon grunted, "Not at all to my liking."

"Nor mine," Hweir agreed, sighting another exit to the kitchens beside the line of ovens. "After you, my Paldridian prince."

Nalcon did not bother to answer, but ran toward the door that led to the garden outside. A scream, a man's scream, filled with tortured agony, tore through the night. Oisia had collected her tribute. Nalcon shivered despite himself, remembering the scene he

115

glimpsed in the altar chamber — Oisia's hand sinking inti Kartorka-Shyn's chest, pulling free with a still living, beating heart in her palm.

Another scream resounded, that of a woman.

"This way," Hweir called to him, darting under a low hanging willow.

No more than twenty strides later, they discovered the source of the scream. Cyreanna lay still on the grass, her nakedness more than deadly pale in the moonlight. The Mask of Karmik was beside her. Its ebony case, the lid still open, lay a few feet away, as if tossed in a moment of horrible surprise.

"She's dead." Hweir stared up to his companion, as he knelt beside the woman.

"She didn't give me time to tell her about the mask's guard," Nalcon answered, pointing to the thrashing scorpion still securely anchored to the gold in the box.

The dark-skinned Kessak shuddered, moving from the dead sorceress and lifting the mask of the ancient wizard from the ground. "Not the reward I had anticipated, nor the gold you expected . . . but it should serve us in Anatia."

"Anatia?" Nalcon glanced at his companion.

"Aye, there are five dead this night and Cuculin's lords will demand an investigation. Four men can place us in this house. And there will be those who will scream for a head or two in return for one as prosperous as the fat merchant. Cuculin will be unsafe for either you or me for the next month or two. So, until the city forgets this night — Anatia," Hweir explained.

"Seven dead," Nalcon corrected, recounting the two guards whom he had slain in Velita's room. "Anatia it is . . . until Cuculin forgets."

"Then I suggest we be on our way. Theopoditus'

116

men will regain their wits any time now and when they return, they'll bring soldiers with them," Hweir said.

"Go back to the Silver Wolf and arrange for three horses and weapons," the yellow-haired Paldridian answered. "I'll meet you there shortly and we'll begin our journey east."

Hweir stared at him in puzzlement. "Three horses?"

"Three," Nalcon nodded, waving his friend away. He turned and trotted back to the house of the dead merchant.

A broad grin brightened his face at the thought of the girl who sat waiting for him within the upper chambers of the house, and the treasure she held. One that her master had not collected nor would ever collect. But one Nalcon of Paldrid had no intention of losing this night.

Introduction to "Pride of The Fleet"
by Bruce Jones

Some of us have enjoyed Bruce Jones's graphic art *(usually illustrating his own scripts)* for years, in color and otherwise. His youth, therefore, is astonishing. So is the fact that he dared write this most unusual story — and brought it off. It's Jones who is referred to in the foreword as having done a good job with both story and art for "Red Sonja," in the Marvel lines of . . . magazines that really can't be called "comic books." Graphic-story magazines?

This is the only story in this volume that doesn't take place in the past. All this guy over in Kansas wants to do is write and draw his fingers to nubs — and break every dam' rule in this genre. Here go a few . . .

PRIDE OF THE FLEET
by
Bruce Jones

The Colifax she wore at her girdle and she didn't like it. It pulled the wrong way. It hurt. It looked ugly.

The stunner she had thrown away hours ago. She could always claim that she'd lost it in the underbrush. It would cost her, of course, but she'd rather pay a fine than be humiliated by the presence of a stunner. She would have thrown away the Colifax too, even earlier, but it happened to be worth several million credits base value and much more than that to the prestige of Colony Six and its Commander; if she had any intention of staying with the Fleet, she'd better hang on to that particular piece of equipment.

All right, she'd put up with it. Even if it did get in her way, slow her down and (most importantly) unforgivably disfigure her newly designed combat uniform. She'd put up with it.

But damned if she'd use it. She'd flit through this mission in record time and bring back her man without a scratch — to either of them. And she didn't need any new technological wonders to accomplish it. Dangers? Threats? Sure, there were always those. But she'd run into them before, in more jungles on more planets than she could remember. She could handle them.

She had her sword.

Her sword.

She touched it now, lightly on the jeweled hilt as she stepped over a moss-laden log, and she couldn't supress the smile of pride tugging at her cheek. Now here was a sword!

The uniform may have been merely showy, true; the flaming hair, moisture-gloss lips, choker, diamond slippers — all decoration, all for effect. Granted. Even the sweep and design of the blade itself may have been opulently histrionic — but that's where the distinction ended. Once that ivory hand wrapped around that ebony grip and the blinding sabre-length sang from its scabbard, all the tinsel ended, all the glitter stopped.

She was lightning, she was whirlwind, she was blur — everywhere her opponent should have been just one nth of a second before he got there — all slash and gleam and awful whining, wind-screaming death, until he got dizzy just watching and probably never felt the incredible razor incisions even after the ground was soaking red around him and his knees were buckling of their own accord. Oh, she was good. She was the best, sex distinction notwithstanding.

120

She knew it too, and enjoyed the reputation that went with it. Men were at once intensely enamoured and terrified of her. She simply could not be bested with a sword — not at Colony Six anyway — and in a place where the men outnumbered the women three to one, well, it made life interesting.

They were all in love with her; all of the men and many of the women. She was beautiful, exotic, talented, lethal. It's easy to love people like that. Even the Colony Commander wasn't immune; him with his stuffy little paneled office and stuffier little shirt . . .

"Come in, Sheffield, yes . . . "

"Thank you, sir."

"Sit down, please." *My god, is that her uniform? Is she running around the halls like that?*

"I prefer to stand, thank you, sir." *It shows me off better.*

"As you wish. (A-hem!) Now, as you've no doubt heard, we've got an AWOL as of last night, Sheffield. A private . . . uh . . . paper's here somewhere . . . "

"Leakwood, sir."

"Leakwood, yes. Private Leakwood. AWOL at 0728. Our *first* AWOL in seven years, Sheffield. *My* first ever. I don't like it. Not a bit. I want him back. I want him alive. I want him recycled."

"Yes, sir."

"It's a blemish, Sheffield. You can appreciate that."

"Yes, sir."

"We don't want blemishes at Colony Six. No one does."

"No, sir."

"We can rectify this thing, Sheffield; clearly, efficiently. I know we can. We have the training, the facility, the man-power, the expertise. We're one of the best, Sheffield, one of the very best. I want us to remain that way. I don't want a blemish like this to upset everything Fleet has built us for. No one does." He paused, gazing at her without approval.

"That . . . ah, uniform you're wearing, has it been officially recognized?"

"It has, sir. I designed it myself after the Princess Dejah Thoris."

"Who?"

"Dejah Thoris, a fictional character of Edgar Rice Burroughs."

"Burroughs . . . "

"A Twentieth Century novelist, sir. He's all the rage now."

"Dear Lord, what they're passing these days. You'll wear something less . . . revealing on the mission, of course."

"Sir, I prefer to go as I am. This was designed as a combat uniform."

"But the . . . your bosom, it's unprotected."

"Bare breasts are quite common on Cylis 4 now, sir."

"I'm aware of that, but surely — "

"Sir, I believe my present uniform will afford me with the greatest amount of comfort and familiarity and therefore serve as the best possible asset to my abilities."

Clever, that speech. But then, she'd rehearsed it thirty or forty times before entering his office, in anticipation of his remarks. Self-designed combat uniforms were commonplace in the Fleet now but this one was almost too radical. Like everything else about Sheffield.

She smiled a little as she moved through the trees. Every woman at Colony Six was jealous of her ability to handle the Commander. If they only realized how simple it was ... how, under all the brass and bluff, he was just like all men.

Ahead and to the right a twig snapped.

She was on Leakwood's trail to be sure; he had, in fact, made little attempt to cover it. But an ambush in this clearing? No. Leakwood just wasn't the type. Besides, unless she was wrong, Leakwood liked her.

It wasn't surprising then, to find a stranger confronting her when she rounded the next tree. What was surprising was to find a member of Fleet. As far as she knew, Colony Six had exclusive privileges on this planet. Could this be another AWOL from another Colony?

She strode politely if confidently up to the man and took in his bearing in a single sweep of her eyes: tall, husky, yellow Fleet stripe on his arm like hers, buccaneer pants and boots (very vogue these days), tank top, series seven sword, no stunner, unnaturally curly hair. That last item was egocentric. Any man who had his hair set regularly was obviously glued on himself; this one was probably into an Errol Flynn thing (also very vogue these days). It *could* be all swagger, but then, she was flamboyant too — and she was *good!* It was always wise to be prudent, even when you're the best.

"Station?" It was a universal greeting.

"Colony Twelve."

She didn't like the way he said it: snobbish. She didn't like what his mouth did when it formed the words. But she was on official business, in a hurry. She'd give him the benefit. "I'm Sheffield, Colony Six, on Fleet Apprehension Orders. Do you wish to assist?"

"No."

It was the way he said it again. Ohh, this one was a

smartass all right. That conceited little patronizing smile. Probably a sexist to boot. She knew she should get about her business, leave this jerk to himself, but she couldn't help adding one last item. "Are you aware that this planet is restricted to Colony Six personnel?"

"Is that a fact?"

"What is your business here?"

"I came to bag a Rhunk. With my sword."

With his sword. Cute the way he added that at the end to let her know he didn't need a stunner to kill a Rhunk. Ohh, a real smartass all right. She knew what reaction her next words would elicit and she said them deliberately. "That's against Fleet Law."

He smiled, widening the conceit, and his hand touched his sword hilt as she knew it would. "And you're going to report me," he filled in for her.

"Yes."

"Klete!" It was what she expected, one of the universal words for "on guard" followed by the swift unsheathing of the challenger's sword. There were other words, but "Klete" was the most widely used. Either she followed suit now or faced ridicule.

"Hhan!" Her word. Oriental, like her swordsmanship. Neither was widely known and rarely practiced, which was why she chose them. Her sword literally sang from its scabbard — Shhingggg! — a phenomenon caused by the friction of the cutting edge running past two minute wheeled sharpeners employed within the case. It wasn't impossible to buy such a scabbard but they were known only to the elite.

His sword, she noticed, made a sound like Shuunk! No sharpeners. He might be flamboyant but he wasn't in her league.

She stepped in immediately, not wasting time, with

a deliberately slowed English shoulder thrust, sacrificing style now to see what he could do. He parried nicely — anyone could have — but still, his movements were quite fast, even admirable. She pivoted next, went low and tried a Cyrnian volupe to the solar plexus. Again, he blocked with ease, adding a quick counter slice when he jerked back his weapon that was supposed to put her off balance. It didn't, of course, but he *was* above average, definitely.

She played with him for a time, letting him get in some false scores, until she knew his every strength and weakness. And, although the latter far outnumbered the former, she found him a splendid swordsman with the potential to be even better . . . if he didn't spend all his time in the beauty salon. It would be a pity, she decided, for her to waste someone who could be so valuable to Fleet.

She stepped back, clicked her heels together, and pointed her sword hand stiffly to the ground at her right side. It meant either "I yield" or "Let's reconsider."

"You're a fine swordsman. I don't wish you harm. Leave the planet now and I see no reason to report you."

The vain smile. He thought she was bluffing out of fear. Oh, boy. There was just no help for this kid. All right then, she'd tried. The fun was over. She had to get back to work.

"Klete!" he answered, and threw himself into an excessively ostentatious fight pose.

Now it was her turn to smile. "Hhan," she said calmly, and slowly, ever so slowly drew the sword level to and horizontal with her breasts. It was a maneuver she savored. They were splendid breasts; large and round and pink-nipple firm. Few men could watch them

125

and the sword simultaneously. He was no exception.

Her next movement was so lightning fast, he had only time to feel the breeze her John Carter blade made in passing in front of him. He started to counter but she was frozen now at the completion of her swing, staring fixedly at his chest.

But she had missed! He glanced down at himself. He'd felt nothing!

Then the ribbons of crimson appeared magically across his tank top, delayed seconds by the impossible keenness of her blade. His mouth fell open. Before he could shut it again, she was behind him, sending the slashed tank top swishing from his body and over his head with two precisely placed thrusts. Together they watched the material arc high into the air and drape quietly over a leafy branch.

When he whirled in humiliated fury to lash at her, she was gone, pirouetting gracefully to his right — no, to his left — no, no she was behind him again! — pulling tentatively at his wide swashbuckler's belt with her sword point, then effortlessly slicing through like butter to the ankles. The pants fell away like faded petals. Then she feinted to the right — he followed — and the pants about his ankles brought him down with a crash as she'd planned. He had to let go his sword to prevent impaling himself.

She kicked the sword away and stuck her own blade beneath his terrified chin. His Adam's apple moved convulsively and he was suddenly swimming in perspiration.

"Up."

He obeyed immediately, propelled airlessly by the stinging tip of the magic sword. She stood grinning grimly at his nakedness, letting the razor point trace a

126

tickly, not-quite-skin-piercing line down his throat, chest, belly . . .

She lowered the sword between his legs and cocked her head speculatively. She had castrated only one man before in swordplay, although it was quite commonly the loser's lot among Fleet swordsmen; indeed, many half expected it. But she found no satisfaction in needlessly maiming someone or in the rapidly growing fad of "gathering nuts." In her book, you either killed your opponent outright or let him go the way he came.

She looked up at his dripping face: eyes squeezed tight, teeth clenched. "Turn around, pig, while I decide how to kill you."

He turned drunkenly, legs calcified with fear, and stood trembling before the sun. He was standing there still, an hour later, long after she had faded silently into the tangled jungle.

Alone again in the forest, she was still on Leakwood's trail and still remembering what the Commander had said about him . . .

"Now then, Sheffield, my reports say you knew this . . . ah . . . "

"Leakwood, Commander."

" . . . knew him personally. Is that true?"

"It's unofficially true, yes sir. 'Acquainted' is, perhaps, a better word."

"Acquainted. Would you care to clarify that term, Sheffield?"

"We ran into each other at the library occasionally and had lunch together once or twice."

"Once or twice."

"Twice."

"What kind of lunches, Sheffield?"

127

"Just . . . lunch. At the cafeteria."

"I see. What else?"

"Let's see . . . I believe he took me to the movies once, yes. Several months ago."

"And?"

"Uh, nothing, sir. It was a terrible film as I remember."

"After the film?"

"He took me home — no, I took *him* home. He's . . . small, sir and well, I'm good with a sword, so . . . "

"I see."

"The truth is, sir, we were just friends. There was never anything romantic about our relationship. I don't think Leakwood had romantic inclinations toward anyone. He just wasn't the type. I socialized with him because I enjoyed his company. I could relax around him; he liked me for my mind. It was nice to know you were going to spend a quiet evening without getting physical.

"Leakwood didn't have many friends. He's sort of . . . *funny* looking, to be blunt. I felt a little sorry for him and I knew he liked my paying attention to him, especially around the Colony swordsmen."

"Was he a thief, Sheffield?"

"Sir?"

"Did he ever steal anything to your knowledge?"

"Not that I'm aware of, sir."

"Well, he has now. Something extremely valuable, extremely expensive and extremely important to Colony Six."

"I see, sir."

"We want it back, Sheffield."

"Yes, sir."

"Pronto."

"Yes, sir."

Pause . . .

128

"Uh, what would that be, sir?"

"How's that?"

"The stolen property, what was it, sir?"

"I can't provide you with that information, Sheffield."

"Can't provide . . ."

"It's Top Secret, Sheffield. You can appreciate that. Colony Six is a Top Secret installation. Half of these buildings house classified information. The object this man stole is highly confidential. I understand there are no more than two in existence and both of them are here at Colony Six. Or *were* here. I want it back."

"Yes, sir, but how will I be sure of bringing back the object if I don't . . . if I can't — "

"I'll grant you that's a problem. That's why you were chosen, Sheffield. My reports say you're one of the best. Are you game, Sheffield?"

"Of course, sir."

Of course she was game. Like the best swordsmen in the Colony, she'd been itching to get a look at what lay outside those walls. Now she had her chance.

Evening was coming fast. In a few minutes she'd have difficulty discerning Leakwood's trail, clear as it was.

The dangleflies were out, zeroing in on her like an attacking airforce, rolling their crystal wings deliriously in her sweat glands. She found a Mulinaw bush without effort, broke one of its berries between her fingers and spread the glistening oil over her limbs. The dangleflies buzzed off in resentment.

The ground beneath her slippers grew steadily softer, damper, as it always did toward evening. The Rhunks would be pushing up any time now. She fingered the hilt of her sword nervously.

129

A species of bird-lizard she was unfamiliar with screeched abruptly above her head. She twisted around and caught sight of its yellow-blue feathers spiraling swiftly across the mauve sky, arrowing gracefully to a nearby tree, landing not so gracefully with a light plop. As she watched, it began kicking convulsively, then stiffened and faded rapidly into the trunk as the tree absorbed it hungrily.

She knelt down beside Leakwood's latest bootprint and took a reading with the pocket trackometer snapped to her girdle. To her amazement the little red needle hovered just over the seven minute mark. Leakwood must be very close. According to her rate of pursuit, he must have slowed considerably within the last hour. Odd. He couldn't have tired this early. Was it indeed to be an ambush? Or had he finally come to his senses?

She produced a food tab from her belt and chewed it reflectively. Leakwood was a hard one to figure all right; cautious, introvertive, rarely talking at all during the few times she'd been with him. Still, she couldn't believe he'd do her any harm. He may not have shared the other men's passion for her, but she'd always seen affection in his eyes.

He *was* an odd one, though.

She twitched spasmodically as a pungent odor assailed her nostrils. Her nose wrinkled in revulsion. She cast about for the source, right hand gripping the dark hilt of her blade. Behind her a soft plopping noise became evident. She whirled in time to see the brownish snout of a female Rhunk poking through the surface soil amid clumps of its own excrement.

She stepped back gingerly, eyes riveted on the enormous block-like head, twitching ears and blinking yellow pupils. The smell became overpowering now. It hadn't seen her yet, so she merely merged with the surrounding undergrowth and watched in repugnant fascination as it heaved its titanic bulk out of the wet earth and yawned enormously.

It was everything the manual and the Commander had described . . .

"Now, I'm sure you're familiar with the wildlife on this planet from your manual, Sheffield. Let me emphasize that these three hundred and sixty-eight pages before you do not exaggerate in describing the ferocity of these creatures. They are many and varied and nearly all lethal. I realize that swordplay is very much the fashion these days — that some of you young people are quite proficient with a blade. However, I'm going to insist you take a stunner."

"But sir —"

"Please. I'm well aware of your prowess and reputation, Sheffield, and that the blade has recently been recognized as an official Fleet weapon. But this planet is different. Aside from this AWOL, only seven men have ever been outside these walls. We lost two of them because we weren't prepared. I don't intend to let that happen again."

"Yes, sir."

"Take a look at page twenty-nine of your manual, Sheffield. Tell me what you see."

"A Rhunk, sir."

"Ugly bastard, isn't he?"

"Extremely, sir."

"Ugly and huge and deadly. You've heard stories of how they can tear animals twice their size to shreds with those claws while holding them securely with those ghastly, tenacious tentacles. You've heard and read how their hide is comparable to the finest chrome armor, how in fact, a certain percent of their chemical make-up is alloy. You know they're virtually indestructible."

"Yes, sir."

"They can't be killed, Sheffield. We've *tried*. We've lost men trying, spent millions. It's not within our present technical scope. They simply can't be stopped."

"I see, sir."

"But they can be fooled!"

"Fooled, sir?"

"Hoaxed, conned! There's only one animal on this planet a full grown Rhunk won't attack and immediately disembowel. Do you know what that animal is, Sheffield?"

"Another Rhunk, sir?"

"That's very good, Sheffield, very astute. Yes, another Rhunk. And we can make another Rhunk . . . we *have* made another Rhunk in our labs here in the Colony. With this instrument in my hands."

"What is it, sir?"

"It's called a Colifax."

A Colifax. It hung now from the gold chain of her G-string, the cold metal pressing uncomfortably against her bare tummy, banging against it when she walked. Until this moment, it had been a heavy, unwanted burden that she'd have given a week's pay to be rid of, Top Secret or not.

Now she wasn't so sure. If it could somehow protect her from this incredible creature before her . . .

For it was obvious now that nothing else could. The emerging Rhunk was an awe-inspiring study in armor-

132

plated destruction. Nothing short of a T-3 bomb could bring it down, of that she was sure. The sword in her hand felt, for the first time in her life, totally ineffectual. That guy from Colony Twelve must have been an idiot; or, like her, he'd never seen a real Rhunk in the flesh before.

She stumbled back through the creepers as it lifted its nose to sniff, and emerged into a clearing on the other side. As she turned to step clear, she came face to face with another Rhunk. A big one this time. A male.

She stiffened. It was staring directly at her, had heard her coming, in fact. There was no place to run, no place to turn. For the first time, real fear found her.

With palsied fingers she tore the Colifax from her waist and knelt slowly to the wet earth, setting it in front of her — eyes never leaving the bloated form of the Rhunk. Its nose was in the air now as the female's had been, taking in the full scent of her with the aid of the strong evening breeze wafting directly toward it. The thin, veined membranes of its four nostrils flared red simultaneously and she thought she detected a sudden tremor pass along the ridges of its back.

Methodically then, as if confident of the helplessness of its prey, it advanced on her, muscles riding in sensuous rhythm along its shoulders, tentacles twitching in anticipation.

She reached out and poked a red button.

The hotness that flooded her body was immediate and not altogether pleasant. Not painful either, really, but leaving her with the distinct feeling that she was being pulled slowly apart from all sides, like heated taffy. She refused to panic; she knew, as Colony Command had told her, the process would reverse itself the moment she stepped on the green button. Even now, her fear was subsiding as she took on the proportions and character of her new body . . . and the approaching Rhunk was appearing much less menacing with the advent of her new height and girth.

Its nostrils didn't flare any less, however, and the tremors along its back increased, if anything. It was still intensely interested in her for some reason. But if not as food . . . then what?

Even before it moved over and deliberately crushed flat the Colifax with its massive hoof, sealing her fate forever, she knew; even before it wrapped its twenty tentacles about her ardently and adjusted her to a mounting position, she knew. For she had looked close into its eyes and they told her everything. Perfect as the Colifax was it couldn't quite disguise the familiar personality behind those eyes, the quiet, introvertive but highly imaginative brain. And in that instant, she knew exactly why Leakwood had led her this merry chase and what was the piece of equipment he'd stolen.

She'd miss her friends, of course, and life at the Colony. But most of all, she'd miss her sword. Even with the highly sensitive tentacles at her command, with seven thousand pounds of Rhunk behind it, it was difficult to be as graceful as Dejah Thoris.

Introduction to "Straggler From Atlantis"
by Manly Wade Wellman

*Manly Wade Wellman really is Manly Wade
Wellman's name.*

*Though he's a great huge bear of a North Carolin-
ian (who could have played Jeremiah Johnson better
than Robert Redford) of three hundred sixty-leben
years, you'd probably be calling him Manly a couple
of minutes after you met him. In writing him for a
story, we mentioned having been a fan of his more
than twenty years ago and cited a specific title
("Sojarr of Titan"). Wellman probably didn't remember. He's written a bunch. In recent years his yarns
have been of the mountain folk of his state — who
could be the mountain people of your editor's*

Kentucky — that marvelously combined the lovely and picturesque with the weird and eerie. The Wellman story collection Worse Things Waiting *received the Best Book award (a bust of H. P. Love-craft created by that maniac Gahan Wilson) at the very first World Fantasy Convention, held in Providence Rhode Island over the '75 Hallowe'en weekend. (Samain, to those who know.)*

And about time. He's been quietly contributing highly entertaining stories to magazines — and thus us — for half a century.

He answered the invitation to submit here like a boy, with questions about length and whether this idea/subject was OK — and nary a word about money. He also advised he's been wanting and waiting to write about the last survivor of Atlantis for forty-five years . . . but that some fella named Howard got a lock on the Atlantean board and no one wanted Wellman's Atlantean *tales back then. Actually, Kardios is rather a better, more likable and thoughtful fellow than Howard's Kull.*

So is Manly Wade Wellman.

STRAGGLER FROM ATLANTIS
by
Manly Wade Wellman

Then he knew, or maybe he dreamed he knew, that he wasn't sea-driven, wind-driven, any more. Those hours or eternities that had thrown him high like a stone from a sling, plunged him into strangling abysses of ocean, hurtled him in a drench and rattle of rain with the wreckage to which he clung, they were past. He was alive and out of the sea, lying peacefully face down on sand and pebbles. The waves only murmured, as though to comfort him.

He could feel the sun's warm caress on his naked back, after the wind and storm and dark clouds like smothering robes. He had not died and gone wherever

137

one goes when one dies. He was alive and ashore — somewhere. He might even be safe.

Rolling over, he opened his eyes to see where he had been flung by the tempest that couldn't kill him. He sprawled on a white beach. Inland showed clumps of rich-leaved trees; in the sky overhead were scattered soft clouds, green and rose and pearl, like the feathers of softly tinted birds. Almost within reach of his hand lodged the splintered wooden gate that had served him in some measure as a raft, the great gate that had earlier stood in the garden wall of Theona, queen of Atlantis.

Of Atlantis. He, too, was of Atlantis — wait; of Atlantis no more. For Atlantis was lost Atlantis now, sunk to ocean's deep bottom, with Queen Theona and all her people. How he had survived he could not imagine, nor where, nor on what unknown shore.

Shakily, creakily he stood up, feeling the soreness in his battered muscles. He wore only sandals and a drenched rag of blue loincloth. His tanned flesh was soaked into ridges on his lean legs, his broad, panting chest, the bunchy brawn of his arms. He put up a hand to shove back his mane of dark, drenched hair. That hand shook, like an old man's. He sensed hunger within him. How long since he had eaten the delicately roasted bird and white bread and drunk the perfumed wine in Queen Theona's garden? Days ago, a lifetime ago?

Among a scatter of shoreside rocks, limpets clung. Stooping, he managed to pry loose two of them. With a big stone he broke their shells and ate them. Almost at once, they seemed to give him back a trifle of strength. He knelt to tug more strongly at a third limpet — and a shadow slid across him.

He started up. A foot was planted beside him, a vast, flat foot clad in laced leather. Its leg was like a tree trunk, meaty of calf, knuckle-kneed. Over him leaned a huge face, set on shoulders twice the height of his. Its bearded lips drew back from square cobbles of teeth. It leaned almost down on him.

"Where did you come from?" asked a thundering voice, in a language he knew.

A mighty hand fell upon his arm.

Gathering the strength from somewhere, he whirled free of it. The great head still hung close to him, and he threw a fist, with all the boxer's skill that was his. It slammed home on the bearded jaw and he heard the giant howl out in surprised pain. But then his quivering legs gave under him and he fell down, not even feeling the sand as it came up to meet him. Something like sleep flowed over him.

Again he roused, to a tingling taste of wine in his mouth. He made himself sit up, rubbing his eyes. The giant was there; no, half a dozen were there, looming around him like crags. They were all twice as broad as he and, sitting, were as tall as he would be standing. They were leather-clad, shaggy, staring. One of them propped him against a monstrous upflung knee and proffered a big stone bottle. He drank again, deeply. His head cleared.

"Thank you," he said huskily. "What people are you?"

A giant leaned forward. His shield-wide face was tufted with coarse black hair. His lower lip looked puffy, as though bruised.

"We ask you the same, little one," he rumbled. "What people are you, and what are you doing in

139

our country where little ones dare not come for fear of us?"

"My name is Kardios."

"Kardios," repeated the one who held him against that big knee. A free hand, big as a basket, clamped a ruddy-bearded chin. "What sort of name is that?"

Kardios grinned. "I was brought up to think it was a good one. It means the heart."

The bruise-lipped giant grunted, and Kardios looked at him. "When it comes to that, what about your name?"

"I am Yod," boomed the other. "Kardios — the heart, eh? A heart can be wounded."

"I've the head and the hand to protect my heart," said Kardios, feeling better with every moment.

"Ha!" Yod roared his gigantic scorn. "A head no bigger than a fist, a hand like a forked twig."

Kardios shoved aside the bottle and made himself stand up quickly. He glared into Yod's big, bulging eyes.

"Get a weapon to fit your hand and give me one to fit mine," he said evenly. "You're a giant, but you're clumsy to the look. I'll wager that before you raised your arm to strike, I'd have you cut open and your tripes shed out on the ground."

Silence all around at that. The giants squatted and gazed at him. He made a show of ignoring them, glancing this way and that beyond the circle to see where they had brought him. He must have been carried well inland, for the sea was not visible at all. Grass grew richly underfoot, with here and there a tuft of trees, palms and what seemed to be orchard growth. At some distance loomed a row of tawny

140

bluffs, in which he thought he saw flecks of darkness like caves. Then he gazed all around at the giants, and grinned, showing his teeth to the gum.

"Bold words, dwarf," said another of the group at last. This one sat on a lump of rock, as though he presided. His great face was deeply folded in wrinkles, but there was no weakness of age in it. His white beard flowed like a blizzard. Over his shoulders hung a cloak of shaggy black skin, perhaps from an immense wild bull. On the knuckly hand that stroked his beard shone a gold ring set with jewels — this people knew metals and the fashioning of them. He gazed at Kardios from under white-tufted brows.

"Bold words," he said again, "from a man all alone among many bigger than he."

"I've spoken bolder than that, against dangers more worth fearing," replied Kardios. "What will you do to punish my boldness? Kill me and eat me, or just kill me? There are enough of you to try."

A grumble went up from several, but the white-bearded one lifted a spadelike hand.

"Be patient, you know we may need him," he quieted his companions. Then, not unkindly: "Think, Kardios, if you know how. My name is Enek, and these people of mine, the Nephol, look to me for command and judgment. Why should we give you wine to strengthen you if we meant to kill you?"

"Wine," Kardios said after him. "Let me help my wits with more of it."

The bottle was given him. He took a long pull and wiped his mouth.

"You've said that people my size are afraid to

come here," he reminded them. "I didn't come here, I was washed here by the sea. Now you say that there's a reason to keep me alive. That sounds as if my size will be of help, though you're all about eight times bigger than I am, and think bigness is a good thing."

"Not always good," said Enek gravely. "You've guessed wisely, Kardios. There's a place the smallest of us can't go, and we want you to go there."

Kardios sat down again in the midst of them. Yod still scowled, and Kardios cocked his head and grinned.

"Yod doesn't seem anxious for anything I can do," he suggested.

"Leave Yod alone," Enek bade him. "It was Yod who found you fainting, and brought you here to us after you'd hit him when he tried to help."

"Then stop trying to frighten me, Yod," said Kardios. "I didn't live through the swallowing of Atlantis by the sea to be frightened by anything."

"We've heard speak of Atlantis," said the red-bearded giant who had given Kardios wine. "Some sort of strange, shining island kingdom, they say."

"It was," amended Kardios. "You Nephol are looking at a rare specimen. Maybe a few of our ships were out in safe waters, but I doubt if anyone other than myself got away from the end of Atlantis itself."

They all goggled again, and Kardios laughed. He was feeling better all the time.

"What are you trying to tell us?" asked Enek. "What happened?"

"Well," said Kardios, "I suppose I was more or less responsible."

At that, they stared at him the more fixedly, and he laughed again.

"I wasn't a citizen of the capitol at the shore," he said. "I lived back in the hills, cutting wood and growing grapes, and I was young enough to want to better myself. So I strapped on my sword and slung my harp on my shoulder. I took the trail right down to the gold and jasper palace of Queen Theona, where she'd ruled longer than anybody ever could accurately tell. I thought she might want me for her palace guard, or to make music for her, or perhaps both."

"So you're a harper, too," grumbled Yod. "You seem to value yourself for that as well as for being a fighter."

"I've always done what I could to harp and fight well. I had surpassed all the country harpers and fighters I knew, and in my part of Atlantis there are — there were good harpers and fighters. But at the palace, and it was big enough to be a palace even for people your size, the guards at the gate laughed at me. After I'd stopped them from laughing —"

"How did you stop them?" broke in one of the listeners.

"The only way. Queen Theona came out on a balcony and watched me stop the laughter of the second one. Then she ordered the bodies carried away and the widows comforted. And she said for me to come into her garden and show if I was equally good with my harp."

"Perhaps Kardios should have a harp," said Enek. "His story sounds as if it should be sung, here and there."

A harp appeared from somewhere and was thrust into Kardios's hand. It was a big one, of course, made from the horned skull of an antelope, with strings of silver wire. Kardios tuned it expertly and struck a chord. It sounded well.

"In her garden, her women and her advisers listened while I played and sang," he said. "After a while, Theona told them they could go and leave me alone with her. She poured wine — good wine, though I'm not disparaging the wine you've given me — and offered me some food."

"This queen, older than anyone could remember," put in Enek. "What was she like?"

"I can say only that she was more beautiful than the stars or the moon," said Kardios. "Than the sun at morning or evening. Than the jewels and gold she wore. She looked at me and told me she would like me to make a song about her."

"Did you?" prompted Enek. "What was the song?"

"I'll try to remember."

Kardios plucked the strings until he found his tune. He cleared his throat and sang:

"Atlantis, Atlantis has flowered forever,
Forever Theona has reigned as her queen,
Worshipped and honored and loved,
    but kissed never —
So is Theona, and always has been.

"Fairer Theona than moon or than sun,
Fairer than stars in the vault of the skies;
No man can say when her reign was begun,
Lovely and queenly and regal and wise.

"So it was told by the gods in high heaven,
Atlantis shall live and forever prevail
Until her sweet lips in a love-kiss are given;

144

So runs the prophecy, so says the tale.
"Forever Atlantis has flowered, but this
Is told of Theona — the moment that she
Grants to a lover the boon of a kiss,
Atlantis, Theona, will drown in the sea."

He muted the strings. "I'm afraid I'm not in my best voice," he apologized.

"That was a good song, and well sung," Enek praised him. "What then, Kardios? What when you'd finished?"

"Theona sat beside me and said, 'Kiss me.' "

All their great lungs breathed deeply, drawing air like bellows.

"I told her to remember the prophecy. She laughed, more sweetly than music, and again she said, 'Kiss me.' So I kissed her."

"Huh?" grunted Yod. "You kissed her."

"And Atlantis sank," said Kardios.

"If that's true, how did you live?" Enek demanded.

"Ask the gods," replied Kardios. "Ask the sea and the storm. But don't ask me. If some god was making a joke on me, it was a rough one. I got hold of the garden gate somehow, and I don't know how long I spun and churned over the sea, in rain, in hail. Days? It must have been days. I don't know. But here I am."

"Do you believe him, Enek?" asked Yod.

"I believe him," Enek made answer, so quietly that he sounded almost casual. "It's a strange story, but it sounds true. It was no joke of a god, Kardios. You lived and came here because there's something here for you to do."

"You've already said that," Kardios reminded him. "What is it, and why should I do it?"

145

"Because we helped you back to life," Enek answered at once. "We came out today, to see in what state the storm had left our shore. It was Yod who was going ahead, found you half fainting, and got his lip bruised for his pains. Now, if you're not grateful enough to help us in return for helping you, be practical enough to think how we'd act if we were ungrateful for anything."

Kardios laughed, and this time several of the giants laughed with him. It was like rolling thunder.

"What is it I am to do?" he asked again.

"You'll need strength to hear about it," said Enek. "It's nearly sundown, and night hasn't been a happy time hereabouts in recent months. Come home with us and eat and sleep."

"I'll be grateful for those chances, at least."

They all got up and walked ponderously toward the distant bluffs.

Kardios walked among them. His first impression had been a correct one. These giants were powerful creatures, but they moved slowly. Even in his weakened condition he could have run from them easily, but he did not. As they tramped along together, Enek told Kardios what troubled them.

Moons ago, there had been a great bolt of fire from heaven, and the Nephol were sure the gods spoke to them. Some of them saw the bolt strike, not far from where they lived in caves. These reported that it seemed to burst into a great shattered spray of blazing embers, which flew in all directions. But from its very midst, a living, moving thing came away safe.

"We call him Fith," said Enek.

"Why?" asked Kardios.

"It is like the noise he makes," said the ruddy-bearded giant who had given Kardios wine, and whose name was Jipi.

Enek continued the story. Fith had seemed to be daunted, or at least uncomfortable in the light of day, and had scrambled shapelessly away to where an ancient dry well opened. He slid himself into it, out of sight. That well, said Enek, had been thought enchanted, once the home of spirits. The Nephol had come at twilight to sing and burn sweet herbs at the well's opening, to honor what surely must be something sent from the gods.

"Then Fith came out," said Enek. "He flowed out — I saw him flow out like a torrent of foam. He pulled one of us down and . . . *flowed* over him. We ran, we were sick with fear. We did not come back until the next sunrise. There were only bones there, as clean and dry as though they had lain beside the well for a year."

"Now you're telling a story as strange to me as my story of the drowning of Atlantis seemed to you," said Kardios. "You thought this Fith was heaven-sent —"

"Did he not come from the sky?" Enek pointed out. "Isn't that the home of gods?"

"I've heard our priests say there isn't any particular home of gods," Kardios remembered. "Anyway, Fith went into a well that you thought of as a sort of home of underground spirits."

"And he makes his home there."

"Where is that well?"

"There," said Enek, pointing with a finger like a bludgeon.

They were approaching a stream, with the cave-

147

pocked bluffs on its far side. A grassless level lay before them, extending to the near bank. Upon this lay what appeared to be a tumble of pale rocks, around a dark blotch of emptiness. Two spotted goats were tethered to pegs nearby.

"You will understand," said Enek, "that, however Fith's flying chariot was destroyed, he managed to land safely at a convenient place for him. That well was very close to where he came free of the wreck."

"Do you think he knew it would be there?" suggested Kardios.

"Possibly, even though he came here from the stars. It didn't seem haphazard."

The giants sidled away from the place as they walked, and Kardios suddenly broke from among them and trotted toward the dark spot. As he came close, he saw that the strew of pale objects was made up of bones — animal bones, great and small. The goats bleated plaintively and Kardios smiled at them, for he liked animals. At the very brink of the hole he knelt. Enek was right, it was a smallish round opening. Kardios might slide his own sinewy body into it, but it was too narrow for any of the giants. He peered down. Far below, like a distant coin of silver, showed a disk of pallid light. It reminded Kardios of the phosphorescent glow of certain kinds of fungus.

He rose and came quickly back to the giants as they approached the stream. "What are those goats doing there?" he asked.

"They are for Fith," replied Enek. "Living things are what he wants. Offerings keep him from hunting us. But dead meat he will not touch."

"At least you haven't made a god of him as yet, with these sacrifices," said Kardios.

Enek sighed unhappily, and Jipi and Yod sighed with him.

"For all practical purposes, he might as well be a god, and a downright evil one at that," said Jipi. "He's here. He takes prey. But let's get on to the caves. The sun has almost set."

So it had, somewhere to seaward behind them. The giants speeded their heavy feet to the margin of the stream and crossed, one by one, on an arrangement of rough rocks. On the other side stretched a level open space, tramped hard by big feet, below the bluffs and their tiers of caves. Kardios saw fires at the mouths of those caves above and below, and giant heads peered out, like dwellers at the windows of a great tenement building such as Atlantis had known.

His escorting party split up, heading for caves here and there. Enek and Jipi guided Kardios to a ladder. Its sides were great treetrunks with the bark long worn away. Up went Enek, then Kardios, and Jipi last of all.

They reached a shelf of rock. Enek led the way along it, to a tall, broad cave opening. Inside glowed a fire. The cave was a tall roomy one and appeared to have been enlarged by powerful chippings into the rock. A giant woman leaned above the fire, clad in loose garment of rough weave that fell to her feet. She had gray hair, in two cable-like braids, and Kardios thought her seamed face was a kindly one. She looked up from her cooking.

"Enek," she cried. "I'm glad you've come back safe." Then she stared down at Kardios. "Who's this small one?"

"He's Kardios, a friend and a helper," said Enek.

"Kardios, my wife's name is Lotay. She's going to give us some supper. You eat with us, Jipi."

Lotay brought out wide clay platters. From the fire she lifted a spit with savory-smelling collops of roast meat strung on it, and poked in the ashes for roots backed in wrappings of charred leaves. Enek drew a bronze knife as long as a sword and sliced meat into a dish for Kardios. Lotay filled pottery cups with wine from a leather bag. But before they sat down to eat, Enek and Jipi went to the door of the cave. Kardios watched as they carefully lifted into place a sort of barrier, of thorny branches and tendrils woven into a close network. It filled the opening from side to side and from top to bottom. They pegged it stoutly, making sure that no gaps were left anywhere. Then, at last, all four sat down at the fireside and took up their well-filled plates.

"This meat is excellent," said Kardios. "What is it, Enek?"

"The hind foot of an elephant, if you know what elephants are."

"We had them in Atlantis, for parades and for hauling stones and timbers, but I never ate elephant before." Kardios took another mouthful. "It's as tender and juicy as fine pork."

The baked root, when broken open, presented a tasty accompaniment. The wine was better than what Kardios had awakened to among the giants. As they ate, Enek told Kardios more things. The Nephol were an ancient people but not a numerous one; those in this cave community numbered perhaps fifty. But other human races, peoples of Kardios's size, feared them and left them alone. Only on certain days were there meetings at the boundaries of the

Nephol territory, where the giants traded tanned hides and uncut gems for woven fabrics and tools of bronze and polished stone.

"You see, those other peoples know that we are heaven-born," put in Jipi. "We are descended from the sons of the gods, who mated with the strongest and most beautiful daughters of men."

After the meal was finished, Lotay shyly asked Kardios to take off his salt-encrusted sandals. She sat beside the fire with them, rubbing them with pieces of fat and working them back to suppleness. Enek and Jipi and Kardios found seats on blocks of stone near a rear wall. A great store of various weapons was kept there. They were stacked against the rock or hung from pegs driven into cracks. Enek found a beautifully tanned leopard skin.

"Perhaps this can replace that poor rag of a loincloth," he said.

"Thank you." Kardios put it on, admiring the spots on the fur. "Now, suppose you tell me more about how I am supposed to deal with Fith."

"Which means your mind is made up to do it," said Jipi, smiling.

"I made it up almost at once. You've said that Fith eats the living sacrifices you put out there."

"He would rather catch us to eat, but he takes the beasts we give him every night," said Enek. "We've given him very many of those. Goats, hogs, cows — he takes them, even bears and tigers we have trapped and tied up at the doorway of his hole. Once even an elephant, though he spent a while sucking the flesh from that."

"I've been wondering why you never just stopped

151

up that hole, by daytime, with him inside it," said Kardios.

"We've done that. With earth and rocks. He throws them out, or somehow burrows through them. When he wants to come out and eat, he comes out."

"I see. All right, when you've given him all your beasts, what's going to happen then?"

"How often we've taken council about that," said Enek sadly. "Fith will come for us then. I've said that when that happens, I must be the first to be given him." He stroked his white beard. "I'll go out to him. Jipi will be chief after me."

"As the chief, I'd have to be the prey for him on the next night," declared Jipi.

The two boulderlike heads nodded at each other. It had been agreed upon, then, long ago.

"And you've never been able to fight him," said Kardios.

"Oh, we've tried fighting," said Enek. "Our bravest have tried. But he moves too quickly for any of the Nephol. And he — he's of no shape, and of all shapes. He changes like a cloud, like a bad dream."

"That's a new sort of creature to me," confessed Kardios. "Indeed, he must be from the stars. We had monsters on Atlantis, but they kept honestly to one shape. You Nephol have had advantages we haven't. But you say he can devour big beasts, big men. What teeth he must have."

"No teeth," declared Jipi. "We told you that he flows away on the other side, leaving the bones."

Kardios grinned drily. "Are you sure you're not offering me as a sacrifice?"

Enek shook his great head. "If we began to give him men, even men of your size, then I'm afraid he'd truly

152

become a god. And what benefit would that sacrifice be to us? He'd only come back the next night, seeing his way by the light he himself sheds."

"Can he climb as high as this cave?"

Enek nodded. Lotay, working on the sandals, seemed to shudder.

"We can't have Fith for a god," said Jipi stubbornly. "The sun has been our god, and Fith stays out of the sun's light. The sun is kind. Kindness is stronger than fear."

"Not always," Kardios told him. "Fear doesn't have pity. I feel like saying, you're lucky I'm here to dispose of Fith for you."

"How will you do that?" wondered Jipi. "You've said you'd go down into his hole to him, but what then?"

"Leave that to me," said Kardios, wondering in his own heart how he would manage. "I'll need a good weapon of course. The best."

"Ah," and Enek actually smiled with his great teeth, "now you bargain."

"I'm in a position where I must bargain. Look at me, I wasn't left more than a rag or two by that ride through the stormy ocean."

"Clothes, too?" asked Enek. "All right, Kardios, our women will make clothes for you. And take any weapon you want." He pointed to the arsenal stacked against the wall. "Just what sort of a weapon would hurt Fith?"

"He knows what pain is," said Kardios, gazing toward the front of the cave. "Your fabric of thorns yonder seems to keep him out. In other words, thorns pain him. And if he has a sense of pain, it's there to warn him away from injury."

153

"That's true," said Jipi. "You're wise, Kardios."

"I'm practical," amended Kardios.

Enek tramped over to the weapons and fumbled among them. "Here, Kardios," he said. "If you think thorns may be bad for him, how about this?"

He held it out. A great, stout pole of dark wood, and from the end hung, on a length of plaited leather cord, a ball as big as Kardios's two fists. This was cased in rawhide, and all over it projected ugly bronze spikes. Enek wagged it in his hand. The spiked ball swung like the end of a flail.

"Could you strike him with that?" he asked. "And another stroke, and more strokes until — "

But Kardios was not watching the play with the flail-weapon. He had come quickly to Enek's side. Stooping, he picked up something else from the display.

"This sword," he said.

Its icy-blue blade was as long as his leg, and three fingers broad at the point where it was set in a handle of leather lashings. He inspected it carefully. It was not of bronze, not of silver. Its two edges, his practised eye told him, were keen enough to shave with. Its point tapered leanly as a needle.

"That's a curiosity," said Jipi, joining them. "It came out of the fire when Fith's chariot smashed and flamed up on the ground."

"And the heat blistered all the ground there,"added Enek. "We scouted later, and there lay that blade you're holding. At first we thought it was a snake. But Jipi picked it up and brought it here to work on and sharpen. But it's not big enough for a grown man's weapon, and we don't let children play with it; they can easily cut themselves."

"It's big enough for me," said Kardios, poising it.

The balance was excellent. He took the point in his other hand. The blade bent springily, like a tough withe.

"And the temper of the metal," he said. "This wouldn't break like a bronze sword. It's harder than silver." He held it to his nose and sniffed. "It has a smell like brine. What is it?"

"We never saw any other like it," replied Jipi. "It came out of the earth under that heat. The earth was a red, crumbly sort. Sometimes we use that earth for paint."

Kardios whipped the sword through the air. It sang musically. He whirled it around his head, listening.

"Let me have this to fight Fith," he said.

"Not these thorns?" said Enek, holding out the flail.

"This is a thorn that might spike down your terrible Fith like a beetle on a pin." Kardios tested the point with his thumb. "I like it."

"Remember, Fith is quick," warned Jipi. "We've tried to throw spears at him. He only dodges away."

"Perhaps you don't throw quickly enough. Let him dodge with me. I can dodge, too."

He swept the sword above his head in a twinkle of light from the fire, than slashed it down at his ankles. He leaped over the blade as it slashed, spun it in the air to slash again while he jumped again. Enek grunted. Kardios paced lightly across the rocky floor.

"You," he said suddenly to Jipi, "take a spear and throw it at me."

"What are you asking?" cried Enek, and Lotay, too, looked up in amazement.

"If Jipi can strike me with a thrown spear, I'd be too slow for Fith," said Kardios. He walked out into the center of the floor and stood with bare feet apart, springy-legged, the sword half lifted in his hand. "Throw, Jipi."

Jipi grimaced. From the stand of weapons he selected a spear. It was as long as he, with a shaft made of a tall hardwood sapling, bound with rings of copper wire. The head was of beautifully polished blue flint, as long as Kardios's forearm, bound into the cleft end of the wood with lashings of sinew. Jipi balanced it on his palm and nodded above it as one who knows his weapon.

"You're sure you want this?" he asked Kardios.

"I'm sure, Jipi. Try me, I say."

Jipi's tall body flexed itself smoothly. The spear drove through the firelight.

Kardios writhed to his left. The spear hurtled past. He made a lightning slash with the sword. It bit the shaft in two, and the pieces clattered on the rock. Kardios laughed as he came to salute with his blade.

Enek drew a long amazed breath. "You'll do, Kardios. If you were twice as tall —"

"If I were twice as tall, I'd be about ten times slower. I couldn't go down and fight Fith tomorrow."

He carefully leaned the sword back in its place against the wall and sat down by the fire. He yawned.

"Yes, let's sleep," said Enek. "It will do all of us good to sleep."

"It will do me a good in particular," said Kardios.

Lotay brought him his sandals and spread the spotted hide of a cow for him, then offered him a woolen coverlet. He stretched out gratefully. Enek and Lotay lighted a big candle in a sconce of baked clay and plodded to where a dark opening led to an inner cave, their sleeping quarters. Jipi found bedding and relaxed near where the weapons were gathered. Almost at once,

156

Kardios heard Jipi's deep, regular breathing as he drifted into slumber.

Kardios did not close his own eyes. Stealthily he put on his sandals and stole to where the screen of thorns blocked the mouth of the outer cave. Crouching there, he listened. At last, with the utmost care, he twitched back a corner of the screen and slipped through. A thorn scraped his side, but he did not care. He tucked the screen in place and tiptoed along the ledge to the ladder, swung quickly down, and stood up in the open space before the caves.

Half a moon hovered above the eastern horizon. That was light enough. Kardios stole across the hard earth to the stream. He could make out the rocks at the crossing, and he stepped carefully from each to the next until he had gained the far bank. He stood and looked toward the place where bones littered the ground at the mouth of the well, and where the two goats had been tethered.

But he could not see the goats. They seemed to be cloaked in a softly glowing mist. It lay over them, a sort of half-defined clump of it. As Kardios watched, the mist stirred and churned. It seemed to thicken, to become more solid there. Then it rolled across the earth; it stole as though with a rhythmic motion. It came clear of where the goats had been. And where the goats had been there showed only another scatter of bones in the moonlight.

That had been Fith, in the act of feeding.

Even as Kardios told himself these things, Fith also seemed to come to a conclusion. Fith's substance stirred and humped itself. A point rose in the midst of that substance, grew taller and made a lumpy ball at the top. The lump swung around toward Kardios,

157

like a head looking at him. In that lump glowed a rosy light, stronger than the blur of Fith's radiance.

"Here I am, Fith!" cried Kardios.

Instantly the luminous mass rushed at him, ponderously swift.

Kardios whirled and ran. If he had brought a weapon — but he had not. Ahead of him showed a dark, brushy clump, and into it he dived like a rabbit, exulting as he felt the rake of brambles. Fith was there close behind him, but stopped as Kardios wallowed out on the other side of the brush.

Goats eaten or not, Fith wanted Kardios. Kardios ran again, to the streamside this time, straddling quickly from rock to rock. He had barely gained the far bank before Fith was catching up. Fith had changed shape, as Enek said that shapeless shape could be changed. Kardios heard a panting behind him. The pallid mass had lengthened itself, to come writhing along like a snake after a lizard.

Like a lizard Kardios ran, as fast as he had ever run. None of the big Nephol could outrun Fith, but Kardios could. He reached the bluffs, the big ladder, and lizard-like he swarmed up. Fith was at the bottom. Kardios dashed along the ledge, slid in past the thorny screen, feeling the rake of more sharp points. He worked the screen back into place. Outside, Fith slithered along the ledge and scraped and panted, but could not come in.

"Your dark world must be a sad world," Kardios addressed Fith. "You must go out at night and hunt for food. I'm glad I'm not you."

Fith subsided. Maybe Fith went away. Kardios paid no more attention. Again he sought his cowskin pallet and pulled the coverlet over himself. Jipi, sound asleep, did not stir. Kardios stretched at full length and crossed his arms behind his head.

He had seen Fith, he had tested Fith's speed and, to some extent, Fith's pursuit methods. He wondered again if he could have made a stand in the night if he had brought along that sword Enek had granted him. Maybe. He drew deep breaths, and went sound asleep.

Sleeping, he dreamed. He was back in the palace garden on Atlantis. Theona sat on the bench with him. Her beauty was music, there so close and so sweet. Her mouth closed on his, a yearning, seeking mouth, as though she found in him the perfect triumph of her timeless existence. Then came the abrupt rush and churning of water all around, and the water fell away and became Fith, a flow and wriggle of pursuing movement. After that came wakening, to the sound of heavy feet. Enek was awake in the cave and so was Lotay, who stooped by the fire to brown flat cakes on a tilted stone.

"Good morning," said Kardios, coming to his feet. "When do we go after Fith?"

"Eat first," said Enek, beckoning also to the wakened Jipi.

"A little," agreed Kardios. "I eat lightly before a fight, and perhaps I have reason to feast later."

He washed his face in a clay pot of water.

Breakfast was grilled fish and those cakes. They were of barley meal, coarse but palatable. Lotay gave him a dish of honey to trickle upon them. Kardios was hungry but he took only a few mouthfuls, and a sip or two of wine.

"If you are ready now — " said Enek.

"I'm ready." Kardios took the sword from its place.

"Let me have cord, to swing this to my wrist so I won't lose it."

The cord was given him.

"And what kind of light for the bottom of that well? I don't mean to trust Fith's light, it might go out."

Enek brought a chunk of green cane, as long as Kardios's arm. Within it were nested live coals, closely swaddled in dry moss. The open end was plugged with clay, and holes had been bored through the tough outer substance of the cane. Kardios took it, examined it, then swung it through the air. Tiny flames burst out through the holes, then died down as he held it still.

"That will be splendid," Kardios approved.

Outside the cave, the bright morning was around them. Enek and Jipi went down the ladder with Kardios. Lofty shapes of the Nephol were abroad and came after them — men only, perhaps all the men of the community. Kardios estimated about twenty. They followed Kardios and his companions across the stepping stones. Their journey was watched by women, and by children small only by comparison with their mothers.

They reached the mouth of the well, strewn around with polished bones. Kardios peered down again, and again he saw the coinlike spot of soft light far below. He made fast the lanyard from the sword hilt to his right wrist, took the torch in his left, and sat down. "Now," he told them, "I want to go down head first. Tie a cord to my left ankle."

A coil of line, braided of tanned leather thongs, was produced by Jipi. "We'd better tie both ankles," he said. "This cord will cut deep into one ankle."

"No, only my left," demurred Kardios. "I don't want to land down there with my feet tied together, and Fith coming. Do as I say, Jipi."

Jipi shrugged. He tore a furred strip from the edge of his mantle and wound it around Kardios's left ankle. Around this padding he drew a loop of the cord and knotted it. Kardios stood up. Enek touched his shoulder, with fingers like great ridged roots.

"Luck go with you, Kardios," he said solemnly. "You're small enough to go into the well, but your heart is as great as any of ours." He considered the praise he had spoken. "Greater," he amended.

"Thank you," said Kardios. "Hold fast to the cord and let me go down fairly fast."

He rose to his knees and yet again he looked into the deep shaft. Once more he saw, seeping from far below, the ghost of light.

"Here I go," he said.

He thrust in both torch and sword and slid after them head first, like a fox gliding into its burrow.

The noose clutched bitingly at his ankle. They were lowering him like a bucket. He twiddled the torch into a rosy glow. The shaft, he saw, was like a chimney, a straight, perpendicular tube into which his body could slide, easily but not roomily. The sides of it were almost glossily smooth. The rock looked volcanic, but its smoothness must be something that Fith had done. He had had months in which to accomplish it, for his own sliding ease.

Down. Down. Kardios wondered how many lengths of his own body he had descended. Blood beat in his ears, but he felt no fuzziness of the wits. He was healthy, thank whatever gods must be thanked. He remembered men he had seen, men called wise in Atlantis back when anybody called things anything in Atlantis. They stood on their heads for long spaces, bringing the blood there to spur their minds. Then they sat up and prophesied or gave advice. Kardios could not remember anything that any of them said that was worth remembering.

The pale patch of light grew wider below him. He must be approaching it. Where that light would be, Fith would be. Kardios let the sword dangle from the lanyard and put out his right hand to touch the smooth wall of the tubelike shaft. The touch slowed his descent a trifle, so that the drag of the cord on his ankle slackened. Now, there, down there, he caught a glimpse of slaty rock flooring. That was where he was coming to, where he was to meet Fith and make a battle.

"I'll do it," he promised himself, half aloud.

And then he was coming into open space at the bottom of the well. As his head cleared the bottom of the shaft, he saw that here was a considerable grotto of some sort. He came to the bottom, landing on one hand and the free foot. Writhing around, he caught the hilt of the sword again and with a flick of it severed the rope that was tied to his left ankle. He stood up quickly in the middle of the floor, and whirled the torch for light to see better where he was.

There was already light to show him that, without the torch. It was a place of rough rock, plenty of level expanse underfoot, as much as a fairsized hall. All around were jagged, dull walls, slanting inward to where, overhead, they came into a curved roof like the inside of a slipshod dome. As much room here, Kardios thought, as had been in the garden of Theona, now sunk to where it was sunken. Looking swiftly this way and that, he judged that this place had been fashioned somehow, though he could not guess just now what that somehow was. The hazy light showed him a darker blotch to the side, where a corridor seemed to lead away. Opposite this, in a jagged corner, lay the light's source.

It looked like a bank of soft sand heaped in among the rocks, palely glowing, as an unpolished jewel might glow under a directed radiance. That softness spread widely, farther across than the tallest of the Nephol people. He thought the glow pulsated, then wondered if this was not a sort of motion, a stir in that substance. There was sound, too, like breathing: *fith, fith*. Then it was Fith, plainer to see here than last night by the glow of half a moon. As Kardios looked, Fith paid attention to him in turn.

For the mass moved, it defined itself. It was not slackness, giving off that blur of light. It began to move itself out from among the rocks where it nested, and it seemed to take on form. It spread like a great, flattened ray, such as once he had seen swimming under water, when he had looked over the side of a fishing boat off his home shore that was shore no longer. Fith crept on outflung projections like flukes that reached right and left. At the center, the expanse rose into a crest. Deep within that center shone the stronger light Kardios had seen the night before, rosy-tinged with a thought of green. Even as Kardios stared, the central light moved within the inner mass, moved forward in it as though to face him.

"Here I am again, Fith," Kardios addressed it. "They sent me down here to fight you. Let's make it a good one."

It seemed able to hear him. It crept toward him

163

across the floor. Its inner bulk humped forward. Its flukes moved gropingly ahead, its substance flowed into them. It took a new position and headed toward him from that one, coming, coming.

Kardios poised, fencer-fashion, on light feet. He brought his sword to center guard position, point to the fore, ready for thrust or cut. Fith approached faster, rising and swelling and breathing, *fith, fith*. Out came a flaplike projection, like a questing tentacle.

Kardios slid his right foot forward and swiftly stooped his long body into a smooth, skilful lunge. The swordpoint licked out, and at the very wink of the right time he brought the blade down for a sweeping , slicing cut. That extension of pale substance parted before the razory edge like a strand of wool. The severed piece went squirming away. The pale hummock of substance recoiled upon itself, almost as swiftly as Kardios recovered from his lunge, drawing his extended foot backward and falling on guard again.

"Did you taste it, Fith?" he cried. "Can you taste as well as hear? Come on, try me again."

Fith knew what he said. For Fith came on to try him again. This time the pale bulk flowed out like foamy water, seemed to blanket the floor. It stole suddenly into action. As it did so, it bunched again, and now it seemed to be moving on bumpy protuberances beneath, moved on them as on legs. The rosy light within glowed stronger. It pulsed. Other parts of the body extended, questing like feelers, like arms. Kardios nipped one of them off with a quick, slicing cut, ducked low to escape another. Fith came charging.

So fast did Fith squatter forward that for a moment Kardios was backed almost against a jagged wall. He couldn't let himself be trapped there. Again he struck

164

at a questing length of Fith's substance. It barely flicked him as he severed it, and its touch was like a tongue of flame upon his forearm. Desperately he crouched, then hurled himself in a great, flying leap above the oncoming bulk of Fith. He landed on his feet just beyond, ran half a dozen steps and faced around.

"I'm not one of those clumsy giants, Fith," he cried. "You didn't catch me. Here I am. You must keep me amused."

Fith was drawing into a new shape. This shape rose up. It grew to the height of one of the Nephol, higher than that. It was giving itself legs, two clumsy bolsters on which it stood. It put forth arms. It was imitating the form of man. At the top, in the blob that might simulate a head, the rosy glow throbbed at him. *Fith, fith*, the creature panted.

"You've been observing things," said Kardios. "But you're clumsy at sculpture. Well, why do we wait?"

The giant shape came at him in a squattering run.

Kardios thrust, backed away, thrust again, and then Fith was all over him. Fith had shot out in all directions and had fallen upon him like a blanket.

The sword drove into Fith's midmost part and Kardios drew it up, with a strong, full-armed rake of a sweep. The edge divided the enveloping tissue like canvas. Next instant, Kardios scrambled and floundered through that great gash, won clear like a netted bird slipping out at a gap in the mesh. He danced away, tingling as though hot water had been thrown upon him. The mass he had escaped tried to draw itself together again, there almost at his knee. He looked down to where the red light flickered, close within reach.

165

At once he sped his blade in a mighty drawing cut. The edge sank deep into the soft pallor, seemed to grate as it struck something more solid inside. He drew it to him with all his strength, cutting the redness in two.

The close air hummed, shrieked all around them. The red glow of awareness in Fith's tissue blinked out.

Kardios backed clear, his sword ready. But Fith was dying. The panting breath labored, then stopped. The great sprawl of substance seemed to slacken, to shrivel, before Kardios's very eyes. The pale light dimmed, grew faint.

Kardios whirled his torch. The flames jumped out to show that Fith sprawled motionless and shrunken there. The grotto was silent.

Stepping close, Kardios prodded with his sword point, poked again. There was no responding movement.

He had done it.

Moving the torch to keep its flame bright, he looked around him. There hung the cut end of the rope that had let him down. He went to it and drew it into a loop under his arms and knotted it securely. Then he took hold of the slack and tugged on it strongly. After a moment, he pulled again. The rope tightened. High above, at the surface of the ground, they were pulling to lift him.

He hung limp in the noose, barely clutching the torch in his left hand and dangling the sword from his right wrist. He was more weary than he had had time to realize, and he felt blistered and singed from where Fith had touched him. It seemed to take far longer to be drawn up than it had taken to be let down.

They were all there at the top, the Nephol. Enek

166

put out a hand to Kardios, then drew it back. "Fith burnt you," he said.

"He scorched me here and there, but I killed him," announced Kardios, and mustered his grin with it. "He was all you said he was, and more. Killing him, I felt sorry for him a little — that foreign thing, alone and hungry and hunting. But fighting men should be careful about being sorry. Anyway, he's dead, fading into nothing down there. Close up that hole again. This time it will stay closed."

"How did you fight him?" asked Yod.

"As I've fought you, getting out of his way and countering. That's how I'd beat you."

"Of course you could beat me," Yod grated, as though the words were dragged out of him. "How could I raise a hand to you now?"

"How, indeed?" wondered Kardios. "You and I are friends."

They wanted to carry Kardios in triumph back to the caves, but he would not let them. In the space before the bluff, the giant women gathered to anoint his scald-like wounds with pleasant balms. Jipi brought him another stone bottle of what was the best wine Kardios had tasted among the Nephol. When the night came down, all sat fearlessly in the open. They sang, like gigantic birds.

"You may live among us as long as you like, Kardios," said Enek, presiding over a supper cooked on a dozen fires. "Since Atlantis is gone, let this be your home. You will be a chief, as I am. All of us will bow to you."

"That's why I'd better be going somewhere else," said Kardios. "You and I talked about religion yesterday evening, discussed how sometimes ordinary things

167

get to be gods. I don't feel ambitions to be bowed to. Bowing to someone grows into stranger notions about holiness and supreme powers and so on."

"But where will you go?" asked Yod, gnawing the thigh bone of a boar. "We can't tell you much of the countries to inland, except that there are small peoples, like you."

"I'll have to find out for you."

"The sword is yours, as we agreed," said Enek.

That night Kardios slept the sleep of exhaustion and triumph. In the morning the women brought the garments they had made. There was a short tunic of blue with white points, that fitted him as though made to his measure, and a cape of soft black wool worked with gold. He put these things on and Enek offered him the sword, for which overnight had been made a bronze-studded leather scabbard and a belt just right for Kardios's lean waist.

"You'll need provisions," said Jipi, fetching a pouch with a band to sling it to the shoulders. "Here are bread and roast meat and dried fruit. And this flask, you liked our wine. Drink on your journey, and remember us as friends."

There was no visible trail inland. Kardios said his farewells and struck out across a field shagged with coarse grass. On the far side, under the shade of a belt of trees, he stopped and turned.

The Nephol stood back there, a throng of huge men and women, with big children among them. Enek towered to the front of them. When he saw that Kardios was looking, he raised his mighty hand as thought in blessing. The other Nephol flung up their hands, too, a forest of hands.

Kardios waved back to them, full-armed. His heart

felt all the warmer as he plunged in among the unknown trees.

The sword he had won jogged against his thigh as he strode. He dropped his hand to the hilt. That hilt fitted his hand as though made for it. And who could say? Perhaps it had been made for his hand, in readiness for what it had done for him and the Nephol against Fith, in readiness for what it would do in future. No man was alone and friendless if he had a proper sword.

Walking past the trunks, Kardios felt a happy surge of expectation within him, a sense of adventure perhaps waiting in the next clearing. He began to hum a tune. He hummed it again, until he had the melody and the tempo to suit the words he was putting together in his mind. At last he began to sing:

"My sword, what wonders shall we twain not do?
The world is ours, to roam and render clean.
Against whatever peril comes in view
My arm is strong, your point and edge are keen.

"For storming citadels, for holding clear
From soil and sloth, for glory in the sun,
For showing enemies the face of fear,
My good companion, you and I are one."

Introduction to "The Ring of Set"
by Richard L. Tierney

Editorial intrusion. I've tried to avoid my favorite word (I) since the first of these introductions. It's impossible. Heck with it.

I didn't ask Tierney to contribute to this anthology, because I wasn't aware I'd read anything by Richard Tierney. Odd; I had continued the exploits of the REH creation Cormac mac Art for this publisher, in Sword of The Gael. *Cormac's only appearance had been in the four stories composing* Tigers of the Sea, *published in cloth by Donald M. Grant in 1974 and in paper by Zebra Books a year later. Preparing for "my" Cormac, I'd read* Tigers *four-point-three times. And loved the epic poem.*

Dick Tierney edited that book and finished a couple of the stories as well. He wrote the poem. Now I know. But when his agent sent The Ring of Set, *I was a bit put off. "Trying to push his ... clients ... off on m ... wow, this is GOOD!"*

To Tierney and his agent I've said so, and too that Tierney is a serious, more-than-competent practitioner of whose works we should get to see more, and that if he was born in 1936 or just after, REH must have been right about reincarnation.

You're gathering that I really like this story by a man I've never met. You're right. It's told *properly.*

THE RING OF SET
by
Richard L. Tierney

I.

Patroclus folded his pudgy hands across his fat belly and smiled with satisfaction. The crowd that filled the spacious courtyard was large, larger than he had expected. It was composed of a colorfully heterogeneous mass of people, most of whom had come down from Rome for the day. There was an assortment of costumes and skin tones that bespoke representation from at least a dozen countries: tall, blond barbarian chiefs from lands beyond the Alps rubbed elbows with lean, sharp-eyed Jewish and Phoenician merchants; Spaniards and Greeks mingled with the proud, robed forms of high-turbanned Persians and swarthy Egyptians. There were even a few ebony-skinned Ethiopians in the crowd, and the mixed babble of alien tongues made a chaotic blend. A strange group it was to be gathered in such a small, quiet town as Astura, Patroclus reflected — but then, this was a rather special occasion.

There was a flurry by the gate, and a small party of nobles in white togas entered, accompanied by a number of Praetorian Guards. No fanfare announced their entrance, but the crowd was quick to make way for their advance, and Patroclus rose to greet them with anxious haste. For he knew that the tall, lean, white-haired man in their midst was none other than the Emperor Tiberius, on his way back to Campania after a brief visit to Rome.

"Hail, Imperator," he beamed as the group approached. "Your presence is most welcome. Seat yourself here in the shade, I pray you."

"When does this auction begin?" demanded Tiberius, seating himself in the chair provided. The Praetorians drew up behind him in close order along the marble portico.

"Whenever it please you, Imperator — we awaited only your gracious presence."

"Begin, then."

Patroclus signaled, and the auctioneer mounted the platform. His voice rang out in the courtyard, and Patroclus settled back under his awning to watch the proceedings. His fat face assumed a complacent, doughy grin as he contemplated his coming profits. It was not often that such a wealthy client as old Diomed passed away, leaving a huge estate to be auctioned off. Diomed had been a queer old recluse who had spent his later years collecting odd trophies from far corners of the world. Few Romans had suspected his vast wealth but, judging by the crowd present, he was not unknown in stranger parts of the earth.

But even more rare was it for the Emperor Tiberius to visit the area around Rome. Seldom did the old tyrant venture forth from his pleasure-palace on the island of Capri where, it was rumored, he amused himself by torturing women and young boys in strange, monstrous ways.

Patroclus stole a glance at Tiberius, who was watching the auctioneer through half-closed eyes. In some ways the Emperor seemed rather striking: his form, though smitten with more than seventy years of age, was still tall and imposing, and his lined face was not yet devoid of majesty. But his lank, thinning hair hung white and straggled about his ears, and his large eyes seemed somehow replete with cold malice. He seemed bored with the auction. Patroclus found that annoying, but dared say nothing. Something about the old man's half-closed eyes struck him very unpleasantly.

The first item to be auctioned off was a young Persian slave girl whose beauty attracted many bidders. After a long haggle she was purchased for a goodly price by Baius, Tiberius's great-nephew, who sat on the old man's left. He seemed a haughty young man, Patroclus observed, with ugly yet ascetic features and foppish dress. His arms were unusually hairy. He grinned after the Persian girl as his slaves led her away, and the executor noticed that his canines were rather large and wolfish.

As more slaves were led to the block Tiberius began to fidget impatiently.

"Enough of this," he muttered. "Bring out the gold and gems. I can't stay here all day!"

Patroclus made hurried, obsequious apologies and

informed his auctioneer of the Emperor's desires. A large ebony chest was then hauled to the stand by two brawny Ethiopians, who unfastened the cover and turned the whole thing over on its side. A glittering profusion of gold, silver and jeweled ornaments spilled out, making a considerable mound on the platform. The crowd gasped at the sight, but the half-hooded eyes of the Emperor did not alter their expression in the slightest.

The auctioneer picked the topmost ornament from the pile and held it up for all to see.

"What am I bid?" he cried. "This ring is of excellent craftsmanship, and set with fine gems. Who will bid?"

"Let me see it," said Tiberius.

The auctioneer descended and deferentially handed the ring to the Emperor's guard, who conveyed it to the old man himself. It was a strange ornament, fashioned in the shape of a thrice-coiled serpent gripping its tail in its mouth. The eyes were small, bright yellow jewels that seemed almost to twinkle with an inner life of their own. The Emperor seemed fascinated by the bauble. For a long moment he gazed raptly at it, caressing its minutely carved scales with his long fingers, staring into its yellow eyes as if half hypnotized.

"I'll take it," he muttered at last. "Will two hundred sestertia be satisfactory?"

"More than satisfactory," beamed Patroclus, amazed at Tiberius's unusual display of generosity. "Your munificence is most gratifying, O Caesar . . . "

"Never have I seen such a ring as this," mumbled Tiberius, ignoring his host. "Those eyes — they seem to hold lost secrets." Then, tearing his gaze away from the ring, he turned to his great-nephew and said:

"Gaius, pay the man two hundred sestertia."

"I bid three hundred," said a voice from the throng.

Patroclus paled. "What did you say?" he gasped, facing the crowd. "Who said that?"

"I did," replied a tall, dark-complexioned man in the forefront of the press. "I bid three hundred sestertia for the ring."

Patroclus eyed the stranger with disfavor. He seemed a man in his mid twenties and possessed the lithe, compact build of an athlete. Black hair spilled in unruly bangs over his broad forehead, and his deep-sunken eyes glowered from beneath dark brows. The cheekbones were unusually high, the mouth wide and tight-lipped, the chin square and clean-shaven. Patroclus could not decide whether the face was homely or handsome — certainly it was striking. The man's apparel consisted of a long, black cloak and a scarlet tunic bordered with black. At his side hung a curved knife, or *sica*, of a type used by gladiators, and in his right hand he clutched a long, dark staff seemingly carved in the shape of a serpent.

"Fool," hissed Patroclus, "be silent! Do you not know the Emperor Tiberius? The bidding is closed."

The stranger's dark eyes glowered more intensely. "I know the Emperor," he said, with a slight bow of deference in Tiberius' direction. "I also know the law. I am entitled to bid."

Patroclus cringed, expecting an outburst from Tiberius, but the old man only smiled, and his enigmatic eyes narrowed slightly.

"The fellow is right," he said evenly but with a trace of sarcasm in his voice. "I raise my bid to four hundred. What say you to that, young man?"

"Five hundred sestertia," said the stranger tensely.

"Indeed! Is the ring worth so much to you? Then I must go to seven hundred. What say you now?"

The man's grip tightened on his staff and his brows knit grimly. At last, with what seemed a physical effort, he said in a low voice:

"A thousand!"

The crowd gasped. Tiberius grinned and touched the tips of his lean fingers one against another.

"Is that as high as you will go, then?"

The stranger stood silent, scowling darkly.

"Then I say eleven hundred," said Tiberius. "Give Patroclus his money, Gaius, and let us be off."

Patroclus clutched greedily at the treasury notes the Emperor's great-nephew handed to him. But the stranger was not to be silenced.

"Tiberius," he said in a firm, quiet voice, "you must not take that ring."

"How say you?" said the Emperor slowly, and the crowd edged back. "Who are you to speak thusly to the Emperor of Rome?"

"I speak not from insolence, O Caesar, but in warning. The ring is not to be worn by any of a ruling line. For any such to wear it is death."

"And how do you know so much about this ring?" asked Tiberius. There was a tinge of menace in his voice.

The stranger shifted his stance nervously. "It is the ring of Set, the Evil God of the Egyptians. A priest of Ptah once told me of its existence and its powers. Several months ago I learned that old Diomed had had such a ring brought from Egypt, and so I came here — only to learn that Diomed had died."

"Your story is a strange one," remarked the young

177

Gaius haughtily. "Why should the ring bring death to the wearer?"

"Because it has been cursed."

A woman tittered in the crowd, and this set off a tide of swelling laughter. Gaius smiled irksomely.

"I do not jest," said the stranger, his voice tense with anger. "The ring is old, older than all the nations of the earth. It was owned by Thoth-Amon, a sorcerer who lived ten thousand years ago in the land which is now called Egypt. The ring was old even then, but Thoth-Amon learned its powers and used them to call up demons to do his bidding. His enemies died with the marks of fangs and claws on their bodies, and for a time none could resist his power.

"Yet the ring was not all-powerful: once, Thoth-Amon invoked its power to destroy a king — but the king had an ally who was a greater sorcerer than even Thoth-Amon, and the ring's power was turned aside. The king lived, and later Thoth-Amon died, but the curse was still on the ring and has never been lifted. Since then several kings have tried to wear the ring, but each died a terrible death, so that at last the priests of Egypt hid the thing beneath one of their altars — and there it lay for nearly ten thousand years, until Diomed's curiosity brought it to light once more."

The crowd laughed anew as the stranger concluded his tale, but Patroclus noticed that several Egyptians in the crowd remained silent, their faces strangely grave.

"Fool!" snarled the Emperor, his eyes now fully open. "Do you think to frighten me into giving up the ring with this child's tale? Fellow, you stand on the brink of death, so answer civilly: what is your name?"

"Simon, of Gitta."

"Then look you, Simon!" Tiberius rose and slipped the ring on one of his fingers, then held up his hand for all to see. "Behold, I stand unharmed. Let the gods strike me if they will."

The crowd cheered, and Simon flushed at the derision for him in their cries. He turned away, angry and embarrassed, but before he could leave the high, taunting voice of Gaius lanced the air.

"Hold on, there — I've a question!"

Simon turned again to face the portico, his face dark and sullen.

"How came *you* to learn of this ring," Caius continued, "that lures you across half the world in quest of its power?"

"I seek not its power," Simon retorted. "Its power is a threat of bane to all humankind. My mentor was Ka-nephru, high priest of Ptah in Thebes and hereditary guardian of the ring; he was slain by that agent of Diomed who pilfered it. With his last breath he charged me to search out the ring, wherever it might be, and restore it to its proper seclusion — else, he warned, might all mankind be brought down to doom by the misuse of its power."

The eyes of Gaius were scowling coals glaring down into Simon's own — and Simon *knew* in that instant that his story was believed. But then Gaius turned to the nobles beside him and said loudly enough for all to hear:

"What think you, friends, of a man with a story like this, and with no retinue, who carries a thousand

179

sestertia on his person? Do you not find that a bit strange?"

"Did I say I carried it?" retorted Simon. "And is it your business to know how I keep or earn my money?"

"Earn it?" mocked Gaius. "Your profession must be a profitable one. Are you a thief, Simon, or a pimp?"

The crowed roared at the coarse jibe. Simon scowled darkly and answered in a low, even voice: "I am a magician."

"Ah — that would explain your ridiculous cloak and staff. Can you do a trick for us, magician? I suspect you are quite expert at making things vanish — especially money from men's pockets, eh?"

"If you dared step down here," said Simon evenly, "you would learn how swiftly I can make a man's head vanish from his shoulders."

"That's all we need," grinned Gaius to the Praetorian Guards. "Take him!"

Three burly guardsmen detached themselves from the ranks and strode down into the courtyard. The crowd moved back. Simon did not stir, but watched in silence as the soldiers advanced with drawn swords. Suddenly he raised his staff and shouted:
shouted:

"Here's a trick for you, Gaius!"

He hurled the staff, not like a spear, but crosswise. It caught the foremost guard across the breastplate, bending at the impact. And then, abruptly, it was a living, writhing cobra whose coils looped and lashed about the man's form. The black, hooded head darted forward, and the guard reeled and fell to the flagstones, screaming and clawing at his face.

Women shrieked in the crowd. Simon whipped off

180

his cloak and flung it over a second guard like a net, sending the fellow sprawling with a quick jerk. He wheeled and twisted aside just as the third guardsman's sword-point tore through his tunic and nicked the flesh of his flank. Whirling, he snatched out his *sica* and sprang: the curved blade swished in a glittering arc that ended in a spurt of crimson, and the guard flopped heavily to the ground, his neck slashed nearly to the spine.

Simon leapt up the steps of the columned porch. Three bounds carried him to the Emperor's chair. The nobles scattered; Gaius backed away hastily, screaming for the guards, his face twisted into a wolfish snarl. The fleeing Patroclus tripped in his haste and rolled down the marble steps. Simon grabbed Tiberius's arm and began to tug at the hand that held the ring.

"Help!" shrieked the Emperor. "Assassin! Help!"

The Praetorians were already surging forward. Simon sprang back to avoid a guardsman's thrusting *pilum;* the thick shaft of another spear cracked sharply against his wrist, knocking the *sica* spinning from his hand.

"Alive!" screamed Tiberius, scrambling out of danger. "I want him alive!"

Simon ducked a *pilum* swung clubwise, darted a lightning-swift chop to the guardsman's face that crushed the bridge of his nose and sent him sprawling. He whirled — but not quickly enough: a heavy brass-studded shield crashed down on his head and shoulder, and Simon reeled and fell stunned to the marble floor.

"A madman!" exclaimed Tiberius, rubbing his hand. "He would have stopped at nothing to get the

181

ring. You were too slow, you fools — he might have killed me had he tried!"

"Thank the gods who made him mad," drawled Gaius casually, "and trouble yourself about him no more, O Caesar — leave him to me, if you will."

"Remove him from my sight, then," ordered the Emperor. "See that he is crucified. You, Macrobius — kill that snake of his! And as for you, Patroclus," he continued, turning to the cowering executor, "hereafter you will be more careful about whom you admit to your auctions. I'll let you off lightly this time, but the damage to my serenity demands compensation. Guards! Gather up these trinkets and gems, and remove them to the imperial treasury."

Patroclus watched in consternation as the imperial party filed out the gate, bearing with them the chest that contained most of old Diomed's wealth.

"A curse on all magicians and madmen!" he muttered vehemently. "Would that the gods had stifled all such at birth! Slaves! bring me a flagon of wine — I am ill."

II.

"Ho, wretch — here is your dinner. Wake up and eat!"

Simon sputtered back to life as a foul-smelling, semi-liquid mess splashed over his face and chest. Opening his eyes, he saw that he lay on the floor of a small room whose walls were beaded with moisture. Above him stood a hunched, malformed individual bearing an oily, flickering torch in one hand and a dripping pail in the other.

"What is this place?" asked Simon groggily.

"The dungeons at Circeii," croaked the man in a

182

voice as warped and sloppy as his twisted face. "The soldiers brought you here but a moment agone. Eat well, for you'll be fed but once a day."

Simon tried to rise, but found that he was chained to the floor. The crooked man laughed and kicked him in the ribs.

"You'll learn to take life easy here," he jeered. "There's no escaping this place. Lie still now, and eat your bilge."

Simon glared up at the hateful face, wishing he could rise and smash it to a pulp. Certainly that would have improved its appearance. Straggled hair pushed out from beneath a dirty leather cap to hang lankly over an apish forehead, and between the strands peered eyes whose fungus-yellow depths reflected a coarse, brutal sadism. A pendulous nether lip dangled droolingly over a receding chin, exposing a jagged line of rotten gray teeth. The man's garments were nothing more than ragged patches of cloth and leather stitched haphazardly together and held in at the waist by a frayed rope. From this rope hung a bundle of keys on a large, iron ring.

The man laughed hoarsely at the anger in Simon's eyes.

"You'll learn the hard way," he grated. "I know your kind. You think you're tough — but you'll break. Maybe you'll even go mad, but I hope not. The sane ones suffer most!"

He laughed again and spat in Simon's face. Simon surged fiercely against his chains, but his efforts only caused the ragged jailer to laugh the harder. The hunched man gave him a final kick in the side and walked chuckling out of the cell. The metal door clanged shut, and Simon was left in darkness.

183

How long he lay in that dank hole he had no way of knowing, but it seemed many hours. Several times he heard the jailer's rough, raucous laugh, always in connection with sobbing cries and muffled blows, and the memory of that unkempt creature made him grind his teeth in futile rage.

At last the tramp of feet sounded from the corridor outside, and a key grated in the massive lock. The door opened, and when Simon's eyes had adjusted to the torchlight he saw that three men had entered his cell. One was the ragged jailer; the second was a brawny, brutal-faced giant of man clad only in a loin cloth; the third, dressed in an elaborate blue tunic and scarlet cloak, was none other than the Emperor's great-nephew, Gaius.

"Ho, scoundrel," Gaius grinned. "Do you find your new quarters suitable? No, don't bother to rise — our visit will be both short and informal."

Simon scowled at him darkly, but said nothing.

"Ah, you are angry!" said Gaius, bending over Simon in a cocky manner. "Be not so quick to take offense — perhaps I'm not the enemy you seem to think I am. If old Tiberius had had his way, you'd be nailed to a cross this very moment. I had you brought here to Circeii instead."

"What do you want with me, then?"

Gaius turned to the jailer. "Leave us," he ordered, and the repulsive creature shambled out of the cell. Simon glanced uneasily at Gaius's massive companion, wondering what was to follow.

"Don't mind Macrobius," said Gaius, indicating the brutal-faced giant. "He's my bodyguard — used to be a gladiator. I would guess, judging by the way you fought today, that you've seen action in the arena yourself."

"I was trained to use the *sica*," said Simon. "For two years I spilled blood for the amusement of your howling crowds. Some of that blood was my own."

"I can see why you survived, Simon — you are quick as a cat. But what of the man you killed with the snake-staff? You didn't learn *that* trick in the arena."

"The priests of Ptah use serpents in their rituals and have long known how to do many things with them. I was once an acolyte in one of their temples."

"After you escaped from your gladiator school, no doubt," remarked Gaius. "But no matter. Were these same priests the ones who told you of the ring?"

"What is all this to you?" Simon demanded. "Have you come here but to mock me again?"

"I do not mock you, Simon of Gitta," said Gaius, bending forward and speaking in a low, intense voice. There was a strange gleam in his deep-set eyes. "Tiberius pretends to scoff at the hidden powers of magic, but I am not such a fool. Do you know that the Emperor has fallen ill? Aye, it happened but an hour after he had left the auction-place, and though he vows it is but a passing sickness I can see death approaching in his eyes. The ring is responsible, Simon — I know it is the ring!"

"What do you want of me, then?"

"The ring, Simon — and the power to wear it. Old Tiberius has named me his heir, and when he dies I will be Emperor of Rome. Yet an emperor has many enemies — his throne is never secure. With the power of this ring at my command I would never need fear their plots; my enemies would fall to the fangs of demons, and none could ever hope or dare to dispute my rule!"

"But no ruler can wear the ring of Set," Simon protested. "As soon as you became Emperor you would die like old Tiberius."

"That is why I can use your help, Simon. You must tell me how to lift the curse from the ring."

"I know not whether the curse can be removed," said Simon. "I do not even know the ring's full powers. Yet, there is a chance . . ."

"A chance? Tell me!"

Simon gauged the fanatic gleam in the man's eyes. "And what can I expect in return?" he demanded.

"Your freedom, plus ten times the amount of money that was taken from you. I will even make you head magician of my house should you so desire."

Simon laughed shortly. "Your court buffoon? Not I! Besides, what assurance do I have that you will keep your promise?"

"You have my word."

"Your word!" Simon smiled wryly. "What sort of a fool do you take me for? Your word is nothing."

"Yet for you it is all, Simon — it is all you have. Without my help you might rot here forever — or you might end up hanging from a cross. But neither of these things need happen, Simon, if you will but tell me of the means to lift the curse from the ring. I promise you freedom on these terms — and I have always kept my word."

"Free me, first," said Simon, "or you can rot on your throne before I'll tell you the secret of the ring."

"It is you who will rot, Simon — you are in no position to bargain with me. With or without your help I will learn the secret of the ring. My ways are many and devious, as you have doubtless heard, and my agents are everywhere — they can follow back the trail that led you here, or the one that led old Diomed to send his thief to Egypt. Yet if you will make my path easier, I will do likewise for you. Speak quickly, now — or I shall have Macrobius begin to break your bones, one by one."

"It seems I have no choice," said Simon. "Very well, I'll tell you — but your task will not be an easy one."

"Speak," prompted Gaius, his eyes agleam.

"In the temple of Thoth, at Alexandria, there is an ancient scroll called the Book of Thoth. It was first written more than ten thousand years ago by Thoth-Amon, the sorcerer of the ring. Only once have I glimpsed this book, and the priest who guarded it would let me read but a few lines of its faded hiero-glyphs — yet I saw enough to know that Thoth-Amon wrote his most dreadful secrets therein. If a spell can be found to counteract that of the ring, it will be found within the Book of Thoth."

"Good!" said Gaius, grinning wolfishly. "When I am Emperor, those priests shall not dare withhold this book from me. After Tiberius dies I shall journey to Egypt. Until then, you must remain here."

"Liar!" hissed Simon. "What of your word?"

"When the ring is mine and its power will no longer harm me, then perhaps you will go free. Until then, Simon, farewell — and wish me good fortune if you would see the light of day again!"

The pair strode out of the cell and the door clanged shut behind them. Simon cried out after them, rattling his chains, but only the mocking laugh of the

187

jailer answered him. Finally he sank back in frustration, realizing that if he were to escape it must be by means of his own.

Most would have despaired of winning free from such a predicament, but Simon had spent considerable time studying the methods of the Persian escape-artists who awed the courts of Eastern kings, and had acquired some degree of proficiency in their arts. Yet a tactile examination of his chains showed him there was little hope of escape. Actually there was but one chain, which looped round and round his body, passing every so often through iron rings set solidly into the stone floor. Each end of the chain ran through a metal loop on a locked manacle clamping one of his wrists, and his arms were held out from his sides with only about a foot of slack. With his left hand he could just touch the padlock that clinched the ends of his chain together — a huge iron lock that only a sledge might hope to crush.

There seemed no way out, but his mind would not admit defeat. For what seemed hours he lay in silence while futile plans spun ceaselessly within his brain. The stone floor was cold and damp, and the chain galled him increasingly. From the corridor drifted occasional muted screams, and Simon knew that a few more hours of this would have him screaming, too.

His hunger had been mounting for some time, and at last he overcame his repugnance enough to try to eat. The swill his jailer flung over him was now dried to a greasy crust, but many solid and semi-solid lumps of food littered the floor round about. Evidently the prisoners were fed on scraps from the soldiers' tables. But when he tried to eat, Simon

188

found that the chain would not allow his hands to reach his mouth.

He cursed, loudly and bitterly. His voice was hoarse and high-pitched, and he realized that he was close to cracking . . .

Suddenly he quieted, and a strange excitement swept over him. The object he had picked up in his left hand was hard and did not crumble at his touch. It was only the broken drumstick of a fowl, but it brought a wild burst of hope to his soul.

Carefully he shredded away the remaining meat, then worked the slender fibula loose from the heavier tibia, retaining the smaller bone in his hand. Next he the broken end back and forth against the rough stone floor until he had a slender pin of bone not unlike a bodkin. With this feeble weapon, in utter darkness and with grease-smeared fingers, he began to attack the padlock.

Only a madman might have tried such a device, and only an escape artist could have hoped for it to succeed, but Simon by now had many of the traits of both. Time lost all meaning as he picked away, steadying the lock with two fingers while working the bone pin into the keyhole with the other three. His mind became concentrated entirely in his left hand, so that he was unaware of the rest of his body or the rest of the world. The cold, the dampness, the stench and the distant cries of prisoners all went unheeded . . .

And at last there was a click!

Simon hardly dared to breathe. Slowly he pressed up against his chain. The heavy padlock fell off with a dull rattle, the thick chain went slack, and Simon realized he was free.

189

Free of the chain, but not the dungeon. For a moment he rose and stretched his cramped limbs luxuriously. When he had restored his circulation he lay down again and draped the chain artistically over his body. Then, with the patience of an Eastern mystic, he began to wait.

He did not have to wait long. Presently a light appeared beneath the door, and a key grated in the heavy lock. The crooked jailer entered and stood his oily torch in a wall-bracket. In one gnarled hand he carried a rusty bucket brimming over with slop, and Simon realized that he had been confined for a whole day.

"Ho, pig," gargled the jailer, setting down his bucket. "I bring your daily fare. But first, I must give you a taste of the last — I haven't yet heard you scream."

He uncoiled a whip from his belt-rope and crossed the cell with a shambling, bow-legged gait. Simon began to mumble under his breath, making his voice seem weak and half-delirious.

"What say you, wretch?" demanded the hunchback. As Simon continued to babble incoherently, the man bent over him and peered into his face. "Curse me beneath your breath, will you?" he muttered. "By Vulcan, 'I . . . !'"

Simon's right hand shot out like a striking cobra, and his stiffened fingers crunched into the jailer's throat, crumpling the hyoid like brittle cardboard. The jailer reared back and sprawled clumsily to the stone floor, the air hissing in his throat as he tried to scream.

Simon rose and calmly stepped out of his chains as the hunchback writhed and flopped about. The man

190

was strangling to death. His face flushed to a dark gray, then to a dirty purple, while his yellow eyes bulged painfully and his stubby fingers clutched at his throat. Simon regarded his throes in silence, feeling not pity but only a dark, savage satisfaction. Finally the jailer's contortions came to an end; blood bubbled in his throat as his chest collapsed; his feet kicked the stone flags, and he lay still.

Simon peered cautiously into the corridor, but no one was in sight. He turned and hurriedly unlocked his wrist-manacles with the jailer's keys, then began to strip the dead man of his grimy clothes. Peeling off his own filth-spattered tunic, he replaced it with the jailer's rags and knotted the frayed rope about his waist. Finally, removing the corpse's crumpled cap, he placed it over his own dark locks and walked into the corridor, closing the door of the cell behind him.

Within the cell Simon's disguise would have fooled no one — indeed, his tall, compactly muscled frame seemed in ridiculous contrast to the squat, twisted body of the jailer — but no sooner had he stepped into the passageway than his whole form seemed to shrivel and shrink. His shoulders hunched grotesquely, and his angular face warped itself into lopsided hideousness. The same Persian magicians from whom he had garnered his escape artistry had also been masters of disguise, and Simon had not studied their arts in vain. No one would have recognized him as he hobbled along that dark, narrow corridor in the uncertain torchlight.

Once he paused with the idea of liberating some of his fellow prisoners, but a quick glance into some of the cells caused him to change his mind. Gaunt, skeletonlike creatures, white-haired and scaled with festering scabs, glared up at his torch with eyes of horror and lunacy, and he backed away shuddering, knowing that he could do nothing for them. Only death could help those who languished in the dungeons of Tiberius.

The corridor ended at a narrow flight of stone steps, and these led up a long spiral to an iron-barred archway. Simon tried several of his keys on the massive gate, and finally found one that fit. The gate rasped open, and he emerged into a wider passage. Through the archway at its far end he could see sunlight on the flags of a broad courtyard.

A guardsman suddenly entered the corridor, and strode toward him. Simon had no time to conceal himself.

"Ho, jailer," the guard greeted him. "Have you heard the good news?"

"I hear no news in these foul pits," croaked Simon in what he hoped was a good imitation of the jailer's rasping voice.

"Tiberius has left Circeii. His belly ails him, and he yearns for the fresh breezes of Capri. That means our discipline is relaxed! What say you to that, old toad . . .?" By this time he had approached closely enough to peer into Simon's face. "By Pallus!" he exclaimed, "You're not . . ."

Simon's fist cracked sharply on the point of the guard's jaw and the man crumpled without a sound. The magician caught his unconscious body before it could clatter against the floor, and quickly dragged it into the dark stairwell. Moments later he emerged from the shadows clad in the polished metal and leather of an imperial guardsman.

Leisurely he strode to the archway and scanned the courtyard. About the walls stood a half-dozen soldiers in relaxed attitudes. The far wall opened onto a public thoroughfare, but the wide entrance was blocked by a massive iron portcullis.

Simon scowled. But even as he wondered how he was to pass this last obstacle, a sharp cry of command rang out and he saw that a group of six or eight soldiers had gathered outside the gate.

"Open!", cried their officer. "We come for a prisoner."

"Which prisoner?" demanded the warden of the gate. "And by whose orders?"

"Orders of Gaius, the Emperor's ward. Here is the warrant with his seal. We are to crucify one Simon of Gitta, who was brought here yesterday."

The warden raised his arm, and two guards began to turn the wheel that lifted the gate. Simon strode from concealment and began to walk casually across the courtyard.

The gate creaked open, and the officer stepped inside and handed his warrant to the warden. Simon hoped his crested helmet was shading his features sufficiently. As the body of soldiers tramped in, he walked unhurriedly past their left flank in the opposite direction, just as the portcullis began to descend . . .

"You, there!" shouted the warden suddenly. "Where do you think you're going . . .?"

Simon cast aside his heavy shield and spear and ducked under the closing gate. It creaked to a stop and the soldiers cried out behind him. Simon did not even glance back; a quick sprint, and he was across the cobbled street through a knot of astonished citizens and into a narrow alley. He cast away his helmet as he dashed on, hoping to shake his pursuers in the windings ahead.

Circeii was an old town, and its alleys were narrow and twisting. Simon cast off the rest of his armor as he ran. The clatter of pursuit faded into the distance, and at last he darted into a black archway and paused, ed, panting . . .

No footfalls sounded behind him, and he knew he had thrown off the soldiers for the moment. It would be easy to get out of town once he disguised himself. Discarding the rest of his uniform, he retained only the plain linen tunic, the short broad-bladed sword, and a small leather pouch that jingled agreeably.

"Two denarii," he muttered, counting out the coins. "Enough to buy a good meal and start me on my way. Tiberius can't be more than a few hours from Circeii — I can surely catch up with him before he reaches Baiae and embarks for Capri. I've come too far to give up the ring now. So Gaius decided to have me crucified, eh? He must have decided to make sure I wouldn't blab to anyone else about the ring. Well, now I know how he keeps his word. By Baal! I once told him I'd make his head vanish from his shoulders — perhaps someday I'll have an opportunity to prove my word better than his!"

III.

As the sun sank behind the hills of Campania a ragged beggar, whining for alms, hobbled along the darkening streets of a fashionable neighborhood at the edge of the seaside town of Misenum. There were few other people to be seen, as the neighborhood was some distance from the market place. As the old beggar approached the high wall surrounding a rather palatial estate, a Praetorian Guardsman strode from a shadowy archway and blocked his path.

"Alms for the needy," wheezed the old man in a thin, cracked voice. "Alms, I pray you!"

"Silence, old fool," ordered the guardsman. "The Emperor lies ill within this house. Would you disturb his rest with your whinings? Begone!"

"Alas that the Emperor is ill!" quavered the aged one. "Yet the gods look kindly on those who do kind deeds; a pittance from one of his good soldiers would fill an old man's belly, and perhaps cause the gods to smile on the Emperor's health . . ."

"Go, curse you!" shouted the guard, brandishing his pilum. The ragged beggar limped hurriedly away, muttering in his straggled gray beard. The clack of his gnarled staff faded into the distance as he turned and vanished down a dark side street.

No sooner had he passed beyond sight of the guardsman, however, than his bent form assumed an upright posture and his shoulders broadened amazingly. There was no hobble in his step as he strode over to a marble fountain that stood amid a small parklike patch of trees. Here in the shadows he pulled off his beard and ragged garments, and began to count out coins from a leather pouch.

"Ten denarii and an odd sesterce or two," he grinned. "Not bad for a day's loafing. By Baal, the beggars in this town make as much in a day as I've earned in a week of performing!"

With this observation Simon of Gitta seated himself against the bole of a tree and began to wait. It was dark by this time, but he did not intend to enter the estate of Tiberius for several hours, when the streets would be entirely quiet.

From gossip on the road he had learned that the Emperor was now seriously ill, and that he had been taken to the estate at Misenum, being unable to continue on to Capri. Rumor had it that he was expected to die, and Simon knew he must act swiftly if this were true. He would have a hard time indeed trying to pilfer the ring from the crafty Gaius; also (the thought set his spine to tingling), nothing on earth would be able to protect him from the most terrible of dooms, should Gaius ever master the secret of sending forth the demons of the ring.

For half the night he sat, savoring the cool smell of the salt breeze and listening to the distant tumult of the market place. About midnight the streets quieted and Simon decided to wait no longer. Clad only in tunic and sandals, the short Roman sword girdled at his side, he set out for the estate.

The moon-cast shadows offered perfect conceal-ment as he crept along the road to a point opposite the wall. The gates, he knew, were heavily guarded. The wall was only ten feet high and could be scaled easily, yet he did not attempt it immediately. During the day he had made a careful survey of the outer environs of the estate; he knew the positions of the guards and was ready to act accordingly.

Presently a sentry clanked by. As soon as he rounded the far corner, Simon dashed across the stone-paved street and sprang lightly up the wall. His fingers gripped the edge, and his lithe, hard muscles swung him easily to the top. For a moment he lay there, prone and silent, listening. Then, making sure there was nothing below to obstruct his progress, he slid down the inside face of the wall and dropped softly to the ground.

The casement to the right of the balcony was open wide, and Simon thought he saw the means to reach it. Stealing from the shadows, he crept acrosss the lawn and began to shin up one of the two pillars supporting the balcony. It was difficult to climb, being fashioned of smooth marble, and its diameter was such that his arms and legs would not completely encircle it. His progress was slow, and he felt horribly exposed hanging there above the garden, though the balcony shaded him from the moon's direct rays. But at length he felt the roughness of the pillar's Corinthian crown beneath his fingers, and a moment later he had struggled up and over the balustraded edge.

After resting flat for a moment, he rose and crossed to the door. It was slightly ajar, and through it he glimpsed a tiled corridor flanked by high mahogany portals. At the nearest door stood two Praetorians, their armor gleaming in the soft light of the hanging lamps. No entrance was to be gained here. He would have to try the open window.

Swinging himself hand over hand along the narrow ledge was easy compared to climbing the column, but again he had to endure the exposed feeling. In a moment he was beneath the open casement. Pulling himself up slowly, he peered into a spacious chamber whose marble walls were partly covered with thick tapestry. A single lamp burned on a small table, beside which an old man in the robes of a physician sat drowsing in a padded chair. Against the far wall rested a large bed, mahogany-carved and thickly mattressed, and Simon realized that the Roman

Fates had guided him well — for in this bed, pale and emaciated to a startling degree, lay the wan and failing form of the Emperor Tiberius.

Simon's fingers ached. Cautiously he drew himself over the sill and, making sure no one else was present, slid inside. Neither of the sleepers stirred. Sidling away from the window so as not to be seen from the garden, Simon crept softly to the Emperor's bedside and peered down at his inert form. A thrill of exaltation swept over him as he saw a flash of copper on one of the waxen hands. It was the ring of Set!

Slowly he reached for the thing, gripping it gingerly so as not to touch the old man's flesh. The metal felt strangely warm and smooth beneath his fingertips. He tugged at it gently, but it would not slide off the wizened hand.

Simon scowled. When Tiberius had first donned the ring it had seemed to fit loosely. Now its coppery loops clasped the Emperor's finger with a snug, frustrating preciseness. Yet the finger was certainly not swollen. Had Tiberius ordered his metal-smith to alter the ring's dimensions? That seemed unlikely. Almost it appeared as if the coppery serpent had tightened its coils of its own accord, and Simon could imagine that he saw a wicked light gleaming in its tiny yellow eyes.

He tugged at the ring again, harder this time. Tiberius moaned; his head rolled feebly to one side, and his lips began to writhe strangely. Simon drew back a pace.

"The ring!" groaned Tiberius in a scarcely audible voice. "It will not let me go. Oh, take it from me! Those cursed fiery eyes — I cannot bear them! They glare at me from the darkness — they seek to drown my soul . . . Listen!" His voice suddenly altered, tensed. His eyes sprang open, bright and feverish, but Simon sensed that they did not see him. They seemed to look through rather than at him, and his spine tingled as he beheld their weird brilliance.

"Listen!" whispered the voice again. "It is coming. From the blackness beneath the pyramids I hear it crawling. Do you not hear? Do you not *see*? Ah — those cursed fiery eyes!"

Simon started. He *did* hear something, like cloth folds sweeping across a tiled floor. Someone was approaching. Swiftly he crept past the sleeping physician and concealed himself behind a section of the tapestry. With one eye he watched the room, tensed to draw back his head in an instant.

But no one entered the chamber. Instead, the sound grew steadily louder, gathering different overtones as it did so. There was a sinister, rasping quality about it that made Simon think of serpent scales sliding over cold stone. Closer and closer it seemed to come, yet somehow its volume did not increase in the slightest. Strange hollow booms accompanied it, muted and distorted, like thunder echoing down the halls of other dimensions . . .

A slender wisp of smoke began to rise from the Emperor's bed, and Simon's skin prickled as he saw that the ring had undergone a strange alteration. The tiny coppery serpent had released its tail, and from its upward-gaping mouth issued a thin stream of black smoke that coiled and coalesced into a nebulous cloud above the stricken Emperor. Even as Simon watched it thickened and swelled, and its billows writhed like the coils of a monstrous serpent. And then a form took shape in its murky depths — a form

199

black as the blackest caverns beneath the earth, a form whose lambent yellow eyes leered down like glowing spheres of flame into the eyes of Tiberius.

Simon cringed back, scarcely daring to breathe for fear of attracting the gaze of that monstrous shape. Coil after coil looped into being within the hazy cloud. A colossal fanged mouth gaped wide, and a red forked tongue flickered sinuously in the air above the Emperor's face. The thing was like a serpent in shape, but its black scales reflected not a glimmer of light and its luminous eyes seemed to glare with an evil intelligence. Although it filled only the space above Tiberius' bed, it somehow gave an impression of vastness equal to that of the towering pyramids of Khem, and Simon knew that he gazed upon Set, the most ancient and evil god ever worshiped by the race of man.

Tiberius' mouth was stretched wide as if in a scream, but no sound issued forth. His eyes stared frozenly into the flaming orbs poised above him. Simon stood petrified. He had seen men die screaming in the arena, and expiring slowly on Roman crosses under the glaring sun, yet never had he seen such awful fear as that which twisted the features of Tiberius. Somehow he sensed that the Emperor's soul was being drawn from his body and into the slitted depths of those hellish eyes. The old man's form seemed almost to shrink, and he quivered like a puppet dangling on a vibrating string. Then, abruptly, his shakings quieted; his strained features slowly relaxed into an expression of vacant, staring idiocy, and Simon knew that he was dead.

Already the terrible form was fading away, dissolving into the murky cloud that was streaming back through the mouth of the ring. Simon did not

200

stir until the last wisp of that unnatural smoke had vanished. Then he eased himself slowly from behind the curtain, hesitating as to whether he should carry out his original purpose or flee from that chamber of death while he still had the chance.

There was a soft clatter on the tile. Simon started, and saw a gleam of metal on the floor by the Emperor's bed. Tiberius' dead hand hung limply over the side, and Simon realized that the ring had dropped easily from his finger.

The old physician stirred in his sleep. Simon hesitated no longer — after all, he remembered, the curse had power over kings alone, and could not harm him. He quickly crossed the room, snatched up the ring and hurried to the window. The ring appeared to be normal now — it felt reassuringly solid and metallic. Slipping it on his left middle finger, he let himself out the window, hung for a moment from the ledge, and dropped.

He landed in a catlike crouch and was on his feet in an instant. Quickly he sprinted across the moonlit lawn — and almost collided with a burly shape that suddenly emerged from the darkness under the trees.

"Ho, there!" rumbled a deep voice. "What do you in the Emperor's gardens . . .? Oh, it's you, dungeon-rat. By Hercules, you'll not escape this time!"

Simon recognized Macrobius, Gaius's bodyguard. He leaped back barely in time as the gladiator's iron-knobbed club swished past his cheek. Simon's sword flashed out in time to ward off the second blow but the impact shattered the broad blade and sent him staggering back. Macrobius bellowed and charged.

Desperately Simon snatched up a heavy marble urn

201

and flung it with all his strength. It smacked full into the gladiator's broad chest and sent him reeling back with the wind half knocked out of him. Simon charged in and grappled his attacker; Macrobius dropped his mace and enfolded the magician in a strangling bear-hug. Simon gasped — his foe's strength was like that of an ape. Frantically he dug his thumbs into the gladiator's sides below the ribs. Macrobius loosened his grip, bellowing with rage, and as Simon slipped free he delivered a savage chop to the gladiator's thick neck. The blow would have killed an ordinary man — but Macrobius only grunted, shook his head, and charged again.

Simon leaped aside and struck again. His quick footwork baffled the heavy gladiator, but his blows might have fallen against a stone wall for all the effect they produced. In the distance he suddenly heard the voice of Gaius calling for the guards. Then his feet unexpectedly struck the fallen urn, and he fell sprawling to the grass.

Macrobius roared as his thick hands gripped Simon's leg in a bone-breaking hold. Simon strained back frantically — and his flailing touched the handle of the club Macrobius had dropped. With all his strength he swung the weapon; its iron head crunched deep into the gladiator's skull, spattering blood and brains about the grass, and Simon's foe went limp and sprawled full upon him.

Pushing aside the dead hulk, Simon rose and glared about the garden like a trapped beast. From both ends of the estate sounded the clamor of approaching guardsmen, and several other guards were dashing from the front of the mansion. There could be no escape this time — unless . . .

Unless he used the ring!

Yet he knew not the thing's full powers. Whatever came to his call might destroy him as well as his enemies. Yet it was a chance — at least it was better than dying without a struggle . . .

Even as these thoughts flashed through his mind he knelt beside the shattered head of Macrobius and ran his hand through the sticky hair. The formula called for blood — human blood — and there was plenty of that around. With a shaking finger he smeared a drop of it over the yellow eyes of the ring, and then began to recite the Egyptian words of the single chant he had managed to memorize from the Book of Thoth:

"Blind your eyes, O serpent of Set,
Open them wide to the gulfs of Night —
Whose shadow falls on the waning light?
Call him to me, O serpent of Set!"

A dozen Praetorians converged from the house and the garden. Simon leaped up to meet their charge, his club held ready — but even as he rose, the soldiers stopped as one man in their tracks, and their eyes went wide. A simultaneous scream burst from all their throats. Two of them collapsed in a dead faint, and the rest turned and fled in a mad scramble for the house.

Simon shuddered. He felt the presence of something close behind him, but a strange fear kept him from turning around. Some of Set's minions, legend claimed, had shapes that would blast men's sanity, and Simon did not wish to put the old tales to the test.

"Follow me," he muttered, setting out through the trees. *Something* obeyed, for strange clumping footsteps sounded on the grass behind him. The guards at the rear gate dashed away screaming at his approach, and he passed unhindered into the street beyond.

Through the deserted, torchlit lanes of Misenum Simon fled, and beyond the rasping of great claws echoed from the cobbles. No one pursued him or sought to bar his way, yet he did not stop until he had left the village behind him and the sands of the seashore whispered beneath his feet.

There beneath the moon he paused, and wiped the crusted blood from his ring. Now was the crucial moment; if the demon obeyed his final command, all was well; if not . . .

"Go, now," he muttered. "Go — back to the hell you came from!"

The wind sighed along the beach, and Simon felt that he was alone. Slowly he turned around — and was relieved at the sight of the empty seashore in the moonlight. Yet his spine prickled strangely as he saw the line of tracks that paralleled his own in the sand — long, slender, five-fingered prints, like those of a monstrous lizard.

"By Baal, this ring is more than I had bargained on!" he muttered. "Power I would have — but not on these terms. The priests of Egypt were right to keep the thing hidden from the world. Well, it's mine now, for good or ill. I'm for Baiae, and a ship that will carry me to Alexandria; with Gaius in power things will be too hot for me here — yet someday, perhaps, I'll return and pay off the debt I still owe him!"

And, with a brief glance back at the village, he

shrugged his broad shoulders slightly, then turned and set out along the beach toward the distant lights of Baiae.

Introduction to "Largarut's Bane"
by Raul Garcia Capella

When I told Ray Capella that Poul Anderson would like his story, he blushed. By mail, from California.

Raul Garcia Capella started calling himself "Ray" after a strictly ugly-Amurrican schoolteacher persisted in calling the Puerto-Rico-born young artist "RAY-ool." That must have hurt; it's even worse than being Andrew and being called "Ayun-duhrooooo." (Kentuckians care what we say, actually; it's how we pronounce it that's unimportant.)

Capella has been art director — for Sears. And a writer — for a transit company. He had a good story in the de Camp anthology *Warlocks and Warriors*, and he has a good story here. Though people rush to *join Science Fiction Writers of America even before their first short-shorts are sold (your editor has been treasurer and membership chairman since 1972), Ray Capella wouldn't use the application I sent until "i feel i qualify a little better."*

Fascinating. Such humility not only sets him apart from most writers, it shows in the story that follows. And so does empathy, and sensitivity . . .

A fisherman is an unlikely protagonist in an anthology such as this. But read, and think, and take note: Largarut is more brave, especially considering his circumstances and station, than Hernando de Guzman and Simon of Gitta. Largarut is a hero.

Thanks, RAH-ool.

LARGARUT'S BANE
by
Raul Garcia Capella

In the stillness of night, Largarut's daughter nestled in her bed, while a creature out of hell whispered in her ear. The child's brow was untroubled, her breathing imperceptible. She gazed upwards as if she did not see it crouching on one side of the headboard, balanced tautly near her shoulder.

The demon was tall as a galley's anchor, skin a mottled blue-black that blended with the shadows. The face was that of a vulpine old man, whose eyes protruded with malicious wisdom as its heavy mouth bent near her small ear.

Largarut arose from the middle of his sleep. He did not struggle with unresponding muscle: one moment he was on his back, the next he stood with one knee on his bed, a foot on the floor. His body moved, with the grace of a man grown lean at sea, out of his chamber and down the hallway. He shouldered the child's door aside and was at the foot of her bed in one stride.

Birdlike, the creature cocked its head to regard Largarut out of one baleful eye, outraged at the intrusion. Largarut rounded the bed, hands shooting forward to grasp its thin neck.

The demon loosed its hold on the headboard, battering at the man's head with cartilaginous wings. It swung razor claws toward his chest, but Largarut cracked its neck in one deliberate motion and hurled the flapping body across the room.

Now upright on her bed, his daughter screamed: "NO!" as if dismayed at his act. Largarut stood dumb, shaking with fury and revulsion.

The trembling woke his wife and she in turn roused him. Largarut blinked at the pattern of wave-reflected moonlight on the ceiling. Binior placed her head on his chest, her body half across his. His breathing quieted.

"Again?" she asked.

"Aye."

Binior arose and hurried out. He listened to the slap of her bare feet as she crossed to the child's room. When she returned, he did not have to ask. Her concern was all for him.

"Then — will you go tomorrow?"

"I must," he replied, "the creature becomes larger with each nightmare; 'twas almost her size. And if it means he is getting nearer, or even that mere danger threatens —"

So it was that the village launched its fishing boats the following morning without their leader. And Largarut sat at his seaward porch in the dawn, lacing up boots he seldom wore.

Behind him, a happy patter announced his daughter's presence. Abruptly it quieted, and he waited squinting at the sun-tipped sails that dwindled on the horizon. Then Eriel's small hands were cupping his eyes.

She squealed as he suddenly came to his feet, holding her upper arms with calloused hands, her body a squirming weight on his back.

"Papa Largarut, what do you here?" she laughed over his shoulder, hugging his neck. "The fleet has left you behind!"

"Your brothers can do well enough without me for a day," he said, straightening legs and back so she could drop off. "And there's no reason we can't contribute to today's catch, just because I've an errand in the city."

"The city?" she echoed. She had run to the porch edge and turned back, all long hair and gawky limbs. The sun had burst with color over Ocba's horizon. On the curve of the beach, women were already at their chores. A few girls had beckoned to Eriel, but now she ignored them: "To *Gris*? Oh, papa, take me with you!"

"I cannot," he said. He adjusted the plaited belt around his tunic and turned his head in a gesture she knew to be final. But she could not help her persistence.

"But, papa, mother has told me what it was like, that time we went. 'Twas beautiful, grand — and I

210

too young to remember it by now! Will I *ever* get to see it?"

"Beautiful? Not everyone thinks Gris beautiful," he said bitterly. Gris, terraced queen of the seas, sprawled across an isthmus, its canals linking a sea and an ocean. An Irian city, its eastern bastions had grown onto Korpad's headland, several leagues from his village. "There is nothing grand about a city that, not content to rule one country, lords it over two."

Eriel had skipped away to measure a length of net against a brown leg, in a suddenly grown-up gesture. She had once fashioned it herself with the skill of an oldster. She chattered: "How can you pick a length of good cloth for mama, if I'm not along? The merchants who come by the market say Gris is good for Korpad's trade. And has it not been so even ere grandfather was born?"

"You don't understand such things, Eriel," he said, deaf to her questions. Aside from a simple fisherman's distaste for the giant, bustling seaport, he had better reasons for not taking her along. And Largarut, a Korpadian who did not live off Iria's wealth, could keep his pride intact. He added: "Gris is good for Korpad's trade, aye — and its trade controls Korpad. Nay, I must hurry there and back. You fare much better staying here."

She tilted her head, the large dark eyes gazing at him past a lock of brown hair, "How can I know how well I fare here if I know not how bad 'tis there?"

He laughed, slapped her rump off the sea-porch, but did not answer. The Witch of the Isthmus would know more of that than even he. And somehow,

211

visiting the witch was not the same as tying up to a quay abristle with Iria's masts. It was with that consideration in mind that he trudged out of the village.

It was said there had been a Witch of the Isthmus generations ago, before the Wars. Even in ancient times, when Gris itself had been a pirate village whose raiders plied two waters. He knew little of history, but his faith in the abiding power of the witch was renewed when he stood before her.

He had shouldered his way past Gris's crowded gates. There, guards with true metal swords scarcely looked at merchant, warrior or strangely dressed visitors. He had asked instructions but once and hurried past fretted walls, a thousand smells and sounds on the cobbled streets to knock finally upon a wooden grate. He had climbed a railless, dizzy staircase to see the city's tiers and spans stretching away towards the isthmus under a blue sky, and now stood on a balconied terrace, gaping at a flaxen-haired maid. She had a saucy figure and attractive, if square-jawed face.

"Sit, Largarut," she pointed at a stool. He had not spoken yet.

She climbed onto a hammock beneath a tattered awning, and he could see she wore nothing beneath the light-green shift. She kicked barelegged at an empty cradle to propel herself back and forth.

"My mother is dead," she said tonelessly. "Dead in Eloris, a victim of the gryphon. Now I am Witch of the Isthmus. Next year I must beget my own replacement. Would you repay my services in that wise, Largarut, or have you Irian coin?"

Out of a small pouch, the fisherman emptied four

pearls and several bits of Korpadian amber onto a calloused palm.

"Keep three pearls, the rest will do." Eyes dark, her smile a mystery, she accepted payment. And he knew she was indeed a witch. Hopping back onto her perch, she continued: "Nay, I'd not add the burden of siring a witch upon you; you might attach too much responsibility to it. Now to business: how old is your daughter?"

"Scarce twelve." It was the first thing he had uttered. Although slow in thought, Largarut had learned to couple persuasiveness with wisdom. One needed it to be considered a leader of his village. And yet, confronted by this wench, he was a child. Inanely, he blurted: "She is rather young for her age —"

"Years often matter less —" Then the woman interrupted herself: "Well, what makes you believe this weird is upon her, and not you?"

"Because I —" he was startled. The dream, after all, was his. "Perhaps 'tis on both of us, striking at me as a threat to her. With each nightmare the thing grows; does this not mean it approaches and will someday harm her?"

"Do you believe that what occurred brought on this weird? That is — do you believe what you did to be its cause?"

Again, surprise rolled over him like surf on a body grown warm under the sun. It had never struck him that this might be no curse, but his own imagining. He did not pause to contemplate that she had not asked, but launched into his tale:

"'Twas three moons ago, at nightfall. I had sold a good catch at an inland village, but a heavy rain forced me to stop overnight at the Three Gods' Haven. 'Tis but a thatch roof over the shrine of Ocmuco, Krenk and Tia, on the high road to Gris.

"Three strangers came riding *crinnos* from the city. One seemed to know his way and was about to dismount when I challenged them, saying they should pay the gods tribute to merit shelter. Which is not true, but I care not for strangers, specially from —" he stopped. The witch nodded, smiling.

"Well, I thought it a worthwhile jest at the time. But a boy who had been huddling in the corner by the shrine spoke up and told them 'tis a free haven. The strangers elbowed in, mounts and all, so that none of us were comfortable 'til dawn. After they rode off, I kicked the boy's rump once for making me look like a fool. 'Twas not a hard blow, but he said: 'Tia take your brood, man, but you're less honest than I!'

"That was all. But he was standing before the image of Tia when he said it, and there was a fey look about him. Now I wot it was all my perverse sense of humor, and bad temper. But I forgot about it, although we are a superstitious people who know our place.

"A moon later, to the day, I began having the dreams. At first it was of a tiny thing that fluttered through our house; I thought nothing of them. Then it commenced growing. After Eriel's birth-date, it took to visiting her chamber. Now it flies in no other, although it can barely rise for lack of room and must alight on the bedstead . . ."

Largarut moved his head in revulsion, as if he had tasted bad fish. His voice had grown low and tight, and the sun on his neck did not warm him. He realized he had been speaking of a dream-image as if it were a part of his household.

The hammock hung empty and still. Now the witch emerged from the shadows behind the awning. That bold stride of hers, the tilt of her hip . . . her presence dispelled the mood. She held a bulbous flask in one hand, a bow in the other.

"Drink a bit," she said. "That fire will make any man stand up, eh? Now the bow — and these two arrows. You must practice every day, for you will employ but one shaft when the time comes. Eriel will keep the other 'neath her pillow. Should you break or lose yours, you must fashion or buy a new one."

"But the bow —" he protested. "The Korpad baronies forbid the longbow! And I know not —"

"Out east, amid the wilds, where *alco* herdsmen oft become outlaws, the baronies try to forbid the longbows," she said. "Not that the simple folk don't hide them . . . But here, where civilized men pretend their everyday sophistry, there's enough authority to prevent lawlessness. You are allowed, and none will challenge. This is how you must meet your bane. Practice. Every night, when the moon rises 'til it sits straight above your head while you wait on the western ridge. There you'll take your post."

He gazed at her, knowing the value of the bow matched what he had given her. What then, of her advice? Within him, his soul accepted the faith she had dispensed. And all in that same instant, as she turned away, she was again a woman on a sun-dappled terrace.

She said: "Aye, drain the bottle, but leave it. That's Madirian glass, and 'tis not called the Country

215

of the Glass Blowers for naught. Fare you well, Largarut."

The wine made him bold. He slid the arrows through his belt and shouldered the bow, to hasten through the gay, noisy and squalid edge of Gris. None stopped him.

He knew that his people would accept his midnight errands, his allowing the younger men to replace him temporarily. Pain, violence and the struggle for survival had long ago dealt Korpadians a primitive existence. His fishermen understood when a weird was upon a man.

From then on, Largarut doled out decisions on dry land. Sometimes he went out with his men, but he rested. And every night he practised by torchlight or under the sullen blue of Ocba's huge moon. But when he sat upon the ridge he fretted.

Because he knew he was no bowman. And how could a man scarcely broken to the bow place an arrow in the carcass of a flying thing? One arrow: what good in that, if having missed its mark it fell into the water — or even upon that long strand of beach that separated him from the village?

Nightly, anger overcame him and he cursed the witch for placing him so far from Eriel. A man must look after his weird himself, and he could never reach that distance in time in the wake of an airborne demon. Not if he lost his missile.

He let fly a thousand times. He picked up the stone-headed arrow again and again from the sand, and its insensate straightness mocked him. Once he broke it and had to purchase a new one. Largarut swore and fumbled and strung his bow. The surf stretched away, away, where stars glowed above that vast horizon and night whispered that he was but a mote of sand. Could *he* defy the will of night gods whose purposes were beyond his comprehension?

Daylight and the catch became meaningless to him. That half-night which was his post became his hours of toil; the life of the village turned away from him. He came to know that it was not the act of striking a youngster he was being punished for. His pride was being demolished. One night he stood under the ghostly iridescence of Ocba's moon, alone upon the curving strand, and cursed the gods, the bow and the life-giving water that whispered on the sand.

And as he stood unprepared, a shadow flitted across the lonely expanse between him and the village.

For an instant he froze like a coral statue carved atop the ridge. Then the bow was forgotten — his quarry already beyond range — and he had leaped to the sand. He ran.

He cut across the curve of glinting water. He floundered, swore, ran on, tasting salt water. He was wet, the sand tugged insidiously at his bare feet, the village seemed further away. He ran and pain began, stabbing him just above his belt.

Largarut paused; he had to. His legs were hard and heavy as giant oars, his lungs were afire. He hefted a long shell-knife, swallowing at the night air, leaning momentarily on a net rack. Then there was a faint cry and he pounded on, careening off a shack, hurdling some piles. Shadows leaped past him, and suddenly the house was before him. He struck the door and it fell with him. In the child's room the air beat with the sound of fury and the breath of horror.

Again Largarut was up and somehow, he did not know when, he had entered Eriel's room.

Wings battered wall and bed, but the creature was

upon the floor. She had snarled up its talons on the coverlet and had leaped on its squirming form. He fell to his knees, grasped the hideous head in one hand, raised the knife.

The stroke was superfluous. Eriel had pinned the creature's heart to the floorboards with her arrow.

Largarut stood up, swaying as if on the deck of his own craft. Now both wife and daughter nestled under his arms and he could not fall. Both were crying, both laughing. He joined them.

Later, he carried the monster beyond the village in the darkness and buried it in the sand. When he had awoken near noon of the next day, he could not remember where. He did not want to. He crossed to Eriel's room and found Binior had cleaned and aired it out, so that sunlight splashed in through open shutters.

Outside, the sky was clear. Sun-bright spots on the horizon told him where part of the fleet glided. Nearby, women toiled at nets, cleaned fish or went about the village's chores. Children played on the shore, voices mingling with the surf's laughter.

"Eriel?" said Largarut.

"Out there, playing." Binior had come in and stood beside him near the window.

"*She* knew, all right." Largarut smiled.

"Who — Eriel?"

"I mean the Witch. She had me wait at the ridge, for she knew it would be best. She wanted me away from the village. Somehow, she knew Eriel was strong enough to take care of herself. She had more faith in Eriel's common sense than I did."

He strode out to the entrance at the slap of bare feet on the hard-trod sand outside. Binior went about her own chores, singing. The child ran at him, all salt-water and shining, sun-brown limbs.

"Papa Largarut, papa," she said. She kissed him and danced away toward the beach. "The fleet has left you here again."

"It won't, tomorrow," he called after her, "you shall see."

Eriel looked back a moment, head to one side, hair afloat in the wind. She nodded and ran on, and Largarut breathed deep of the salt air. Binior had come to the porch and he turned to her: "Aye, she knows how to handle herself. She'll be a fine strapping girl, like her mother."

Binior colored and added: "And a woman worthy of her father's pride, I'll wager."

Introduction to "Dragons' Teeth"
by David Drake

Each of the next two writers has proven himself
most professional indeed, which is a damsight more
than can be said for a lot of professionals.

To begin with, I rejected David Drake's first submission. It was a bloody shame; the story, set in the
days just before the Roman Empire began to notice
the termites in the foundation, was jampacked with
lore of that time. It also contained a rousing conflict,
and horror. It was also about a small ship, sort of like
a fishing boat, under attack by a huge fish. Poor Drake;
he wrote it before that fair book and terrific movie
Jaws, too!

Unfazed, Drake had his agent send another. Whereupon, meeting him in Providence and noting that he looked little mightier than I — we're both built for speed — I told him that the idea was good, the opening better than good, the ending a whizzer, and — the story sagged in the middle like a hammock under a fat man on a muggy day in July. I was specific about seven pages of blah talkin'. Many writers would have reared, neighing and naying loudly, like a stud mustang under spurs.

Drake — young, slim, handsome, married to this handsome woman and with this *fantastic occupation* we won't go into, nodded, left, came to my party that night, drank pop (!) and talked equably, went home to NC, threw those seven dull pages in the direction of the Atlantic, and sent me one-and-a-half pages to replace 'em. No more sag.

A point has been stretched to include the story; I like its detail and lore and I respect a professional. That *other version* has appeared before in a "little magazine" called *Midnight Sun*, which has a distribution of a thousand or so. This story, by a real professional who knows more Roman detail than any ten others, has appeared nowhere else.

DRAGONS' TEETH
by
David Drake

The sound of squealing axles drifted closer on the freezing wind. The watching Roman raised his eyes an inch above the rim of his brush-screened trench. A dozen Sarmatian wagons were hulking toward him into the twilight. Their wheels of uncured oak, gapped and irregular at the fellies, rumbled complainingly as they smashed stiff grass and bushes into the unyielding soil.

A smile of grim satisfaction brushed Vettius's lips as the Sarmatians approached. He did not touch the bow that lay beside him; it was still too soon.

The enormous weight of the wagons turned every finger's breadth of rise into a steep escarpment up which the oxen had to plod. They grunted out great plumes of breath as they threw their weight into the traces. Sexless, almost lifeless in their poses of stolid acceptance, the drivers hunched on the high wagon seats. Like the oxen, they had been at their killing work since dawn. The wind slashed and eddied about the canopies of aurochs hide that covered the boxes. Tendrils of smoke from heating fires within squirmed through the peaks. They hung for a moment in the sunset before scudding off into invisibility.

The last of the wagons was almost within the defile, Vettius noted. It would be very soon now.

Among the Sarmatians the whole family travelled together, even to war. The children and nursing mothers huddled inside the wagons. So did the warriors; their work, like that of the horses tethered behind each wain, was yet to come. Soon the wagons would halt and laager up in the darkness. Using night as a shroud, the reivers would mount and thunder across the frozen Danube. Laughingly they would return before dawn with booty and fresh Roman ears.

The only picket Vettius could see from where he lay was a single rider slightly ahead and to the left of the wagons. Earlier in the day he might have been guide or outrider. Hours had passed. Wagons had bunched or straggled according to the strength of their teams and the temper of their drivers. Now, while the sun bled like an open wound in the western sky, the rider was almost a part of the jumbled line and no protection for it. Vettius smiled again, and his hand was on the bow.

The wind that moaned around the wagons scuffed up crystals from the snow crusts lying in undulant rills among the brush. The shaggy pony's rump and belly sparkled. The beast's torso, like its rider's, was hidden under armor of broad horn scales, each one painstakingly sewn onto a leather backing by the women of the family. Across his pommel rested a slender lance more than eighteen feet long. The Sarmatian fondled its grip as he nodded over his mount's neck, neglecting to watch the bushes that clawed spiked shadows from the sun.

A sound that trickled through the wind made him straighten; unexpected movement caught his eye. Then the Roman archer rose up from behind a bush far too small to conceal a man the way it had. The Sarmatian, spurring his horse in incredulous panic, heard the slap of the bowstring, heard the loud pop as one scale of his cuirass shattered. After the bodkin-pointed arrow ripped through his chest he heard nothing at all.

"Let's get 'em!" Vettius shouted, nocking another arrow as his first target pitched out of the saddle. The trumpeter crouching behind him set the silver-mounted warhorn to his lips and blasted out the attack. Already the shallow hillsides were spilling soldiers down on the unprepared Sarmatians.

The driver of the lead wagon stood up, screaming a warning. The nearest Roman thrust her through the body with his spear. With two slashes of his short-sword, the legionary cut open the canopy behind her and plunged inside with a howl of triumph.

Sarmatians leaped out the back of the second wagon, trying to reach their horses. Three legionaries met them instead. Vettius had set fifty men in ambush, all picked veterans in full armor. None of the others had bows — the legate had feared a crossfire in the dusk — but sword and spear did the butcher's work on the startled nomads. The Sarmatians were dressed

224

for war in armor of boiled leather or aurochs horn, but they had no shields and their light swords were no match for the heavy Roman cut-and-thrust blades. One at a time the nomads jumped down to be stretched on the ground by a stab, a quick chop, or even the heavy smash of a shield rim. Death trebled, the legionaries stood waiting for each victim. The fading sunlight gleamed from their polished helmets and greaves and touched with fire the wheels of bronze and vermillioned leather that marked their shields.

The legate's practiced eye scanned the fighting. The wrack showed the Sarmatians had battled with futile desperation. A baby lay beside the fourth wagon. Its skull had been dashed in on the wagon box, but its nails were stained with Roman blood. The oxen bellowed, hamstrung in the yoke. One was spurting black jets through a heart-deep channel. This day was Rome's vengeance; retribution for a thousand sudden raids, a thousand comrades crumpled from a chance arrow or a dagger thrust in the night.

Only toward the rear where three wagons had bunched together was there real fighting. Vettius ran down the line of wagons though his quiver was almost emptied when he saw one of his men hurtle through the air in a lifeless somersault. The legionary crashed to the ground like a load of scrap metal. His whole chest and body armor had been caved in by an enormous blow. Measurably later the man's sword completed its own parabola and clanked thirty feet away.

"Get back!" Vettius shouted when he saw the windrow of ruined bodies strewn in front of him. "Stand clear!" Before he could say more, the killer was lumbering toward him around the back of the wagon.

The horsehair crest wobbling in the waning sunlight

increased the figure's titanic height, but even bare-headed the giant would have been half again as tall as the six-foot soldier. Worse, he was much heavier built than a man, a squat dwarf taller than the wagon. Though he carried no shield, his whole body shone with a covering of smooth bronze plates. Both gauntleted hands gripped the haft of an iron-headed mace. The six-foot helve was as thick as a man's calf and the head could have served as an anvil.

The giant strode toward Vettius with terrifying agility.

Vettius arced his bow. The shaft of his arrow splintered on the monster's breastplate. It left only a bright scar on the metal. Vettius stepped back, nocking another missile and shifting his aim to the oddly sloped helmet. The face was completely covered except for a T-shaped slot over the eyes and nose. The light was very dim but the narrow gap stood out dead black against the helmet's luster. As the giant started to swing his mace parallel to the ground, Vettius shot again.

The arrow glanced off the bronze and howled away into the darkness.

Vettius leaped upward and fell across the wagon seat as the giant's mace hurtled toward him. The spiked head smashed into a wheel with awesome force, scattering fragments of wood and making the whole wagon shudder. As it rocked, the driver's hacked corpse tumbled to the ground, leaving the Roman alone on the seat as he sighted along his last arrow. He released it.

The giant had reversed his grip on the mace. Now he swung his weapon upward with no more effort than a man with a flywhisk. As the head came level with the

226

giant's hips, the mace slipped from his fingers to fly forward and burst through the side of the wagon. The titan reeled backwards. A small tuft of feathers was barely visible where the helmet slot crossed the bridge of his nose.

The earth trembled when he fell.

Shaking with reaction himself, Vettius dropped his now-useless bow and craned his neck to peer over the wagon's canopy at the remaining fighting. Some of the wains were already burning. Confusion or the victors had spilled the heating fires from their earthenware pots and scattered coals into the cloth and straw of the bedding.

"Save me a prisoner!" Vettius bellowed against the wind. "For Mithra's sake, save me a prisoner!"

He jumped to the ground and cautiously approached the fallen giant. The helmet came off easily when he grasped it by the crest and yanked. Beneath the bronze the face was almost human. The jaw was square and massive; death's rictus had drawn thin lips back from leonine tushes, yellowed and stark. The nose squatted centrally like a smashed toad, and from it the face rose past high flat eyesockets to enormous ridges of bone. There was virtually no forehead so that the brows sloped shallowly to a point on the back of the skull. Only their short tight coils distinguished the eyebrows from the black strands that covered the rest of the head.

No wonder the helmet looked odd, Vettius thought bleakly. He would believe in the face, in a man so large, because they were there for him to touch; but he would have called another man a liar for claiming the existence of something so impossible. Perhaps believing in the impossible was the secret of the success

227

of the Christians whose god, dead three hundred years, was now beginning to rule the Empire.

The trumpeter approached from behind with his horn slung and a bloody sword in his right hand. The torque he now wore was of gold so pure and soft that he had spread it by hand to get it off a dead nomad and rebent it around his own neck.

"Sir!" he called, "are you all right?"

"Give me a hand here," Vettius grunted unresponsively as he tugged at the mace. Together the men pulled the weapon from the fabric of the wagon. Vettius gave a curt order and hefted it alone as his subordinate stepped back. "Ha!" he snorted in disbelief. The mace weighed at least two talents, the weight of a small man or a fairsized woman.

He let it thud to the ground and walked away from it. "May the Bull bugger me if I don't learn more about this," he swore.

The doorkeeper had difficulty slamming the door against the gust of wind that followed Vettius into the anteroom. Moist air from the baths within condensed to bead the decorated tiles and rime the soldier's cape of black bearskin. He wore the bear's head as a cowl. The beast's glass eyes usually glared out above Vettius's own; now they too were frosted and the doorkeeper, turning, shuddered at the look of blank agony they gave him.

Vettius shrugged off the cape and stamped his muddy boots on the floor. The doorkeeper sighed inwardly and picked up his twig broom. The damned man had been stomping through the muck like a common soldier instead of riding decently in a litter as befit his rank. The slave said nothing aloud as he swept, though; the legate had a reputation for violence and he already wore a dark glower this afternoon.

Walking through the door of the changing room, Vettius tossed his cape to one of the obsequious attendants and began to unlace his boots. While he sat on a bench and stripped off his thick woolen leggings, the other attendant looked delicately at the miry leather and asked with faint disdain, "Will you have these cleaned while you bathe, sir?"

"Dis, why should I?" the soldier snarled. "I've got to wear them out of here, don't I?"

The attendant started at his tone. Vettius chuckled at the man's fear and threw the filthy leggings in his face. Laying both his tunics on the bench, he surveyed the now apprehensive slaves and asked, "Either of you know where Dama is?"

"The Legate Vettius?" called a voice from the inner hallway. A third attendant poked his head into the changing room. "Sir? If you will follow me . . . "

The attendant's sandles slapped nervously down the hallway past steam rooms on the right and the wall of the great pool on the left. Tiles of glaucous gray covered the floors and most of the walls, set off by horizontal bands of mosaic. A craftsman of Naisso who had never been to the coast had inset octopi and dolphins cavorting on a bright green sea. The civilization I protect, Vettius thought disgustedly. The reason I bow to fat fools.

At the corner of the hall the attendant stopped and opened one of the right-hand doors. Steam puffed out. Vettius peered in with his hand on the jamb to keep from slipping on the slick tile. Through the hot fog he could make out the figure of the small man who lay on one of the benches.

"Dama?" the soldier called uncertainly.

"Come on in, Lucius," invited the other. He rose to his elbow and the light on his head of tight blond curls identified him. "How did it go?"

"The interrogation was fine," Vettius answered; but his tone was savage, that of a man used to taking out his frustrations in slaughter and very close to the point of doing so again. "We didn't need much persuasion to get the prisoner to tell us everything he knew about the giant. It came from a tent village called Torgu, and he says the shaman running the place has ten more just like it."

"If one, why not eleven?" Dama mused. "But I didn't think the Sarmatians ever made a shaman chief."

"I didn't either," Vettius agreed darkly, "and that wasn't the last strange thing he told us about this wizard, this Hydaspes. He was at Torgu when the family we ambushed got there late in the fall, nervous as the Emperor's taster and fussing around the village to look over each new arrival. He wasn't claiming much authority, either. Then about two months ago a horseman rode in from the east. Our prisoner didn't talk with the fellow but he saw him give a package the size of his fist to Hydaspes. That was what the wizard had been waiting for. He laughed and capered all the way to his tent and didn't come out again for a week. When he did, he started giving orders like a king. Since now he had a nine-foot giant behind him, everyone obeyed. In back of Hydaspes's tent there was a long trench in the frozen ground and a lot of dirt was missing. Nobody the prisoner knew hung about behind there to see if the wizard really was digging up giants there night after night — they were all scared to death by then."

"So a one-time hedge wizard gets a giant body-

230

guard," the merchant said softly, "and he unites a tribe under him. If he can do that, he may just as easily become king of the whole nation. What would happen, Lucius, if the Sarmatians got a real king, a real leader who stopped their squabbling and sent them across the Danube together?"

The white fear that had been shimmering around the edges of Vettius' mind broke through again and tensed all his muscles. "A century ago the Persians unified Mesopotamia against us," he said. "Constant fighting. Some victories, more losses. But we could accept that on one frontier — it's a big empire. On two at the same time . . . I can't say what would happen."

"We'd better deal with Hydaspes soon," Dama summarized flatly, "or Hydaspes will deal with us. Have you told Celsus?"

"Oh, I told the Count," Vettius snapped, "but he didn't believe me — and besides, he was too busy reaming me out for leading the ambush myself. It was *undignified* for a legate, he said."

Dama crowed, trying to imagine Vettius too dignified for a fight.

"That's the sort he is," the soldier agreed with a rueful smile. "He expects me to keep my cut-throats in line without dirtying my boots. A popular attitude this side of the river, it seems."

Knuckles slammed on the steam-room door. Both men looked up sharply.

"Sirs, quickly!" the attendant hissed from outside.

Dama threw the door open, his face blank.

"Sirs," the frightened slave explained, "the Count has come for the legate Vettius. I misdirected him, thinking you might want to prepare, but he'll be here any moment."

"I'll put on a tunic and meet him in the changing room," the soldier decided. "I've no desire to be arrested in the nude."

The frightened changing room attendants had disappeared into the far reaches of the building, leaving the friends to pull on their linen tunics undisturbed. Celsus burst in on them without ceremony, followed by two of his runners. *He's not here to charge me after all*, Vettius thought, not without at least a squad of troops. Though Mithra knew, his wishes would have supported a treason indictment.

"Where have you been?" the official stormed. His round face was almost the color of his toga's broad maroon hem.

"Right here in the bath, your excellency," Vettius replied without deference.

"Word just came by heliograph," the count sputtered. "There were ten attacks last night, *ten!* Impregnable monsters leading them — Punicum, Novae, Frasuli, Anarti — posts wiped out!"

"I told you there were other attacks planned," the soldier replied calmly. "None of them was in my sector. I told you the why of that, too."

"But you lied when you said you killed a monster, didn't you?" accused Celsus, stamping his foot. "At Novae they hit one with a catapult and the bolt only bounced off!"

"Then they didn't hit him squarely," Vettius retorted. "The armor isn't that heavy. And I told you, I shot mine through the viewslit in his helmet."

The count motioned his runners away. Noticing Dama for the first time he screamed, "Get out! Get out!"

The merchant bowed and exited behind the runners.

232

He stood near the door.

"Listen," Celsus whispered, plucking at the soldier's sleeve to bring his ear lower, "you've got to do something about the giants. It'll look bad if these raids continue."

"Fine," Vettius said in surprise. "Give me my regiment and the Fifth Macedonian, and some cavalry — say the Old Germans. I'll level Torgu and everyone in it."

"Oh no," his pudgy superior gasped, "not so much! The Emperor will hear about it and the gods know what he'll think. Oh, no — fifty men, that was enough before."

"Are you —" Vettius began, then rephrased his thought. "This isn't an ambush for one family, your excellency. This is disposing of a powerful chief and maybe a thousand of his followers, a hundred miles into Sarmatia. I might as well go alone as with fifty men."

"Fifty men," Celsus repeated. Then, beaming as if he were making a promise, he added, "You'll manage, I'm sure."

The two riders were within a few miles of Torgu before they were noticed.

"I shouldn't have let you come," Vettius grumbled to his companion. "Either I should have gone myself or else marched my regiment in and told Celsus to bugger himself."

Dama smiled. "You don't have any curiosity, Lucius. You only see the job to be done. Myself, I want to know where a nine-foot giant comes from."

They eyed the sprawling herd of black cattle finding some unimaginable pasturage beneath the snow crust.

Perhaps they were stripping bark from the brush that scarred the landscape with its black rigidity. A cow scented the unfamiliar horses approaching it. The animal blatted and scrambled to its feet, splashing dung behind it. When it had bustled twenty feet away, the cow regained enough composure to turn and stare at the riders, focusing the ripple of disturbance that moved sluggishly through other bovine minds. Face after drooling, vacant face rotated toward them; after long moments, even the distant herdsman looked up from where he huddled over his fire in the lee of a hill.

Dama's chest grew tight. There was still another moment's silence while the Sarmatian made up his mind that there really were Romans riding through his herd toward Torgu. When at last he grasped that fact, he leaped to his feet yipping his amazement. For an instant he crouched bowlegged, waiting for a hostile move. When the intruders ignored him, the Sarmatian scampered to his horse and lashed it into a startled gallop for home.

The merchant chewed at his cheeks, trying to work saliva into a mouth that had gone dry when he realized they would be noticed. He'd known they were going to meet Sarmatians: that was their whole purpose. But now it was too late to back out. "About time we got an escort," he said with false bravado. "I'm surprised the Sarmatians don't patrol more carefully."

"Why should they?" Vettius snorted. "They know they're safe over here so long as a brainless scut like Celsus is in charge of the border."

They jogged beyond the last of the cattle. Without the Sarmatian's presence the beasts were slowly drifting away from the trampled area where they had been herded. If they wandered far they would be loose at night when the wolves hunted.

"Cows," Vettius muttered. "It's getting hard to find men, my friend."

Half a mile away on the top of the next rolling hill an armored horseman reined up in a spatter of snow. He turned his head and gave a series of short yelps that carried over the plain like bugle calls. Moments later a full score of lancers topped the brow of the hill and pounded down toward the interlopers.

"I think we'll wait here," the soldier said.

"Sure, give them a sitting target," Dama agreed with a tense smile.

Seconds short of slaughter, the leading Sarmatian raised his lance. The rest of the troop followed his signal. The whole group swept around Vettius and Dama to halt in neighing, skidding chaos. One horse lost its footing and spilled its rider on the snow with a clatter of weapons. Cursing, the disgruntled Sarmatian lurched toward the Romans with his short, crooked sword out. From behind Dama, the leader barked a denial and laid his lance in front of the man. The merchant breathed deeply but did not relax his grip on the queerly shaped crossbow resting on his saddle until the glowering Sarmatian had remounted.

The leader rode alongside Vettius and looked up at the soldier on his taller horse. "You come with us to Torgu," he ordered in passable Greek.

"That's right," Vettius agreed in Sarmatian. "We're going to Torgu to see Hydaspes."

There was a murmur from the Sarmatians. One of them leaned forward to shake an amulet bag in the soldier's face, gabbling something too swiftly to be understood.

The leader had frowned when Vettius spoke. He

235

snapped another order and kicked his horse forward. Romans and Sarmatians together jogged up the hill, toward the offal and frozen muck of Torgu.

On the back of a nameless, icebound stream stood the village's central hall and only real building. Dama glanced at it as they rode past. Its roughly squared logs were gray and streaked with odd splits along the twisted grain. Any caulking there might have been in the seams had fallen out over the years. The sides rose to a flaring roof of scummed thatch, open under the eaves to emit smoke and the stink of packed bodies. The hall would have seemed crude in the most stagnant backwaters of the Empire; the merchant could scarcely believe there could be a threat from a people to whom it was the height of civilization.

Around the timber structure sprawled the nomad wagons in filthy confusion. Their sloping canopies were shingled with cow droppings set out to dry in the wan sunlight before being burned for fuel. The light soot that had settled out of thousands of cooking fires permeated the camp with an unclean, sweetish odor. Nothing in the village but the untethered horses watching the patrol looked cared for.

Long lances had been butted into the ground beside each wagon. As he stared back at the flat gazes directed at him by idle Sarmatians, Dama realized what was wrong with the scene. Normally, only a handful of each family group would have been armored lancers. The rest would be horse archers, able to afford only a bow and padded linen protection. Most of their escort hung cased bows from their saddles, but all bore the lance and most wore scale mail.

"Lucius," the merchant whispered in Latin, "are all of these nobles?"

"You noticed that," Vettius replied approvingly. "No, you can see from their looks that almost all of them were merely herdsmen recently. Somebody made them his retainers, paid for their equipment and their keep."

"Hydaspes?" the merchant queried.

"I guess. He must have more personal retainers than the king, then."

"You will be silent!" ordered the Sarmatian leader.

They had ridden almost completely through the camp and were approaching a tent of gaily pennoned furs on the edge of the plains. At each corner squatted an octagonal stump of basalt a few feet high. The stones were unmarked and of uncertain significance, altars or boundary markers or both. No wains had been parked within fifty paces of the tent. A pair of guards stood before its entrance. Dama glanced at the streamers and said, "You know, there really is a market for silk in this forsaken country. A shame that —"

"Silence!" the Sarmatian repeated as he drew up in front of the tent. He threw a rapid greeting to the guards, one of whom bowed and ducked inside. He returned quickly, followed by a tall man in a robe of fine black Spanish wool. The newcomer's face was thin for a Sarmatian and bore a smile that mixed triumph — and something else. On his shoulder, covered by the dark hood, clung a tiny monkey with great brown eyes. From time to time it put its mouth to its master's ear and murmured secretly.

237

"Hydaspes," Vettius whispered. "He always wears black."

"Have they been disarmed?" the wizard questioned. The escort's leader flushed in embarrassment at his oversight and angrily demanded the Roman's weapons. Vettius said nothing as he handed over his bow and the long cavalry sword he carried even now that he commanded an infantry unit. The merchant added his crossbow and a handful of bolts to the collection.

"What is that?" Hydaspes asked, motioning his man to hand him the crossbow.

"It comes from the east where I get my silk," Dama explained, speaking directly to the wizard. "You just drop a bolt into the tall slot on top. That holds it while you pull back on the handle, cocking and firing it all in one motion."

"From the east? I get weapons from the east," the Sarmatian said with a nasty quirk of his lip. "But this, this is only a toy, surely? The arrow is so light and scarcely a handspan long. What could a man do with such a thing?"

Dama shrugged. "I'm not a warrior. For my own part, I wouldn't care to be shot with this or anything else."

The wizard gestured an end to the conversation, setting the weapon inside his tent for later perusal. "Dismount, gentlemen, dismount," he continued in excellent Greek. "Perhaps you have heard of me?"

"Hydaspes the wizard. Yes," Vettius lied, "even within the Empire we think of you when we think

238

of a powerful sorcerer. That's why we've come for help."

"In whose name?" the Sarmatian demanded. "Constantius the emperor?"

"Celsus, Count of Dacia," Vettius snapped back. "The Empire has suffered the bloody absurdities of Constantius and his brothers long enough. Eunuchs run the army, priests rule the state, and the people pray to the tax gatherers. We'll have support when we get started, but first we need some standard to rally to, something to convince everyone that we have more than mere hopes behind us. We want your giants, and we'll pay you a part of the Empire to get them."

"And you, little man?" Hydaspes asked the merchant unexpectedly.

Dama had been imagining the count's face if he learned his name was being linked with raw treason, but he recovered swiftly and fumbled at his sash while replying, "We merchants have little cause to love Constantius. The roads are ruinous, the coinage base, and the rapacity of local officials leaves little profit for even the most daring adventure."

"So you came to add your promise of future gain?"

"Future? Who knows the future?" Dama grunted. Gold gleamed in his hand. A shower of coins arced unerringly from his right palm to his left and back again. "If you can supply what we need, you'll not lament your present payment."

"Ho! Such confidence," the wizard said, laughing cheerfully. The monkey chittered, stroking its master's hair with bulbous fingertips. "You really believe that I can raise giants from the past?

"I can!"

Hydaspes' face became a mask of unreason. Dama shifted nervously from one foot to the other, realizing that the wizard was far from the clever illusionist they had assumed back at Naisso he must be. This man wasn't sane enough to impose successfully on so many people, even ignorant barbarians. Or was the madness a recent thing?

"Subradas, gather the village behind my tent," Hydaspes ordered abruptly, "but leave space in the middle as wide and long as the tent itself."

The leader of the escort dipped his lance in acknowledgment. "The women, Lord?"

"All — women, slaves, everyone. I'm going to show you how I raise the giants."

"Ho!" gasped the listening Sarmatians. The leader saluted again and rode off shouting. Hydaspes turned to re-enter his tent, then paused. "Take the Romans, too," he directed the guards. "Put them by the flap and watch them well.

"Yes," he continued, glancing back at Vettius, "it is a very easy thing to raise giants, if you have the equipment and the knowledge. Like drawing a bow for a man like you."

The Hell-lit afterimage of the wizard's eyes continued to blaze in the soldier's mind when the furs had closed behind the black figure.

As the rest of the Sarmatians dismounted and began to jostle them around the long tent, Dama whispered, "This isn't working. If it gets too tight, break for the tent. You know about my bow?"

Vettius nodded, but his mind was chilled by a foretaste of death.

As the prisoner had said, eleven long trenches bristled outward from the wall of Hydaspes' tent. Each was shallow but too extensive for the wizard to have dug it in the frozen ground in one night. Dama disliked the way the surface slumped over the ditches, as if enormous corpses had clawed their way out of their graves . . .

Which was what the wizard seemed to claim had happened.

The guards positioned the two Romans at the center of the back wall of the tent where laces indicated another entrance. Later comers crowded about anxiously, held back in a rough circle by officers with drawn swords. Twenty feet to either side of the Romans stretched the straight walls of the tent paralleled by a single row of warriors. From the basalt posts at either corner curved the rest of the tribe in milling excitement, warriors in front and women and children squirming as close as they could get before being elbowed back.

The Sarmatians were still pushing for position when Hydaspes entered the cleared space, grinning ironically at Vettius and Dama as he stepped between them. A guard laced the tent back up. In the wizard's left hand was a stoppered copper flask; his right gripped a small packet of supple cowhide.

"The life!" Hydaspes shouted to the goggle-eyed throng, waving the flask above his head from the center of the circle. He set the vessel down on the dirt and carefully unrolled the leather wrappings from the other objects.

"And the seed!" the wizard cried at last. In his palm lay a pair of teeth. They were a dull, stony gray without any of the sheen of ivory. One was a

241

molar, human but inhumanly large. The other tooth, even less credible, seemed to be a canine fully four inches long. With one tooth in either hand, Hydaspes goat-footed about the flask in an impromptu dance of triumph.

His monkey rider clacked its teeth in glee.

The wizard stopped abruptly and faced the Romans. "Oh, yes. The seed. I got them, all thirteen teeth, from the Chinese — the people who sell you your silk, merchant. Dragons' teeth they call them — hee hee! And I plant them just like Cadmus did when he built Thebes. But I'm the greater prince, oh yes, for I'll build an *empire* where he built a city."

Dama licked his lips. "We'll help you build your empire," he began, but the wizard ignored him and spoke only to Vettius.

"You want my giants, Roman, my darlings? Watch!"

Hydaspes plucked a small dagger from his sash and poked a hole in the ground. Like a farmer planting a nut, the wizard popped the molar into the hole and patted the earth back down. When he straightened he shouted a few words at the sky. The villagers gasped, but Dama doubted whether they understood any more of the invocation than he did. Perhaps less—the merchant thought he recognized the language, at least, one he had heard chanted on the shores of the Persian Gulf on a dead, starless night. He shuddered.

Now the wizard was unstoppering his flask and crooning under his breath. His cowl had fallen back to display the monkey clinging fiercely to his long oily hair. When the wizard turned, Dama could see the beast's lips miming its master obscenely.

Droplets spattered from the flask, bloody red and glowing. The merchant guessed wine or blood, changed his mind when the fluid popped and sizzled on the ground. The frozen dirt trembled like a stricken gong.

The monkey leaped from Hydaspes's shoulder, strangely unaffected by the cold. It faced the wizard across the patch of fluid-scarred ground. It was chanting terrible squeaky words that thundered back from Hydaspes.

The ground split.

The monkey collapsed. Hydaspes leaped over the earth's sudden gape and scooped up the little creature, wrapping it in his cloak.

Through the crack in the soil thrust an enormous hand. Earth heaved upward again. The giant's whole torso appeared, dribbling dirt back into the trench. Vettius recognized the same thrusting jaw, the same high flat eyesockets, as those of the giant he had killed.

The eyes were Hydaspes's own.

"Oh yes, Roman," the wizard cackled. "The life and the seed — and the mind too, hey? There must be the mind."

The giant rose carefully in a cascade of earth. Even standing in the trench left by his body, he raised his pointed skull eight feet into the air.

"My mind!" Hydaspes shrieked, oblivious to everyone but the soldier. "Part of me in each of my darlings, you see? Flowing from me through my pet here to them."

One of the wizard's hands caressed the monkey until it murmured lasciviously. The beast's huge eyes were seas of steaming brown mud, barely flecked by pinpoint pupils.

"You said you knew me," continued the wizard.

243

"Well, I know you too, Lucius Vettius. I saw you bend your bow, I saw you kill my darling —

"I saw you kill me, Roman!"

Vettius unclasped his cape, let it slip to the ground. Hydaspes wiped a streak of spittle from his lips and stepped back to lay a hand on the giant's forearm. "Kill me again, Roman," the wizard said softly. "Go ahead; no one will interfere. But this time you don't have a bow. Watch the little one!" he snapped to the guard on Dama's right.

The Sarmatian gripped the merchant's shoulder.

Then the giant charged.

Vettius dived forward at an angle, rolling beyond the torn up section of the clearing. The giant spun, stumbling in a ditch that had cradled one of his brothers. The soldier had gained the room he wanted in the center of the open space and waited in a loose-armed crouch. The giant sidled toward him splay-footed.

"Hey!" the Roman shouted and lunged for his opponent's dangling genitalia. The giant struck with shocking speed, swatting Vettius in midair like a man playing handball. Before the Roman's thrusting fingers could make contact, the giant's open-handed blow had crashed into his ribs and hurled him a dozen feet away. Only the giant's clumsy rush saved Vettius from being pulped before he could jump to his feet again. The soldier was panting heavily but his eyes were fixed on the giant's. A thread of blood dribbled off the point of his jaw. Only a lip split on the hard ground — thus far.

The giant charged.

Two faces in the crowd were not fixed on the one-

sided battle. Dama fingered the hem of his cloak unobtrusively, following the fight only from the corners of his eyes. It would be pointless to watch his friend die. Instead the merchant eyed Hydaspes, who had dug another hole across the clearing and inserted the last and largest tooth into it. The wizard seemed to ignore the fighting. If he watched at all, it was through the giant's eyes as he claimed; surely, mad as he was Hydaspes would not otherwise have turned his back on his revenge. For the first time Dama thought he recognized an unease about the monkey that rode again on the wizard's shoulder. It might only have been fatigue. Certainly Hydaspes seemed to notice nothing unusual as he tamped down the soil and began his thirteenth invocation.
invocation.

Dama's guard was wholly caught up in the fight. He began to pound the merchant on the back in excitement, yelling bloodthirsty curses at Vettius. Dama freed the slender stiletto from his cloak and palmed it. He did not turn his head lest the movement catch the guard's attention. Instead he raised his hand to the Sarmatian's neck, delicately fingered his spine. Before the moth-light touch could register on the enthusiastic Sarmatian, Dama slammed the thin blade into the base of his brain and gave it a twist. The guard died instantly. The merchant supported the slumping body, guiding it back against the tent. Hydaspes continued chanting a litany with the monkey, though the noise of the crowd drowned out his words. The wizard formed the inaudible syllables without noticing either Dama or the stumbling way his beast answered him. There was a look of puzzlement, almost fear, in the monkey's eyes. The crowd continued to cheer as the merchant opened the flap with a quick slash and backed inside Hydaspes's tent.

Inside a pair of chalcedony oil lamps burned with tawny light. The floor was covered with lush furs, some of which draped wooden benches. On a table at one end rested a pair of human skulls, unusually small but adult in proportions. More surprising were the cedar book chests holding parchments and papyri and even the strange pleated leaf-books of India. Dama's crossbow stood beside the front entrance. He ran to it and loosed the bundle of stubby, unfletched darts beside it. From his wallet came a vial of pungent tarry matter into which he jabbed the head of each dart. The uncovered portions of the bronze points began to turn green. Careful not to touch the smears of venom, the merchant slipped all ten missiles into the crossbow's awkward vertical magazine.

Only then did he peer through the tent flap.

Vettius leaped sideways, kicking at the giant's knee. The ragged hobnails scored his opponent's calf, but the giant's deceptively swift hand closed on the Roman's outer tunic. For a heartsick instant the heavy fabric held; then it ripped and Vettius tumbled free. The giant lunged after him. Vettius backpedaled and, as his enemy straightened, launched himself across the intervening space. The heel of his outstretched boot slammed into the pit of the giant's stomach. Again the iron nails made a bloody ruin of the skin. The titan's breath whooshed out, but its half-ton bulk did not falter at the blow. Vettius, thrown back by the futile impact, twisted away from the giant's unchecked rush. The creature's heels grazed past, thudded with mastodonic force. The soldier took a shuddering breath and lurched to his feet. A long arm clawed for his face. The Roman staggered back, barely clear of the spade-like talons. The monster pressed after him relentlessly, and Vettius was forced at last to recognize what should have been hopelessly obvious from the first: he could not possibly kill the giant with his bare hands.

A final strategem took shape. With desperate purpose Vettius began to circle and retreat before his adversary. He should have planned it, measured it, but now he could only trust to luck and the giant's incredible weight. Backed almost against a corner post, he crouched and waited. Arms wide, the giant hesitated — then rushed in for the kill. Vettius met him low, diving straight at his opponent instead of making a vain effort to get clear again. The Roman's arms locked about the great ankles and the giant wavered, then began to topple forward. As he fell his taloned fingers clamped crushingly on Vettius's ribs.

The unyielding basalt altar met the giant's skull with shattering force. Bone slammed dense rock with the sound of a maul on a wedge. Warm fluids spattered the snow while the Sarmatians moaned in disbelief. Hydaspes knelt screaming on the ground, his fists pummeling terror from a mind that had forgotten even the invocation it had just completed. The earth began pitching like an unmastered horse. It split in front of the wizard where the tooth had been planted. The crack raced jaggedly through the crowd and beyond.

"Lucius!" Dama cried, lifting the corner of the tent.

The soldier pulled his leg free from the giant's pinioning body and rolled toward the voice, spilling endwise the only Sarmatian alert enough to try to stop him. Dama dropped the tent wall and nodded toward the front, his hands full of crossbow.

"There're horses waiting out there. I'll slow them up."

Vettius stamped on a hand that thrust into the tent.

"Get out, damn you!" the merchant screamed. "There aren't any more weapons in here."

A Sarmatian rolled under the furs with a feral grimace and a dagger in his hand. The soldier hefted a full case of books and hurled it at his chest. Wood and bone splintered loudly. Vettius turned and ran toward the horses.

The back flap ripped apart in the haste of the Sarmatians who had remembered its existence. The first died with a dart through his eye as Dama jerked the cocking handle of his weapon. The next missile fell into position. The merchant levered back the bow again. At full cock the sear released, snapped the dart out into the throat of the next man. The Sarmatian's life dissolved in a rush of red flame as the bolt pricked his carotid to speed its load of poison to the brain. The third man stumbled over his body, screamed. Two darts pinged off his mail before one caught the armpit he bared when he threw his hands over his face.

Relentless as a falling obelisk, Dama stroked out the full magazine of lethal missiles, shredding six screaming victims in the space of a short breath. The entrance was plugged by a clot of men dying in puling agony. Tossing his empty bow at the writhing chaos behind him, Dama ran through the front flap and vaulted onto his horse.

"We'll never get clear!" Vettius shouted as he whipped his mount. "They'll run us down in relays before we reach the Danube."

Wailing Sarmatians boiled around both ends of the tent, shedding helmets, weapons — any encumbrance. Their voices honed a narrow blade of terror.

"The control," Dama shouted back as the pair dodged among the crazy pattern of wagon tongues. "He used his own mind and a monkey's to control something not quite a man."

"So what?"

"That last tooth didn't come from a man. It didn't come from anything like a man."

Something scaly, savage and huge towered over the wreckage of the tent. It cocked its head to glare at the disappearing riders while scrabbling with one stubby foreleg to stuff a black-robed figure farther into its maw. Vettius twisted in his saddle to stare in amazement at the coffin-long jaws gaping twenty feet in the air and the spined backfin like that of no reptile of the past seventy million years.

The dragon hissed, leaving a scarlet mist of blood to hang in the air as it ducked its head for another victim.

Introduction to "The Sustenance of Hoak"
by Ramsey Campbell

Ramsey Campbell, like Wellman and Drake, I met at that convention in Lovecraft's town, Providence. Campbell went about wearing a strangely hued teeshirt with sleeves, sounding like Ringo Starr or Graeme Edge of Moody Blues or someone putting on that Liverpool accent. Few aside from me understood one in three of his words; I have a thing for the British and prefer the Liverpudlian sound to the strange toothy noises we're more familiar with.

Campbell makes this anthology international; he really does live in Liverpool. He's affable, smiling, good company — and has a horrid mind, as you'll *learn if you find and read his vicious little story "Call First." Lord!*

Campbell outdid Drake; his story was longer. He cut out four thousand words — which is more wordage, for instance, than Capella's whole story contains! Fantastic. Amazing man. A pro. And if you've encountered ere now a shuddery idea such as this story is built on, don't tell me. To me it is unique, brilliant, and that's not mentioning that there are both characterization and humanity here — attributes too often missing in this genre.

Ramsey, I saved it for last. Send me another. I love it.

THE SUSTENANCE OF HOAK
by
Ramsey Campbell

I

"If we ever reach the treasure," Ryre said with
bitter humour, "we'll have earned it and twice again."

Glode's mouth opened, but nothing emerged except a thread of blood. He was trying to raise himself
against the tree where Ryre had propped him; his fists
crushed the earth, his arms trembled like trees, their
thick veins swelled. "Keep down," Ryre said as a
flight of arrows tore through the leaves overhead.
"I'll get you in there if I have to stick the lot of them
on their own arrows," he said, gazing narrow-eyed
through the trees at the gate of the town of Hoak.

And it might come to that, he thought, crawling
through the undergrowth. Heat throbbed through

the forest like blood, slow and viscous. He remembered how they'd decided to come to Hoak.

Like most of the mercenaries who'd helped win the war against the pirates on the Sea of Shouting Islands, they had been drinking their pay and complaining of its meagreness when talk had turned to the treasure of Hoak. The treasure was buried beneath the town; a now long-lost map showing its location had been found attached to the leg of a migrating bird; the people of Hoak (someone had said, trying to outshout jeers) were willing to give the treasure to whoever found it; nobody who had sought it had returned. Silence followed that, quickly broken by bantering. Ryre and Glode had jeered with the rest, but later they'd agreed that the rumours felt more like the truth than did most tales of treasure. And they knew that unless they moved on they would have to vow allegiance to the local lords, or fight those of their companions who had done so. As for the vanished seekers — they must have failed and been too ashamed to return empty-handed. Ryre and Glode had smashed their wine-mugs in the street below the inn, splashing the boots of a cursing sailor, and had made their way to the wharves. Next day they had left the continent of Drobond for Thabbe.

Ryre was at the edge of the forest now, two hundred yards from the gate of Hoak. The trees around him were scraggy; the forest must once have been cut further back from the town. Peering across the parched grass, he saw that the gate beneath the archers had been patched with planks, leaving gaps. The town wall was of growing trees, the gaps plugged with logs. His lips pulled back thinly. It would be enough.

Once on Thabbe they'd bought steeds at the port

of Zizir. The trader had smiled sadly on hearing where they were bound, but had told them the route readily enough. They had been six days into the forest that covers half of Thabbe, and less than a day from Hoak, when in a long avenue bandits had dropped like ripe fruit from the trees. Ryre and Glode had swerved between them, slashing them as they fell. The bandits must have been used to slower and meeker prey. But some had had blowpipes as well as knives; one dart had spilled the last of the water while another, finding a chink in the leaves of Glode's armour, had lodged deep in his guts. Since then he had ridden doubled over, his silence like a cry in Ryre's ears.

He was still propped against the tree, sitting bent low over his stomach, his fist clenched white around a fistful of earth. "I can break the gate," Ryre said, collecting dry twigs and grass and tying them in a bun at the head of a lopped-off branch. He untied their steeds and brought Glode's to him. "Bid him farewell," Ryre said. "He will help save you."

At the edge of the forest he lit the tip of the firebrand with a flint from the pouch at his belt, then slapped Glode's steed out into the open. At once the arrows responded. The few he had time to watch looked too high for an attack, more like a warning. Certainly he thought it was an inexpert bowshot that spiked the animal's neck.

But he was riding, lying low behind his own steed's broad head. Air streamed smarting over his eyes; the brand dwindled into roaring fire at his shoulder. He was squeezing more speed from his mount with his thighs, urging the implacably distant gate closer as the archers swung toward him; he felt the grass beneath his steed's pads hindering him like water. He was there, and the song of the bowstrings had failed. He plunged his blazing club into the gate.

Here his plan was weakest. His steed was rearing now that the fire which had driven it had sprung before its face, dilating furiously. Above him he heard moving stone, grunts of exertion. During the war against the pirates he'd learned how to coax his steed through fire, but this was another steed, *Hakkthu*, he swore between defiant blasphemy and plea, and covered the beast's eyes with his hands, its ears with his forearms.

It quieted uneasily. Overhead he heard the unmistakable sound of heavy stone poised on wood. Then, as a wave of heat surged out from the collapsing gate, Ryre's steed flinched back stumbling, yards clear of the protection of the wall.

He heard the first stones fall. It took him a moment to realize they had fallen within the gate. The defenders didn't want to kill him, only to keep him out. Why? He grinned and shrugged, snarling.

The gate sagged on the dropped stones with a shout of flame. The defenders were scrambling down from scorching branches. One of them was shouting, directing the others to fetch water from a well, to throw earth on the fire, to bring axes; now he was monkey-climbing down a trunk.

He saw Ryre coming at him through the frame of fire: all six and a half feet of him, reflected fire streaming over the predator's mane that widened in a V from his shaved crown to his shoulders, fire pouring down his long grimly grinning face and over his flexed muscles, tensed for an easy spring. The man twisted; his feet found a branch from which to launch him upward again. Ryre chopped the branch from beneath him and catching him as he fell, stunned him with his sword-hilt.

255

"Move again, any of you," Ryre shouted, "and I'll knock you down with his head." They were a sorry-looking lot, even the hostage: grimy, dull-faced, ragged. Their shuffling approach had been disordered, tentative. Behind him another tree snatched the fire, cackling. Their faces flickered like embers as they watched him, their gazes plucked fretfully at the fire; shovelfuls of earth drooped from their hands, narrow-necked vessels of water drained.

"My friend is injured," he shouted above the chorus of fire. "Have your best healer ready for him. I shall bring him in now. This man stays with me until my friend is healed. If I've reason even to suspect any of you, we'll see if this man can walk while he's holding his guts from tripping him up."

The growing crowd, fifty or so of them, now, was milling as if turned up from beneath a stone. "We'll help," a voice said just audibly within the mass; then, as if drawing strength from its concealment, more loudly: "We promise. Don't take him out."

"He stays with me until my friend is well," Ryre shouted.

They were turning uneasily toward someone in the narrow dry earth street between the low square houses: their leader, Ryre thought — then saw that it wasn't a man at all. It was a stump of wood planted in the street, shaped near the top into a fat mouthless face; instead of ears, limp-looking branches hung. The black wood looked wet and was patched with white, as if stretched pale; specks of reflected fire burned in the wide whitish stare. Their god, no doubt.

"Please, not out," someone was muttering; others joined in. "Please."

Ryre had never seen such insularity, not even on the

Sea of Shouting Islands. "I will protect him from anything out there," he shouted, riding toward the leap through the blazing gap. "Keep your word and he is safe. If I think you haven't" (their paling faces showed he had found the words to command them) "I'll leave him out there."

Glode was lying beside the tree. His lips were so pale that Ryre couldn't distinguish the slit between them from their trailing threads of blood. He didn't move when Ryre supported his head. Ryre frowned; he had counted on Glode's being conscious and able to hold onto the hostage before him on Ryre's steed. He pondered, stroking the beast's neck. Heat sank thickly through the branches.

As he pondered, his hostage began to move. The man pushed at the beast's ribcage to raise himself. When he saw where he was, he started to flail his limbs and scream incoherently. He lay draped over the animal's spine, screaming and wriggling wildly, then he fell to the ground.

"Be quiet and listen." Ryre had to push the sword's point into the man's neck before he would stop thrashing about. "We are going back to Hoak now. You will ride this steed. You will carry my friend, who is injured. If you loosen your grip on him, or try to ride faster than I walk, I shall cut you down and leave you outside the wall."

Ryre had once seen one of the steeds set ablaze by the warriors of Gurj and sent screaming into enemy camps to cause injury and demoralization: he had seen its staring eyes, piteously rolling. He had hoped never to see such terror again, but it was here, in the eyes of the hostage. The man's arms gripped Glode and his entire body shook as if caked with ice; he gazed in supplication at the distant wall pacing closer, at the gap where men were chopping away the charred section of the wall. Glode's inert body trembled with him.

Ryre felt himself to be a stretched rein, holding the man back from utter reckless panic. His sword was out and ready; its point winked a warning beside his hostage. He curbed his mind from pondering the source of the man's terror. *Hakkthu*, he thought, *if I'm going to know I'll know without tempting it nearer*. Behind him he felt the hot bright forest and plain, silently poised.

The healer was waiting in the street. He'd brushed away dust from a space and laid planks there. He was an old nearly bald man, scrawny as if he'd melted himself down in losing a long fight; grey hair made a tidemark around his skull. "Put him there," he told Ryre indifferently.

"Haven't you a house of healing?" Ryre demanded.

"Outside is better." Townspeople were clambering exhausted down the singed trunks. Ryre prodded his panting hostage into lowering Glode from the steed.

"Help him, some of you. Now you get down, slowly. And you, hold my steed." As the hostage dismounted the others were still holding Glode's unconscious body. "Give him to your healer," Ryre said with tight control. *Hakkthu*, he thought, *one day they'll forget how to dung until someone tells them*.

"What's wrong with him?" the healer asked.

"A dart in the gut. Bandits attacked us, half a day from here."

Dust eddied around the restless crowd and crept toward Glode. "Keep still," the healer shouted. Ryre felt the beginnings of trust. What he'd taken for indifference in the healer wasn't the apathy that weighed down the watching faces, but harassed weariness. In the man's eyes alertness still glinted faintly.

Someone was murmuring at Ryre, as if in sleep: a large-boned man with a face like a square slab of rock that might once have looked chiselled but now was less weathered than moss-smoothed by beard, and slackly bland. "That's who we thought you were," he was saying. "The bandits. They want our treasure. But you can't get at it from inside the town. We wish they'd take it. It's only trouble for us. We're happy without it. We try to keep the bandits out so they'll search outside and take it."

"What is this treasure?"

"Jewels," another voice said. "A cave full of jewels."

"And how is it reached?"

"There are tunnels," the slab-faced man said. "They're easy to find. We can tell you where."

"You're so anxious to keep people out you've convinced me there's something in here worth defending." Ryre turned his back, dismissing them all. The healer had parted the hard yet flexible leaves of Glode's armour, had lifted the shirt beneath and was probing Glode's stomach.

The crowd was fraying, wandering away; people plodded into the low houses. Ryre disliked the way windows were blocked with old wood. The kneeling hostage shifted gingerly beneath his sword. Ryre prodded him toward a house. "Knock the wood out of that window," he said.

The wood scattered clattering, and Ryre laughed grimly. The scene within seemed so typical of Hoak: a man lying on a plank bed in a bare room, drinking from a long-necked vessel, blinking timidly at the intrusion. Apart from the bed, and dust and tracked-in

259

mud, there was nothing in the low-ceilinged room but a replica of the stumpy god from the street. About two feet high, it stood in a corner as if growing through the floorboards, its eyes closed in sleep. Ryre knew instinctively that nothing more sinister was happening behind the masked windows of the other houses.

A woman was carrying a vessel to the healer. Glode's head turned tottering toward the vessel. "Give me drink," he said, his tongue protruding weakly, dry as a sand-burrower's tail. The healer shrugged sadly, and rose.

Glode took one gulp, Ryre's hand behind his head. Then he coughed the liquor into the dust, mixed with what might have been a stomachful of blood. He fell back, unconscious.

For a moment Ryre dreaded that the healer had never intended to drink. He sniffed at the mouth of the vessel: a sharp vinous smell. The healer and the remnants of the crowd were watching him. He put the mouth to his lips.

He was tipping the vessel against his tongue-stopped lips, watching for their reaction, when the hostage knocked the vessel from his hands. He scrabbled after it on all fours, seized it and began to gulp, his throat working like a climber's hand on a parting rope. By the time Ryre had bullied it from him he knew it couldn't be poisoned. His own throat was chafing and pleading, but he pointed his sword to Glode.

"The dart's lodged deep," the healer said. "It's in his stomach, too deep to get out. All he can do is rest. It may work itself out before he starves."

Ryre felt frustrated anger mass within him. He knew from battles that if the dart had lodged so, there was nothing they could do. He tipped the vessel, gulping.

Thick liquor spread through his throat. A warmth rushed through him, tingling his fingertips.

The healer turned away; he looked disappointed, somehow betrayed. Let him thirst, Ryre thought savagely. His mouth was full of a meadish taste; light sparkled on slow drops of cloudy amber liquid spilling from the vessel's mouth. The squat houses and encircling trees, the dust and dancing ash, seemed to have snapped into closer clarity, as if the light had hardened. "We need a room," he shouted, to halt the retreating crowd.

"We have one," a girl said. Like the rest she was dressed in shapeless rags, almost colourlessly browned by use and the sun; she was thin and stooped as if by an insistent gale. Only a trace of youth in her face, which was shaped like a starved heart, convinced Ryre she was younger than twenty. She stood beside the slab-faced man, no doubt her father. As she gazed at Ryre, he caught sight of a dull glint of desire.

The house was a dozen housefronts away up the street — more accurately, the trudged path. Each house was surrounded by twice its own area of earth, baked to a cracked crust, in which tufts of grass and weeds browned. Apart from the small procession behind which he was leading his steed, the hot flat blinded streets were deserted.

When they reached the house Ryre let the hostage go. If he needed to defend a room he could best do so without the hindrance of the man. He walked through the house, cursing loose boards, knocking the wood from the windows to admit light. Each room was the same: the plank bed, the sleeping god in the corner, the liquor-vessel, bareness. The first room, into which the sagging street door opened, was entirely bare.

261

Ryre chose the fourth room, which could be approached only through all the others. It could be a trap of sorts, but at least there was only one doorway to defend. He beckoned the bearers to lay Glode down, then gestured them out. He draped Glode's cloak and his own over his unconscious friend. He called for a bed to be brought for himself. He tethered his steed outside the window, and propped the wood he'd knocked down so that any attempt at entry through the window would send it clattering.

The girl, whose name was Yoce and whose father's was Vald, peered in while Ryre was eating some of the food his steed had carried. The second time, he held out a chunk of cheese to her. He'd seen no food or plates in the house. But she shook her head and went back into the next room. *She needn't think she'll come to me in the night*, Ryre thought, gazing anxiously at Glode. Later, in the twilight, he heard her sucking at her liquor-vessel.

Darkness muffled the houses. The dry ground breathed out thick heat. Ryre sat on the bed with his back against the door, gazing at the god in the corner. Of everything he'd seen in Hoak he disliked that face most of all. It looked like the face a slow growth on a treetrunk might have: fat and somnolently sated. Beneath the eyes it swelled featurelessly, like a bladder. The branches hanging limply looked obscene, as if flaunting their impotence. It summed up Hoak. He couldn't truthfully believe he would be attacked during the night. He sipped at the liquor-vessel, pondering the contradictions of Hoak. Before him the mouthless face sank sleepily into the embrace of night.

II

It was late next day when he awoke, and Glode was dead.

Glode's faded eyes stared into a glare of sunlight. His face was slack as melting fat. On his cheeks and beneath his head were the marks of a last bloody cough.

There was no mark of further violence, no culprit on whom Ryre could take revenge; he could only rage dully. Sweat had gathered within the leaves of his armour; they felt close and clammy, he felt closed in upon himself, his emotions muffled. He strained to mourn Glode. But as he gazed at the limp face his grief seemed dulled.

He grabbed the liquor-vessel. Glode would have a mercenary's mourning. Ryre laughed harshly, staring out at the desiccated street. Sometimes an unwary passer-by would scoff at a mercenary's tears, and die for it; such deaths were a tribute to the mourned. Ryre hoped someone of Hoak would dare to scoff. He sucked the vessel, which someone had refilled.

He was still trying to drink grief into himself when footsteps sounded in the outer room. Vald and three other men appeared, peering warily; beside them Yoce gazed. Vald thrust the girl into the room. Ryre's nearness quickened her breath; her eyes were wide with awe of him. "They've come to bury your friend," she said too loudly, nervously.

Burial ought to be swift, in this heat. Ryre gestured brusquely to the men. They hefted Glode as if he were a heavy plank, and hurried him out; his sword lay on his chest. Ryre followed, gulping liquor to hasten his mourning. Yoce hung back, in the house.

He hurried after the bearers. Hakkthu, they were

anxious to be done with the burying! Hot dust puffed up from their scurrying feet and settled over figures squatting beside the path. All the figures were blankly intent on their hands, which were whittling arrows. It was the only occupation Ryre had seen practiced here. Once, so the trader in Zizir had told him, Hoak had been renowned for the skill of its carvers.

None of the whittlers glanced at the burial-party. Ryre felt numb rage at their indifference, all the more because it seemed to have infected him: he stared at Glode, at the sword jogging on his friend's chest, and could feel nothing.

The town was infecting him. Everywhere he saw slumped apathy: in the parched streets, the senile houses, the whittlers like hollow jerking dummies draped with sacking. Even the well from which water had been drawn to douse the fire was used as a communal cloaca. Yet once, the trader had told him, Hoak had been a station on a trade route between the coast and the interior, until its people had grown sullenly hostile.

It must be the liquor that had brought apathy. Ryre had seen no other food or drink. He supposed it was brewed from the trees in the town walls – there seemed to be no other healthy growth. No wonder the people were dull, if liquor were their only food. He would drink no more of it once Glode was buried. He'd need all his wits to find the treasure.

The bearers stumbled rapidly onward. They had carried Glode almost half a mile; they were nearly at the centre of Hoak. Ahead Ryre saw a group of small figures scattered among the whittlers, dressed in torn knotted rags of larger clothes. He had to peer closely to tell they were children.

They were the only children he'd seen here — hardly three dozen of them. On their faces, which looked already pinched and old, apathy was set like identical masks. They sat or lay in the dust; one child stared flatly from a window. When their muddy eyes moved, it was always to a liquor-vessel standing near them. They drank mechanically. Beside a dull-eyed mother, Ryre saw an infant sucking at a vessel as though it were a breast.

Fury swelled in him; he trembled. Behind the child in the window he saw a stump and its sleepy contented face, the flaccid branches dangling. Perhaps all the drinking was a religious tribute to their self-satisfied god. He would storm into the house and lop off the mouthless head —

He checked himself. However deplorable they were, gods were something whose revenge one couldn't fight. But he smashed his own vessel to the ground.

Some of the children watched the swiftly dwindling stain; a few of the adults gave him a glance like a faint sad shrug. The bearers were trudging ahead indifferently. He stamped angrily in pursuit.

Above the roofs he saw a shiny dome, swaying closer in imitation of his stride. Here at the centre the houses were even more dilapidated. Among them he saw bare patches where houses had stood. In each patch was a deep socket; had that housed a god-stump? The bearers had halted in a wider space. Ryre hurried there.

It was the old market-place. Remnants of stalls and tethering-rails poked from the ground, like bones from a boneyard. At the centre of the space a patch of dark moist earth, no more than twenty yards square, stood out from the dry surround. From this earth protruded a pillar whose crown was the shiny dome.

The pillar wriggled with heat-haze. Ryre gaped at it, breathing harshly.

It stood twice his height, half again as broad as his chest. Its domed crown was a pale bubble swelling up through the black cracking mud of its bark. On the side nearest him, formed of the same lividly patched substance, was the flabby contented face, several times enlarged. Its left cheek was bloated out of shape by a large fibroid growth, giving it a fattened cheek-pouched appearance. Ryre felt grubs of disgust crawling over him.

There were no branches sprouting beside the face, nor any room for them. Four faces bulged at various heights on the pillar, identical except for blemishes and variations in size. That on the north side — the one he'd first seen — looked to be encroached upon by the larger fibroid eastern face, which seemed to be eating into its cheek.

Ryre felt passionately that the entire festering thing ought not to be here in the sunlight, but buried beneath tons of earth. He had a sudden crawling notion that the substance of the thing had not ceased growing. He clutched his sword-hilt to feel cold metal amid the soft sticky embrace of the heat.

Vald and the others were digging. Glode lay in the dust, his loose face upturned. They meant to bury him beneath the bunch of swollen faces. Ryre felt harsh rage — but wherever Glode lay in Hoak he would be overlooked by the omnipresent stump. Better he should lie here in this rich tended earth than in the parched ground. He stood over his friend's body, sword bared in tribute, as they dug.

They were digging hastily, exhaustingly, near the foot of the pillar. Ryre had time to wonder at the size of the burial ground, which seemed bewilderingly small, before the diggers turned up a flat rock. The top of it looked like a fleshless hand. Peering, Ryre saw that it was indeed a hand, rotted at the wrist and stuck to the rock. One man scraped it off with his spade and threw it back into the hole. Then they grounded their spades and picking up Glode's body, carried him across to roll him, sword and all, into the hole.

"Not like that!" Ryre roared. His sword trembled between them, darting at their throats. "Make him a coffin!"

They gazed blankly. "A box for him to lie in!" he shouted, prodding them with their burden to the edge of the ground. "Make him a box," he said with cold fury, "and bring it here."

He waited, glaring at the introverted faces on the pillar. Heat rose from the moist ground, fluttering about them; the edge of the fibroid face seemed to bulge, creeping like a grub across its neighbour's cheek. As they had made to drop Glode into the hole Ryre had imagined he glimpsed the eyes of the northward face opening, a blink, closing before he'd glared at them. It must have been the antics of the heat.

He gazed across the market-place. On the side which he had yet to explore stood a house full of piled timber. Some of the wood looked delicate. Crushed between stacked planks he saw elaborate ladles, stringed instruments, minute figures. One figure lay in a niche between planks, almost unharmed: the figure of a swordsman, poised in easy but assured defense. Its tiny perfect face, hardly the size of Ryre's smallest fingernail, was stern yet peaceful. Ryre slid the figure from its niche. Rough handling had crippled it; one leg was snapped off at the knee.

267

The burial party returned, carrying a crude box from which protruded bent and rusty nails. They lifted Glode into the box and nailed down a plank for a lid. Then they dropped the box into the hole.

Ryre's fury drained quickly. He saw how they must feel about death. He gestured them back and nicking his forearm with his sword-blade, held his fist above the coffin as his blood dripped. He lifted earth from the grave and sprinkling it over the wound, let the mud of blood fall on the coffin. When they had filled in the grave, he stood the carved swordsman on the mound and watched over it while they wandered away.

Still he had not mourned Glode. His mind seemed to have lost its grasp on his friend. When he managed to recapture a few of their exploits — Glode saving him from a knife-thrust in a dark temple; Ryre trying to swing himself onto Glode's shoulders to snag the ropes that were lowering them into a pit of snakes — they seemed flat, unconvincing. Now the liquor was making him feel light, unconcerned, unburdened. He would mourn Glode when he was free of Hoak — when he had made sure their journey had not been in vain. He must find the treasure.

The sun was low. The shadow of the pillar lay across the glistening patch, like the shadow of a cankered tree. It pointed toward the far side of Hoak. The treasure must be there, where he hadn't explored.

He searched, trying to outdistance night. The earth was grey and cracked as the skin of a senile corpse. Few of the windows were blocked; these he knocked open. He stared into room after room, at fallen planks, at the hole like a burrow in the corner of each floor. The rooms were dimming; twilight rose in them like a mist with which the dark burrows merged. The twilight was heavy with silence, the silence of midnight in a dead and windless forest.

The heads of the surrounding still trees peered at Ryre over the nearby wall. Desolation waited silently behind him wherever he turned. His mind was chattering: it isn't here, not in these houses, there's nothing here, go back.

And this was all that was left of Hoak: scarcely a hundred people, isolated on this barren island amid the enormous forest. Then he realized something else. The vanished population must be buried in the square, all of them, piled up and rotting beneath the contented pillar. He shrugged off a shudder at the thought of the earth in which Glode lay, and hurried back toward the centre. He had words to scare the truth of the treasure out of slab-faced Vald.

The faces on the pillar were set in the twilight as in plush. Ryre spat in the dust. Corpse-candle of a god, he blasphemed the pillar. He glanced toward Glode's grave. At once he was striding across the yielding ground, clutching his sword. The mound had vanished.

The carved swordsman still lay on the earth. As he snatched it up he heard a faint muffled creaking. It came from the grave. Was Glode pushing his way out of the box, rising up through the soil to punish Ryre's negligence? Blotting out his terror with anger, he began to gouge out the grave with his hands.

The grave was shallow, but his progress seemed slow as the creeping twilight. As the soil squeezed through his fingers he remembered the hand that had been thrown into the hole. At last he reached the box. The lid had split open; soil had widened the split and fallen through. Cursing the makeshift coffin, Ryre lifted the pieces of the lid.

At first, in the twilight, he couldn't distinguish what was in the box. A mixture of earth and pale objects: the pale things were entangled — there were large glistening pale surfaces and paler forms coiled about them. The pale thick tendrils were dragging the larger object, or objects, through the bottom of the coffin. One extremity of the large object slipped an inch lower in the hole, amid a strained creaking and a rattling of earth. Although the large object was losing its form, as if melting, it had Glode's face.

Ryre screamed in fury and brought his sword crashing down on the tangle within the coffin. Tendrils parted and whipped into the earth like pale worms. When Ryre had finished chopping, there was nothing recognizable in he hole. Weeping, ablaze with shame, he kicked earth into the grave.

The cancerous faces loomed above him, at his back. He rushed at the pillar, brandishing his sword. The faces waited, untroubled. Suddenly full of panic and nausea, Ryre fled toward the gate.

His steed waited outside Vald's house, chewing in its foodsling. Ryre reined back his panic; he must retrieve his satchel of food, which was lying beneath the plank bed. In the dim deserted street that throbbed wakefully with the sound of his heart, Ryre felt the need for stealth. Somewhere he could hear a slow muffled trickling. He shook his head impatiently and paced around to the outer door.

Vald was prostrate on his bed, fingers hanging limply to the floor. Ryre thought he was dead until his nails scraped the boards feebly. Padding softly, Ryre had almost crossed the room before he saw Yoce. She was standing with her back to him, in the corner where the

270

face stood. As Ryre strode loudly toward her, she turned.

The branches dangling from the head were swollen, pale, almost transparent. They glimmered in the dimness. Yoce had been thrusting the neck of a liquor-vessel over one branch; now she pulled the vessel away. Snatching it, Ryre saw that it was brimming with liquor. A drop hung at the tip of the branch.

Yoce grabbed the vessel before he could smash it, and carried it to Vald. Ryre was less horrified by his discovery than by the yearning of his own parched throat for the liquor. "You do that!" he shouted through his nausea, hand at his sword.

"What else can I do for him?" Yoce said furiously. "Where's another food?"

When her words reached him, his hand slumped on the hilt. "What is this town?" he demanded thickly.

Liquor was spilling from Vald's mouth. She stood the vessel beside him, then she took Ryre's hand simply and led him into the inner room. Her fingers read the moist earth on his hand. "You've seen what it does," she said. "To your friend."

The face hung like a clot of the dimness, inscrutable eyelids swollen. "It can't hear us," she said reassuringly. "Anyway, it's dead. It died when my mother did. That's what happens when you die. This was her room. She died a few days ago, I think. I can't remember time very well."

Ryre sat on the bed, away from the face. He shook himself; this wasn't what he wanted to know. "That thing in the burial ground," he snarled.

"Nobody knows what it is. You know it's the same as the ones in the houses. They grow from it."

He felt the dimness closing about him as though it

271

were the heavy exhalation of the faces. "Why do you need to drink that filth?" he shouted, then answered himself dully "Because you need more and more of it."

"I don't," Yoce said indignantly.

That explained her comparative vitality. "Yes. But there must have been a time once when someone could have killed that thing," he said impatiently. "When it first began growing."

"We could never kill it. It wouldn't let us."

He felt her words giving power to the face. Ripping a splinter from the wood beneath the window, he lit it with his flint. He thrust the flame into the corner, peering. But the face hung on the stump, slack and puffy.

He was about to shake out the flame when the eyes opened.

The lids rose heavily, with the faintest of moist creaks. The widening crescents of dull white looked to Ryre exactly the colour of the marsh-fungus he'd once seen growing on a corpse in a swamp. The eyes were open now, swollen globes of thick white in which he could see no life at all. They seemed to watch the flame. All at once he caught up a stick, lit it from the splinter and thrust it into the face.

The wood, if such it were, of the stump began to sputter. Threads of fire squirmed across it, and vanished. The eyes were still, but the lids shivered. Then the stump caught fire; a spot of flame grew and flared up across the face. The eyes burst. In a minute the stump was a dwarf of fire, twisting and writhing as it crumpled into ash.

Ryre kicked the ash down the hole in the floor, laughing harshly. Hot ash crawled on the sides of the hole, and he glimpsed a charred stump retreating,

272

dousing itself with earth. "What can the rest of it do now?" he demanded.

Yoce was sitting unmoved on Glode's bed. "It won't do anything. It only does if you attack it in the burial ground. That one was dying, anyway. If it had anyone to feed it would have grown again."

He grinned into the darkness. He was the thing's master now. He could destroy it whenever he wanted to, and he would. But first — "It must have made your people forget where they'd hidden the treasure," he said. "Do you know where it is?"

"There isn't any. There never was."

"There is. You've just forgotten, if you ever knew."

"I haven't! I remember that! They made up the treasure so people would come from outside. To kill the eater."

"Then why did your men try to keep us *out*?"

"Because you can't kill it from inside the wall. You have to go underneath. And when people came here they'd drink the milk, even if our people tried to stop them. Then they'd stay and not be able to go out. That's why the men keep people out. Only they've forgotten why. They think there really is a treasure."

Everything he'd seen confirmed her words. He felt too defeated by Hoak even to be angry. "If you managed to keep some people out," he said desultorily, "why didn't they kill it?"

"Maybe they didn't get far enough. Or maybe they were frightened. You have to go all the way under the burial ground. There was a map that said the treasure was there."

"Why can't you kill it from up here?"

"Someone tried, a long time ago." She had lowered

her voice; the darkness leaned closer. "It ate his woman. He set fire to the one in her room. He was sleeping there, so it grew again for him. Then he tried to set fire to it at the burial ground, but it reached out of the ground and ate him while he was still alive."

"How do you know all this?" Ryre demanded.

"Trome the healer told me. He tries not to drink much, like me. He helps babies to come and gives them names, and he tries to teach people how to do things. The man you took out, he was one Trome taught. He helped me to remember all the things he'd told me, so I could tell you. He said you wouldn't kill me."

Ryre was silent. Heat and darkness and Hoak gathered on him like mud. Yoce came and sat beside him. "I'm sorry there isn't a treasure for you," she said. "I never liked stories that weren't true. Vald used to tell me when I was little that I'd be able to go outside the wall, to stop me crying." She took his hand and pressed herself against his side.

"Does your healer expect me to kill that thing for you?" Ryre asked, letting the disbelief of his words soak into him.

"You could do it for us," she said, gripping his hand. "For your friend."

Suddenly he grabbed her shoulders and threw her against the wall. "You called the men to bury my friend!" he shouted.

"I didn't," she said. "It calls in your head when it wants its food." She began sobbing like an exhausted child — exhausted perhaps by the effort of talking to him. Irritably he grabbed her and pulled her roughly to him until she ceased shaking. All of a sudden she was straddling him, her hips gulping. "Have me," she said plaintively. "Nobody else can."

His body was shouting yes, yet he hesitated. Had they reached the true reason why Trome had sent her? Ryre didn't object to even so meagre a bribe, nor did his feeling that she was still a child trouble him. But he felt insulted by her eagerness, in a sense; he could be any man except a eunuch.

"Please," she said. "I always used to wonder. I knew it made some girls happy, until they stopped feeling it. Trome said the milk did that. So I didn't drink much, only as much as I had to. But all the boys did, so they couldn't have me, they didn't work. Trome tried when I asked him, but he was too old."

Even with Yoce's clothing laid over them the floorboards were harsh against Ryre's knees. But once she'd closed around him he felt nothing but their union. She was eager as a parched throat; his heart seemed to be pounding all his blood into his genitals. It was quickly over. Both of them cried out.

They lay together until dawn. "You weren't a virgin," he said drowsily; then, sensing her blankness: "Not sealed."

"I did that myself," she said proudly.

III

As they neared the gate Trome formally wished Ryre "Your day of triumph." At the gate Yoce said "Good fortune. What's your name?"

He was unwilling to leave his name where it might be at the mercy of Hoak. "You don't need my name. You want the deed," he said and, reaching into his pouch, handed her the carved swordsman. "Say that was me," he said.

Waiting for Trome to wrench open the repaired

wall, he felt a cancer of panic growing within him swiftly as fire. It was the effect of the liquor; it infuriated him. Yet it was only a taste of the panic that ruled Hoak. He averted his face from Yoce as he rode out. He wouldn't betray his fear to her. She had enough of it already.

The baked plain drank his sweat avidly. The forest took him with a slow suffocating hiss of leaves. Foliage swayed like drowned tentacles, luring him in. When he closed his eyes he felt the cooler moist air settle over him like a clammy shroud. His breath racked his throat. He breathed harder, to distract himself. By the time his steed led him to a stream he was a flayed tube of thirst.

The soothing drink felt distant, merely a concept separate from the dull unchanging panic. But the very dullness of the panic helped him by enraging him. He must act. He had dreaded tunnelling beneath the eater; now this seemed less daunting. He had come out of Hoak: he could do anything.

Even the sight of the tunnel entrance failed to daunt him. He passed it once, covered as it was by a tangle of green shoots. But a large mound of earth and a pile of timber showed its position. Beneath the shoots the tunnel descended for a few feet at a steep angle, eased by steps of wood driven into the earth, then levelled into darkness.

Ryre filled his satchel with faggots and dry grass. He lifted the two rusty spades from his steed. Strapping the satchel to his back, he gazed through the trees at Hoak. Trome had left the gap open. Ryre gazed at it, then he climbed down into the earth.

He had made tapers in Hoak. He lit one with his flint and peered ahead. The taper burned feebly, sputtering. At least the flame was slow. The light plucked at the tunnel: a quivering hole of darkness that drew the walls and roof into itself. The roof was roughly but adequately shored with a thick length of timber, supported by two others forced beneath it, against the walls. It was too low for him to stand upright.

He clambered out and began to collect shoring from the pile. Birdsong was scattered over the forest like light on water. His panic at leaving Hoak was ebbing somewhat, baffled.

He climbed down with an armful of props, grinning sourly. Whoever had opened the tunnel must have believed they were outwitting the guardians of the treasure. He would make sure, he vowed grimly, that they were among those who had outwitted the eater of Hoak.

He stuck a burning taper in the earth near the entrance, then hefted his shoring. The burden hardly taxed him, but this was only the first journey. He debated taking off his armour. But it was light, though few blades could cut its flexible leaves, which grew harder under pressure. It might save him — from what, he refused to think. He pulled the taper from the earth and holding it before the pile of shoring on his arms, stooped quickly into the tunnel.

The taper was burning more steadily now, though feebly. He had to walk slowly for fear of extinguishing it. His view ahead was cramped by the pile of wood, which was almost as broad as the tunnel; he could see a dim box surrounding him and keeping pace, shaking as if crumpled by the weight of earth above. At least it was excellent wood, he reassured himself; neither the shoring around him nor the pile outside had rotted.

The dim box swung slightly about him. Its featurelessness lulled him, stealing his sense of time and of how far he'd come. He strained to look back. His shadow flickered forward from the blinding darkness. Within it he thought he could see a tiny point of light, the tunnel entrance. Then it was gone.

He drove himself onward, trying to measure his distance from Hoak by the count of his steps. He had to trust the judgment of those who had dug the tunnel. Assuming that they had followed the original map, the course of the tunnel should lead to a point directly beneath the eater — unless the thing had grown downwards since.

His back was beginning to resent its cramping. In the dim browned light his eyes felt as if mud were gathering on them. His hearing felt muffled, suffocated. Even his legs felt hobbled, for he had to tread carefully on the uneven floor.

He dreaded that the thing knew he was approaching. He felt its vast bulk somewhere above him, and it seemed impossible that it could not sense him. He was struggling so fiercely with his unease that he had almost touched the tendril with the taper before he saw it.

It was a limply coiled pale thread, drooping through a crack between the shoring of the roof. As the flame approached, the tendril drew itself up jerkily and flattened against the wood, groping about convulsively. Ryre flinched back, almost dropping taper and props. Surrounding him beyond his cage of faint light, he heard a muffled creaking whose rhythms imitated the convulsions of the tendril. He lowered his pile of wood to the floor and kneeling, rested on it, willing the spasms of the tendril to subside.

At last they did so, and the creaking faded: but not until half the taper had burned. Ryre walked more deliberately now, his strained gaze urging forward the dim sluggish wave of light. Darkness swelled up solidly beyond it, but yielded only darkness. When something more solid loomed into the glow, he was prepared and hardly started. It was a white root, blocking the centre of the tunnel.

It had forced its way between the shoring, bulging itself a hole. Earth was sprinkled on the floor beneath, but the root had plugged the gap it had made. It spanned the tunnel, fat and glistening white.

He planted the taper. Then he slid the props past the root on their edges, letting them down gently beyond. He pulled up the taper and holding it beyond the root, inched himself past. The root might have felt him if he'd touched it. In any case, he couldn't bear the thought of doing so.

The darkness ahead bobbed closer, thickening, bulging between the props, refusing to give way to the advancing light. He had reached the end of the tunnel, a couple of hundred yards past the root. Ahead sloped a ragged wall of earth, somewhat smoothed by time.

He dropped the timber from his aching arms. After a while he took a taper from his pouch and lighting it from the first, stuck the latter in the floor. He glanced back at the light as he made his way toward the entrance.

There he rested. Light lapped the swaying foliage above him. Should he have left the taper? Wouldn't a flame left underground starve the air? He was arguing himself out of going down again, he knew.

He saw himself spading out the tunnel, carrying

back the earth, spading out, trying to prop the tunnel
— But was he exaggerating the task? It might have
been his fear confusing his feelings, yet he felt the
tunnel had almost reached its goal. He'd lost count of
his steps at the tendril.

He remembered the carving he'd given Yoce. But
his words didn't require him to be like the carving.
He though of Yoce and Trome, trapped within the
open wall. He thought of the children, and of Glode. If
Ryre succeeded, he would have a tale in which to
hold Glode fast and give him power. Already Glode
must feel nothingness closing about him as Ryre's
words of him slipped away, dwindling to nothing.
Ryre refilled his satchel and picked up the spades,
then walked into the tunnel.

He'd hoped the taper he had left would look en-
couraging. But its glimmer swam forward like marsh-
gas, emphasizing the enormous darkness. He set the
two tapers at opposite sides of the tunnel. The darkness massed behind him, seeping into his brain,
reminding him of the deceptive stillness of the white
tendril, of the way the plump root seemed to have
moved and swollen since the first time he'd passed it.
He began to dig.

A taper burned down to the floor, and another.
He filled his satchel with earth, which he scattered in
the dark beyond the flames: again, again. His breath
felt rougher than the earth; muddy sweat poured
over him; pain clamped his muscles, tightening. He
had been digging until the dark felt thickened by
midnight when the creaking began.

It was all about him, muffled. It grew, a dull
immense writhing mass of sound. Ryre felt as if the
darkness were pressing down on him, as if the flimsy

tunnel were sinking into depths where the pressure would burst the walls, flooding him with tons of earth, letting in the insidious source of the creaking.

This must be what had scared the dung out of his predecessors. As a youth he'd suffered the lightless hold of a ship for days; if this were the eater's defence it was already defeated. He dug.

The creaking trailed away, leaving the silence thick and close. There was no sound except a sprinkling of earth, ahead of him. The hard earth roof, which had held up uncomplainingly while he dug the softer earth below, was cracking.

He grabbed a length of shoring and swung it up against the roof. He ground his shoulders against it and reaching back, forced lengths of timber into place alongside him, propping the roof. Beyond it a shadow reached out for him, glistening with earth. He hurried back and brought the tapers forward.

He dug and shored another length of tunnel. Then panic flooded him. He was suddenly sure that the next thrust of the spade would touch the eater. It was waiting for that moment, to close on him. Or it might play him, filling the tunnel with hungry tendrils, until it chose to block his way entirely.

Perhaps the thing was stealing these fears into his mind, or perhaps the darkness was thinking for him. He thrust the spade in furiously, but couldn't help closing his eyes. Glode and Yoce and the rest had fled his mind, leaving him alone.

The spade gouged the earth. Another spilling spadeful of earth for his satchel; another. Then the spade plunged into softness. Ryre fell forward, then threw himself back, wrenching out the spade. But a sliding of earth had already begun. The end of the tunnel was collapsing. He had turned to flee in case the props gave way, or before something emerged, when he realized that the wall was collapsing away from him. He had dug his way into a hollow.

When the sound of scattering earth had ceased he lit a new taper and held it low through the gap. Within was a hollow of moist earth, about seven feet high and twenty feet in diameter. Its walls sloped up to a pale ceiling, a soil-smudged whitish object swollen with dozens of almost translucent veins. He was beneath the eater.

Appalled fascination paralyzed him. The surface was bloated like a great veined belly. Amber liquid coursed through some of the veins, others were empty and flabby. He forced himself away, back to his satchel. Emptying it of earth, he stuffed it with faggots and dry grass, and strapped it on.

He bullied himself into leaving the taper in the entrance to the hollow. If he took it in, the thing might act to defend itself. He scrambled down into the hollow, disliking the moistness of the earth. It was only ordinary good earth, he told himself, unlike the dry earth above, which the thing's hunger had drained. But he couldn't forget that the burial ground was above him. Liquor pumped through the whitish ceiling.

He piled the kindling at the centre, wondering uneasily why the hollow was there at all. It didn't matter. One last trudge to collect kindling, then he would lay a fuse to the hollow. At last all the effort which had led here would be justified; Glode would live in tale. Ryre was making for the taper, thinking of words that would preserve the power of the deed, when the tunnel collapsed.

There was a violent splintering, and a heavy fall of earth. When he seized the taper he saw that the walls of the tunnel twenty yards away had been crushed. Among the debris writhed thick whitish tubes. He kicked at the collapsed wall, and the tubes closed about it, squeezing the earth. He knew that they would crush him even if he managed to broach the barrier.

Now that it was open battle the darkness lost some of its power. He felt it, solid on every side, but he could plan. The thing blocked the tunnel, but could he distract it? He grinned hungrily. He knew what the thing feared.

He slid down into the hollow, carrying a taper. He was about to throw the taper into the kindling — but no, the flame might not catch. Better to venture all the way in. He had almost reached the pile when he heard air moving in the tunnel, a hollow muttering. Suddenly the dim tunnel mouth was a black hole. Air swept across his face, and the taper he was holding went out.

The darkness rushed into his lungs, choking him. Above him he heard a vast creaking, no longer muffled. He scrabbled in his pouch and found the flint. He struck it, struck it again; the creaking lowered toward him. The taper flamed.

When he looked up he saw why there had been a hollow. At some time the eater, perhaps not content to feed through its tendrils, had raised itself bodily toward the burial ground. Now it was descending on him, having trapped him at last. A few tendrils crept down from the edge of the dwindling hollow. The cold moist belly sank and touched his forehead.

Ryre roared wordlessly. He ran, cramped and stooping, to the fuel and thrust in the taper..

A flame groped over the pile. In a minute it was a mound of fire. The fire rushed at the white belly, which sputtered and crackled, blackening. What happened then, hideous as it was, filled Ryre with grim triumph. The thing was raising itself on its roots, which its haste exposed all round the hollow, as if it were a vast bloated spider raising itself on its web. But its retreat worked the fire like a bellows, and the flames followed it up, flaring higher, roaring.

Fire sprang out from the midst of the belly, snatching whitish fuel that writhed. Veins popped, hissing. A whole piece of the thing fell on the edge of the hollow, torn away by an arc of fire that had charred through its roots. Clods tumbled through the torn gap, smoking, blocking the gap as Ryre considered dashing toward it.

The thing had raised itself above the level of the tunnel. Falling earth had closed the tunnel mouth, but there was still a small gap, and the wall of earth looked weak. Ryre scrambled over the shifting floor. Above him the centre of the belly was drawing up and in, trying to flee its agony; fire rushed into the drawn-in pit, splitting it open. Fire was dividing the eater along its veins, consuming each patch.

Ryre launched himself at the tunnel mouth, but slithered back. As he gathered himself to spring again the fire above him shouted, crackling and popping. It rushed above him, embracing a patch. He heard it give way, and the blazing chunk fell toward him. He tried to throw himself out of its way, but it fell full on him, smashing him into darkness.

IV

He was buried alive. His face was full of earth. A crushing weight lay on him. He clawed at the earth, which squeezed beneath his nails, and the weight moved. His shoulders felt like an open sore, but when he raised them the weight toppled away. It was the fallen wood, quenched by soil. Propping himself on all fours, he looked about.

He was at the bottom of the hollow perhaps fifteen feet deep, open to the sky. Its sides had collapsed, and within it lay mounds of fallen earth and chunks of smouldering wood. Ash flocked over all; he beat away a settling cloud. Opposite him, where most of the earth had slid, leaned the central pillar. It was little more now than smouldering ash that retained its shape. Empty sockets smoked; a face of ash was crumbling in the wind.

Ryre dragged himself upward. His body throbbed with bruises, his mane was charred, but the fallen wood and his armour had protected him from the fire. He reached the lip of the hollow. The people of Hoak were milling about nearby, wandering blankly, halting, starting constantly as if from traps of sleep. He groped for a hold to pull himself up. Suddenly Yoce and Trome were lifting him.

The girl's left foot was bound — in a shirt patterned with swords, that Glode had worn. His fury faded quickly: Glode would have given it to her, and they must need cloth. "What's wrong with your foot?" he asked.

"Someone smashed it," Trome said.

"I broke all the milk vessels," Yoce interrupted, so swiftly Ryre could tell she didn't want revenge. "So we couldn't save any milk. Now we'll have to go outside." She saw Ryre's hunger for vengeance, gleaming in his eyes. "You mustn't kill anyone," she said. "There are too few of us."

Trome hurried to fetch ointment. Ryre hobbled to a window and, knocking out the wood, began to chop brands. "Come here," he shouted at the wandering crowd. "All of you! Here!" He handed out the brands and lit them. The crowd stood gazing; nothing about them but the flames. "Wherever you find that thing's head," he shouted, "burn it. Let one live and by Hakkthu, I'll feed you to it in pieces. When I'm gone, Trome has a sword to rule you. Quickly!" he shouted as they stumbled away.

Trome was staring uneasily at him. "Haven't you my friend's sword?" Ryre demanded. "Then use it as wisely as he did."

Trome fussed about him, salving and binding.

"Enough, enough. I'll live, unless you smother me to death. Bring the children to the gate," he said to Yoce.

Ryre felt no qualms as he passed the wall. The power of the eater was dead. At the tunnel mouth he untethered his steed, then he filled his scorched satchel with fruit. Some hard-shelled fruit were as big as his head; the halves of the shell could be used to carry water.

Yoce was standing with the children just inside the gate. Adults stood nearby, restless and threatening; Trome was holding them back with the sword. Ryre piled the fruit a few feet outside the gate. He chop your arms off with an axe just to see what you looked like with no arms.'

Tony's anxiety began to infect Billy. 'Yeah. But any trouble, you'd help me out. Wouldn't you?'

Tony laughed grimly. 'Do I look like a pillock? I've got a wife and kids, mate. Listen. I'll tell you a story about how brave I am. Yesterday I was on my own in the squad car and I saw someone park in a disabled space. It didn't look like a disabled driver and, sure enough, out steps this big guy, broken nose, shoulders a mile wide.

'I flashed my badge and said, "I think you'd better move your car, sir." And he says, "One more word out of you, sonny, and I'll break your fucking neck." I looked around. There was no one watching. So what did I do? I got back into my little car and drove away. And, Billy, any other copper would have done exactly the same.'

'What are you saying?'

'That if you've got a bad case of flu, I'll go to the chemist for you. If you go on holiday, I'll feed the cat for you. But if you want to pick fights with Mal Priest, you're on your own.'

Afterwards, while Billy was waiting for his bus, an old gypsy woman tried to sell him some lucky heather. He declined politely, but not politely enough

23

to stop her black tiny eyes narrowing in malice. 'You'll have bad luck in the new year,' she promised darkly.

Like most writers, Billy was superstitious. He immediately began to wonder what form the bad luck would take. Then he remembered Tony's warning. It had genuinely not occurred to him that the Priest article might create problems. Indeed, in composing the piece, Billy had exercised considerable restraint. He had quoted Priest accurately and faithfully, refraining from his usual habit of fabricating facts and putting words into the mouth of the interviewee. Priest's lawyers couldn't touch him. But someone else might.

When he arrived home, there was a fresh dog turd lying on the doormat. Someone had posted it through the letter box in his absence. In Billy's neighbourhood, it was quite common to receive turds, condoms and tampons from anonymous well-wishers. Billy didn't know who had delivered this particular turd. But he was fairly certain it wasn't a dog.

Perhaps it was a message from Priest. Indeed, Billy almost hoped it was. A man who has paid £2.50 to send you a dog turd is hardly likely to fork out an extra five thousand to have your legs broken.

Billy rolled up the doormat, turd and all, and took it outside to the bin. A thick yellowish fog was descending. When he re-entered the house, he noticed a strong smell of gas. This was nothing new. He'd bit into the largest and juiciest fruit. Then he held it out to Yoce.

She stepped forward hesitantly. As she reached the wall fear clamped over her face like a mask. Behind it he could see her struggling. The mask's forehead puckered. Sweat streamed from it. Then she stumbled forward, eyes closed, across the boundary. She gripped Ryre's arm, bruising it, and opened her eyes.

Fear still pinched her face like a claw, but she managed to smile. She bit into the fruit. Juice trickled from her mouth, tears from her eyes. She held out the fruit to the children.

They shuffled, glancing away. Suddenly the youngest ran out and grabbed the fruit. Her sister ran to drag her back. The older girl halted abruptly, gaping, as she realized where she was. But Yoce stuffed a fruit into her open mouth.

Ryre showed Yoce the use of the half-shells, and pointed toward the stream. In time they would venture there. Trome forced himself to emerge, breathing heavily, and exchanged swords for a moment with Ryre in farewell. All the children were out now; their parents were scurrying timidly to rescue them, glancing suspiciously at the pile of fruit, sniffing at it, snatching a fruit and nibbling like rodents afraid of a trap. Ryre looked at Yoce, but she was rounding up the children, who were laughing hysterically, discovering their voices. He rode away.

Just within the forest he halted on a rise. By a caprice of the heat he could see Hoak vividly, minute and detailed. A group of people were lustily smashing the pillar of ash, while near the gate the guardian stump was ablaze. Some old men sat obstinately by the burial ground, arms huddled over their head refusing to move. Yoce was leading the children into the town, pointing in the direction in which he'd ridden, showing them a small object. It was the carved swordsman. He turned and rode into the forest, toward the sea.